DEAD TO THE WORLD

DEAD TO THE WORLD

An E.J. Pugh Mystery

Susan Rogers Cooper

Severn House Large Print
London & New York

This first large print edition published 2015
in Great Britain and the USA by
SEVERN HOUSE PUBLISHERS LTD of
19 Cedar Road, Sutton, Surrey, England, SM2 5DA.
First world regular print edition published 2014 by
Severn House Publishers Ltd., London and New York.

British Library Cataloguing in Publication Data

Cooper, Susan Rogers author.
Dead to the world. – (An E.J. Pugh mystery)
1. Pugh, E. J. (Fictitious character)–Fiction.
2. Murder--Investigation--Texas–Fiction. 3. Psychics–
Fiction. 4. Women novelists–Fiction. 5. Women private
investigators–United States–Fiction. 6. Detective and
mystery stories. 7. Large type books.
I. Title II. Series
813.6-dc23

ISBN-13: 9780727872616

Severn House Publishers support the Forest Stewardship Council™
[FSC™], the leading international forest certification organisation. All
our titles that are printed on FSC certified paper carry the FSC logo.

MIX
Paper from
responsible sources
FSC
www.fsc.org   FSC® C013056

Typeset by Palimpsest Book Production Ltd.,
Falkirk, Stirlingshire, Scotland.
Printed and bound in Great Britain by
T J International, Padstow, Cornwall.

This book is dedicated to the late Warrant Officer George Rogers, USMC, Rt., my dad, who was a China Marine.

ACKNOWLEDGEMENTS

I'd like to thank the *Leatherneck* archives and the *Marine Corps Gazette* for the history lesson. Any change in fact was for the story, or my own fault. I'd also like to thank Joan Hess for her invaluable assistance during gab fests, Jan Grape for her invaluable input, and my daughter Evin Cooper for keeping me on track. As always, thanks to my agent, Vicky Bijur, and my editor, Sara Porter.

PROLOGUE

DECEMBER, 1947

Carrie Marie Hutchins came home from school that day full of gossip to tell her mother. Mama loved to hear the goings-on at the school, especially about the teachers and the lunch-room ladies, even though Mama had taken to her bed with the vapors. She'd been up in her room ever since they'd got that telegram from the War Office telling them how Daddy had been killed on D-Day.

Home was a two-and-a-half story, gingerbread Victorian that had belonged to Mama's mama and her mama before her, built by Carrie Marie's great-great-great grandfather, who had come to Texas from Tennessee when he was only eighteen and Texas was still its own country. Carrie Marie loved the high ceilings that echoed and the wood floors that made her shoes sound like tap shoes. She loved that Mama didn't mind if she rode the bannister down from the second floor, as long as she didn't do it in front of company.

But they hadn't had company for a while now, not since the telegram from the War Office. People had come by at first with food and stuff; one man had mowed the lawn, and another used his own coupons to fill Daddy's car up with gasoline. But since Mama didn't drive, Carrie

1

Marie figured it was sort of a waste of good ration coupons.

That day Carrie Marie ran up the long flight of stairs two at a time, even though Mama said it wasn't lady-like. She called her mama's name a couple of times, and was surprised when Mama didn't call back to her. She rushed into her mama's bedroom and stopped short.

Carrie Marie's mama was lying in a bloody heap on the floor next to the bed, her throat slashed. Standing over her was a man with a shiny, bloody thing in his hand. Unfortunately for Carrie Marie's future, that man was her daddy.

Of course nobody believed her, but the sheriff of Toledo County, Texas, where Carrie Marie's hometown of Peaceful was, checked with the War Office anyway. They said that not only was Norris Manford Hutchins dead, but they'd sent his dog tags to his widow, Mrs Helen Bishop Hutchins, on January 4, 1945. So word got around and Carrie Marie started getting teased by some of the boys and ostrasized by most of the girls in school. Her only living relative was her daddy's younger brother, Herbert, who was 4F – medically disqualified – and didn't serve. He came to live in the old Victorian to look after Carrie Marie, not that he ever did much of that. Mostly he drank whiskey and listened to the radio.

At fifteen, five years after her mama's death, Carrie Marie couldn't take school anymore and got her Uncle Herbert to sign the papers for her to quit. She got a job at the Goldman's Five & Ten in downtown Peaceful, and worked there for twenty-two years, until Mr Goldman died and his children decided to sell the store. But five and dimes were rapidly disappearing by 1972, and the dollar stores were taking over. The one moving into Peaceful was simply called '$$', and Carrie Marie got in line fast and told the person hiring that she'd been the manager of Goldman's Five & Ten store. Since Mr Goldman's children had taken the money and gotten the hell out of Peaceful, Carrie Marie figured her little white lie wasn't going to hurt anybody. She got the job as assistant manager, which was OK with Carrie Marie, because she wasn't sure exactly what an actual manager did.

And so life went on. Having been born with what they called in those days a 'withered arm,' caused by what Carrie Marie finally learned was a birth injury called shoulder dystocia, she hadn't been real popular with the boys. Add the fact that she had small breasts and a big butt to the withered arm, and there weren't many – if any – gentleman callers.

Carrie Marie never married, and lived with her Uncle Herbert until he died. He was ninety-seven at the time and Carrie Marie was seventy-four. It was then that she discovered that living off Carrie Marie had been a fairly good thing for her uncle Herbert. Since he didn't pay rent or buy groceries – other than whiskey – he had managed to squirrel away a hefty sum from his disability payments. When he died he didn't leave a will, but as Carrie Marie was his only living relative she got everything that was his. And what was his amounted to $74,352.75. It was at this point that Carrie Marie decided to give up her job at the $$ store and add yet another B&B to the town of Peaceful.

And she did OK. She actually made money because of her beautiful home full of the treasures of four generations. That is, until Daddy started showing up again.

One

Willis and I take turns planning our anniversary celebration every year. This year was my turn, and since it was the big two-oh – yes, folks, twenty years married to the same man – I was pulling out all the stops. Knowing that in five years it would be our truly significant twenty-fifth, I decided this would be great, yet a little understated. Travel, but within reason. Since we both loved the Texas hill country, that would be my destination. Doing my research, I found the small town of Peaceful, Texas, north of San Antonio, west of Austin and just a smidgen away from Bourne. It was full of antique stores, boutiques and restaurants. All the goodies.

I wanted this to be a surprise, so I packed a suitcase for the two of us and stashed it in the trunk of my Audi TT Roadster (a two-seater I bought with an extra-big book check), and told him we were going for a drive. This was on a Friday afternoon.

Things were OK at home – my three girls are all seventeen now, and my college-aged son has been living with my mother-in-law. We were just going to be gone Friday and Saturday, back on Sunday, and with Elena Luna, our police detective next-door neighbor on the alert, I figured I didn't need to worry about them getting into too much trouble.

Willis and I got in my beautiful sports car with me driving and headed west. I call him Grandma Willis for his less-than-stellar driving skills. He calls me a stunt driver – which I think is grossly unfair. I never go more than five to ten miles over the speed limit – unless I'm really in a hurry. He sets the cruise control on his Texas clown truck (one of those big trucks balanced on way too big tires that means you have to have a ladder to climb into the damn thing) to the exact speed limit. He also stops at green lights. Not necessarily a complete stop, but irritating none the less. I, on the other hand, spent my formative driving years in Austin at the University of Texas and picked up the Austin rule of thumb concerning traffic lights: it doesn't matter at what point in the yellow light sequence you are – run it. And a red light is really only slightly more than a suggestion.

Once we were west of Austin, getting into the hill country and its winding roads up and down steep hills, I hit the accelerator and got into some serious driving. It infuriates me when people in front of me have to slam on their brakes for a rolling turn or going down a barely steep hill. I mean, come on folks, you *accelerate* into a turn, and why do you have to stop to go downhill, for God's sake? Willis, of course, spent the entire time with one hand clutching the door and his left foot raised to the dashboard – which is a feat and a half for a guy who's six foot three and most of that's leg.

The convertible top on my Audi was down, the spring sun was shining on us and the wind was kissing my cheeks. I had had my curly

6

copper-red hair chopped off recently so the wind wasn't going to do much damage on that score. I loved the new do – definitely wash and wear. Get out of the shower, towel it dry, hand comb it, give it a toss and there you go. Willis said it made me look like Little Orphan Annie, but I think he's just jealous because there's more hair on the floor of the tub after his shower than on his head.

Being April, the sides of the back roads I was taking had sprung to life with bluebonnets, Indian paint brush, primroses and other Texas wild flowers whose names I didn't know. Suffice it to say there was a riot of color on both sides of the road, interrupted only by a steep, rocky hill or a large-limbed oak tree, and there was a plethora of both. In front of us we could see hills of all shapes and sizes and, like clouds, you could identify a dog or a rabbit or a guy with a flat-top. The roads swooped up and down, a hair-pen curve here, a ninety-degree turn there. And I made them all going somewhere between seventy and eighty miles an hour. Which, personally, I just don't think is all that excessive.

At about four in the afternoon we pulled into the outskirts of Peaceful. Like many a small town in Texas (and I'm sure other states as well), the outskirts were scattered with car graveyards, junk dealers, auto repair shops and the like, but once past those we found ourselves in a quaint little village of Sunday houses and ornate cisterns. I knew from my reading that Peaceful was founded by German immigrants, and the ornate cisterns were straight out of the old country. They had stored water before the town had its own reservoir, but were now home to small shops and tea rooms. Some were shaped like small windmills, others patterned after the Sunday house they'd belonged to. For those not in the know on Sunday houses, that was a tradition where wealthy farmers and ranchers would buy a house 'in town' and the family would drive in on Saturday, buy whatever supplies they needed, spend the night in their second home and go to church on Sunday.

Our destination, The Bishop's Inn, was on a street called Post Oak, two blocks off the main thoroughfare, which, strangely enough, was called Main Street and looked just like the pictures I'd seen on their website. The house was a beautiful Victorian in excellent condition, with a garden my black-thumbed self envied beyond reason. We parked in the small parking lot adjacent to the house, and I confessed all to Willis.

'But I was supposed to play handball with Jim tomorrow!'

'I told his wife that you had to cancel.'

'You what?'

I sighed. 'Willis, this is our twentieth wedding anniversary! Cut me some slack here, OK?' Had the asshole forgotten it was our anniversary? Was he that big a douche? All the fun was slipping out, quickly replaced with a building anger – and, I'll admit, a little sadness with a touch of embarrassment.

Then my husband of twenty years grinned at me. 'Good thing I decided to bring this along on our, excuse the expression, "drive."' And he pulled a small box out of one of the pockets of

8

his cargo pants and handed it to me. He did remember! He was just giving me grief, like only he could. I leaned over and kissed him, and he kissed me back, putting a little more into it than you'd think after twenty years. Which was a good thing.

Once that had ceased, I unwrapped the box and opened it. Winking at me from the depths of a ring box was a diamond. I'm not well versed in diamonds, having never had one, but this looked to be at least a full karat. I stared at it – a baguette-shaped solitaire – then up at my husband. Then back at the ring.

'Wha—' I started, then stopped.

Willis was shaking his head and laughing. 'E.J. Pugh, speechless! I never thought I'd live to see the day!'

'But . . .'

He took the box out of my hand, removed the ring and held up my left hand. 'When I asked you to marry me twenty years ago, all I had to give you was that stupid friendship bracelet that your roommate made into a ring for me. And still you said yes. I was looking for something in our bedroom the other day and happened to open that big old jewelry box of yours. There it was – that friendship ring – all the threads losing their color, just sitting there. I couldn't believe you'd kept it all these years. That's when I decided it was about time you got a real engagement ring.'

He lifted my ring finger and slid the ring on it. The gold of my wedding band matched the gold of the engagement ring perfectly. And, as if in on a private joke, the diamond winked at me. 'I

9

love this, Willis,' I said, and kissed him again, 'but it doesn't mean you can touch my original engagement ring! That stays right where it is, you hear?'

He put up his hands in surrender. 'Jeez, I thought you were only sentimental about the kids!'

I really wasn't paying that much attention. I was staring at my hand with the beautiful new ring. I really needed to do my nails.

It took a little longer than would seem necessary to get out of the car, grab our one bag and head up the seven steps to the front door of the Bishop's Inn. The inn itself was painted a subtle gray-blue, with wine-red shutters and white accents. The floor of the deep front porch had been fairly recently painted white and held white rocking chairs and two porch swings, one on each side of the porch. Willis went up to the wine-red door and used the lion's head knocker.

There was no answer, so he knocked again. Still no answer. He turned and looked at me.

'We have reservations,' I said. 'Try the knob.'

He did and the door swung open into a wide foyer, empty of people but well-appointed with an ornate antique coat rack, an antique grandfather clock and an antique half-circle pedestal table with a cut-glass vase atop it. The vase contained multicolored roses that were beginning to all turn the same shade of dead brown.

'Hello?' Willis called out.

'Miss Hutchins?' I said. Miss Hutchins, the

10

owner, and I had corresponded through email about the reservation weeks ago.

There were rooms to the right and to the left of the foyer. The room on the right appeared to be a living room/parlor; the one on the left was outfitted as a library. Coming off the library was another room – a formal dining room. As we stepped toward that, we saw the staircase on the right, with a hall between it and the living room that led to more rooms. We heard steps on the staircase and looked up. That's when we heard a tiny squeak come out of the mouth of the woman descending the stairs.

She was an older lady, probably in her seventies or eighties, with a halo of thinning white hair, fading blue eyes, thin, and with a handicapped right arm. 'You startled me!' she said, stopping on the landing, her left hand clutching the area around her heart. 'Who are you?'

Her voice was thin and reedy, and a little trembly. I said, 'Miss Hutchins? I'm E.J. Pugh. I emailed about reservations?'

She continued to stare at me for a full minute, then turned to stare at Willis for another minute. Then said: 'Well.' She continued to stand where she was – on the landing – still clutching the material of her blouse above her heart.

'Is there a problem, Miss Hutchins?' I asked.

'Problem?' she said. 'Well, yes, I guess you might say that.'

'May we do something to help?' I asked.

Another minute of staring. Then she said, 'Thank you, but I don't really see how you could.' Tears sprang to her eyes. 'I don't think anyone can help.'

I slowly walked up the stairs to the landing and took her by the arm. 'Let's go to the kitchen and make some tea, shall we?' I asked.

We slowly descended the stairs and she replied, 'I'd prefer a shot of whiskey, but I know you mean well.'

The kitchen was bright yellow with new appliances but old painted cabinets and bright white Formica counter tops. There was a large round claw-foot table in the middle of the room (I'd mention it was an antique, but I have a feeling that word's going to be a description for almost everything in the house), and we sat down on old ladder-back chairs. She pointed at a cabinet in which I found a bottle of Tennessee sipping whiskey and three glasses, and brought it all to the table. I poured each of us two fingers, then the old lady took the bottle from me and added two more to her glass.

'I'm not much of a drinker,' she said and downed the glass. 'But lately it seems like the best solution.'

I lifted my glass and smelled the whiskey. It made me want to throw up. I set it back down. Give me a nice daiquiri or a tequila sunrise, but straight whiskey? Not my poison of choice.

I touched the old lady's hand. 'What's the problem, Miss Hutchins?' I asked.

She squeezed my hand. 'Call me Carrie Marie,' she said, and tried a tentative smile. Her false teeth were an awesome white even against her pale skin. 'Well, you see, my daddy has come back. Which is a hell of a problem.'

Willis and I looked at each other – both thinking the obvious, I'm sure. At her age, her 'daddy' had to be in his hundreds, right?

'Your daddy?' Willis said. 'You mean your father or your husband?'

Carrie Marie gave him a horrified look. 'My father, of course! That's just sick!'

'Oh, no, ma'am,' Willis started, 'I mean—'

'Young man, I think you've said enough,' the old woman said, and turned her face away from Willis.

'He meant no disrespect,' I said quietly. 'It's just that some women call their husbands daddy.'

She looked from me to Willis and back to me. 'Why in the world would they do that?' she asked, her faded blue eyes big and round.

I shrugged. 'I have no idea, but some do.'

'Well, I've never married,' she said, and pointed at her disfigured arm. 'Men don't like girls who aren't whole, you know.'

I started to open my mouth to confront her with the political incorrectness of her statement, then thought better of it. 'So let's get back to your daddy being back,' I suggested.

'Certainly,' she said. 'Well, first, you know, he killed Mama back in 'forty-five—'

'Excuse me?' Willis said.

Carrie Marie looked at my husband and proceeded to repeat herself slowly and succinctly. 'He. Killed. My. Mother. In nineteen forty-five.'

'I'm so sorry, Carrie Marie!' I said. 'That must have been awful!'

'Oh, it was,' she said, filling her glass yet again

13

with the Tennessee sipping whiskey. 'I found her body and him standing over her with a knife or something in his hand.' She took a long sip and nodded her head. 'Yep. Awful is a good word for it.'

'Is he out of prison now?' Willis asked.

'Prison?' she repeated. 'Oh, no! He didn't go to prison. Nobody believed me when I told 'em my daddy killed her.'

'Why not?' I asked.

She drained her second glass (I was losing track of the finger amount) and said, ''Cause he got killed on D-Day. We were sent his dog tags and everything. Still got 'em. And they say there was no mistake.'

'So he went to war after he killed your mother?' Willis asked, a frown on his handsome face.

'No, no,' she said. 'Mama died after we got the telegram from the War Office. Gosh, it had to have been close to eighteen months since D-Day.'

'Then how—' Willis started.

Carrie Marie looked around the room, as if to make sure we weren't going to be overheard, and whispered, ''Cause it's my daddy's spirit, y'all! He'd come back from the dead. And now he's back again!'

Not much later we were in a suite on the second floor. There was a sitting room with a camel-backed sofa and an easy chair, both covered in a blue willow-patterned brocade. Two paintings of blue bonnets graced one wall, while a second held large windows and a French door leading

14

to a balcony overlooking the back garden. The bedroom held an antique four-poster bed that had been adjusted to queen-size, and covered with a blue willow-patterned comforter. A second wall of windows overlooked a side garden. The bathroom was one door down and contained the largest claw-footed bathtub I'd ever seen, with a toilet that had a chain one used to flush. Being early spring, Miss Bishop had opened the windows to air the room out before leaving us alone.

Before leaving, however, she'd said, 'I've lost so many customers to daddy's shenanigans that I had to let my helper go. I don't climb these stairs often, so if you need something you might want to come downstairs to tell me.'

'We'll be fine,' I assured her as I closed the door behind her. Leaning against it, I looked at my husband. 'Well,' I said.

'So get your phone out and find us another place to stay,' Willis said.

I pushed away from the door and shook my head. 'Can't. There's a big bicycle ride going on this weekend and every room in three towns is in use.'

'So you took the last room available?' he said, giving me the evil eye. 'Didn't you wonder why nobody else wanted it?'

I sank down on the camel-backed sofa. 'Honey, I didn't know about the ride when I made the reservations three weeks ago! I wanted to make reservations for dinner and I tried calling the only restaurant in the area fancy enough to take reservations but the guy told me they were full up the entire weekend, and that all the hotels, B&Bs

15

and motels were too. I just felt lucky that I got this reservation when I did.'

Willis sank down beside me. 'Oh, yeah, boy are we lucky. In a haunted house with a crazy lady.'

I leaned my head against his shoulder. 'Babe, you can't have it both ways. Either she's sane and the house is haunted, or it isn't and she's crazy.'

'Point taken,' he said. He was quiet for a minute, then asked: 'Do you believe in ghosts?'

'No,' I said emphatically. Then backed down a smidge. 'Mostly no.'

'Yeah, me, too,' he said. 'Mostly no.' Then: 'But . . .'

I looked up at him. 'But what?'

'When I was a kid, about twelve or thirteen, my grandfather was really sick and my parents took us to my grandparents' place in Waxahatchie. They lived out in the country and had this big front porch. My grandmother loved wind chimes, so there were bunches of 'em lining the whole length of the porch. Grandma Pugh and Daddy were both at the hospital and Mama and me and Rusty were sitting on that front porch soaking up some sun. The place was real still. Not a leaf was stirring on the trees. Then all of a sudden, starting from the left and going all the way down the line, the wind chimes starting making their songs, one after the other. Mama looked at us boys and said, "Grandpa Pugh is saying goodbye, boys."'

He stopped and I just looked at him. 'I've never heard this story,' I said, thinking fondly of Rusty, my deceased brother-in-law.

16

'That's because my mother denies it ever happened and I decided that was probably for the best. But I heard her that night telling Daddy about it and she told him what time it happened, and Daddy said that was exactly when Grandpa Pugh passed away.'

I shuddered. 'Wow,' was all I could say. Then, 'So you *do* believe in ghosts?'

Willis shrugged. 'Maybe. Maybe not. But either way you look at it, I don't think Miss Hutchins' daddy came back from the dead and killed her mother. If there are such things as spirits, I doubt they can wield a knife.'

1915–1934

Clayton Delaware Hutchins and his wife, Lydia Marie Hutchins, were blessed with three sons: Norris and Herbert, born within eighteen months of each other, and then the youngest, Edgar, at which point Lydia Marie died in childbirth. The three boys were raised by their father and a string of housekeepers/lovers that Clayton Hutchins would bring into the home. Young Edgar, the comeliest of the three, was barely thirteen when he was seduced by the then current housekeeper, a girl of nineteen, although she later claimed it wasn't she who did the seducing. She was sent packing and Clayton refused to speak to his youngest son from that day forward.

Norris, the eldest, was a big, strapping young man and his father's odds-on favorite. Since he no longer spoke to his youngest, and his middle son, Herbert, was a sickly, and therefore – in Clayton's mind – inferior specimen, it was only

17

natural – in Clayton's mind – that Norris would shine. And he did. In the year 1928, Norris excelled at the newish game of football that had been bulldozing through small Texas towns and was revered in his hometown of Peaceful, Texas.

It was in 1932, at the age of seventeen, that young Edgar fell in love with the comely Helen Bishop, the daughter of the richest family in town. Being the daughter of the richest family in town had a lot to do with young Edgar falling in love. Had she been poor it may never have happened. That year in Peaceful was a hard one for most people. Well into the depression, many stores had closed on Main Street, including Clayton Hutchins' haberdashery shop. Times were lean, and since Clayton still did not bear credence to his youngest son's existence, Edgar's pleas for certain food items would often go unanswered. This only made Edgar all the more determined to win the hand of the fair Helen and move into the grand old house on Post Oak Street, where he believed food to be abundant. There were also rumors of treasure within its four walls.

As Edgar set about wooing Helen, he found himself a job at the Rexhall Drugstore, one of the few remaining establishments on Main Street, as a soda jerk. Although his pay was a pittance, the occasional tip enabled him to eat more steadily than he did at home, and he even saved up enough to buy Helen a small bottle of Evening in Paris cologne and take her to an occasional picture show.

The summer he graduated high school, he was working behind the counter, while Helen sat in *front of him, sipping on a Coca-Cola and smiling at him, when his brother, Norris, walked in. Helen was a pretty girl, which was immediately noticed by Norris. On her part, Helen also observed that big brother Norris was fetching in his own way. While all three brothers looked much alike in the face, Norris was bigger, with muscles, square shoulders and thin hips, while Edgar was slender and almost feminine in physique. Poor Herbert, on the other hand, was scrawny and slump shoul- dered, and the only one of the three with hypo- thyridic eyes.*

Edgar continued to see Helen throughout that summer, but in the fall she was off to Mary-Hardin Baylor College in Waco, while his older brother Norris was off to fulfill his scholarship require- ments at Baylor University, also in Waco. Edgar, who considered himself quite a catch, never thought of his clumsier big brother as a threat. Until, that is, that Christmas break.

It was then, at the tender age of nineteen, that Edgar Hutchins received the third and final blow that would color the rest of his life. The first being, of course, the death of his mother at his own birth, the second his father's emotional abandonment, and the third the announcement on Christmas Eve that his brother Norris and his true love Helen were to be married in the spring.

In the wee hours of Christmas morning, Edgar went into his brother Norris's room with intent to do bodily harm. Unfortunately Norris was awake.

'Come to try to beat the shit out of me?' Norris inquired, sitting up in his bed.

'You son of a bitch!' Edgar said in a harsh whisper.

'Didn't mean to step on your toes, but it just sorta happened,' Norris said.

'You just sorta happened to go to her all-girls school and just sorta happened to ask her out on a date? Is that what you're saying?'

'Yeah, more or less,' Norris agreed.

'Bullshit!' Edgar hissed. 'You're after the treasure! That's all you want—'

Norris laughed. 'Treasure? Jesus, Ed, are you still hung up on that old chestnut? There's no treasure at the Bishop house! That's just something kids tell each other!'

'No, it's not! I know for a fact there's a treasure in that house!'

Norris smirked. 'Yeah? So what is it?'

'I'll know when I find it!'

'Guess you're not going to find it now, huh? Since the only time you'll be in that house is when I invite you in! Which may be never!'

Three days after Christmas, Edgar joined the Marines and left town – permanently, he hoped.

Two

BACK HOME

There were different reactions to being left home on their own, each according to the particular sister's views and personality. Alicia, the foster sister and newest member of the family, had been left alone on many occasions in her foster career and barely noticed; Bess was stoic about it. Being left alone meant responsibilities, but she was a responsible person and could totally handle it; but Megan . . . Megan was delighted, if not downright joyful. She could think of a million things to be done in the two days her parents would be gone that would otherwise never be accomplished. She even played with the thought of losing her virginity, but didn't have a boy in mind for the honor, so nixed the idea. But that didn't mean they couldn't stay out late, find someone to buy them beer, or find an adult station on cable . . . like, there were *so* many temptations to choose from!

There aren't a lot of rules in the Pugh household: don't hit if you can help it; if you're male, put the seat down in the bathroom; if you're female, keep sanitary products out of sight; if it's on the floor anybody can use it (like a sweater, scarf, pen, whatever); and the newest one (and mandatory to all), knock before entering a room with a closed door. Megan had that one half

21

down. She knocked on her sister Bess's door that Saturday *as* she opened it.

Bess had half a second to slam shut her newly acquired yearbook and shove it under her pillow before Megan was upon her.

'You're supposed to knock!' Bess said.

'I did!' Megan answered, flopping on Bess's bed.

'*Before* you enter the room, stupid!'

'Don't call me stupid!'

'Then don't do stupid things!'

'Whatever. Are you going to the dance?' Megan asked.

'What dance?'

Megan sighed. 'The spring dance. Now who's stupid?'

'No,' Bess said emphatically.

Megan turned from her stomach to her side so she could look her sister in the eye. 'Why the hell not?'

Bess shrugged. 'Don't want to.'

'Bullshit.'

Bess did not reply. She rolled off the bed and headed out the door of her room.

'Where are you going?' Megan demanded.

'To the kitchen. I'm hungry.'

'You're never hungry between meals, Miss Goody-Two-Shoes!' Megan said, following her sister out the door.

'Whatever.'

'You're up to something!'

Bess sighed long and hard. 'Get over yourself! You always think something's up when nothing is! You're an idiot!'

There was also a rule about name-calling, but it was widely ignored.

'You're the idiot!' Megan shot back as they headed down the stairs.

'Bite me,' Bess said.

'No way. Your skinny ass would taste awful!'

'God, you are soooooo funny.'

They found their other sister in the large kitchen sitting at the table, eating a slice of cold pizza. 'Breakfast,' Alicia said with her mouth full.

'Any left?' Megan asked, beating Bess to the refrigerator.

'Yeah. Couple of pieces. Should we put something out for dinner tonight?' Alicia asked.

'Naw. We've got plenty of money. Let's go out!' Megan said.

Bess snorted. 'We *do not* have plenty of money! They're gone for three days and Mom left us fifty dollars. We spent seventeen on the pizza and breadsticks last night. Going out for the three of us would be at least twenty to twenty-five dollars. And this is the first full day. Which would mean we'd only have like eight to ten dollars left for all day tomorrow!'

'So we're going to church with Grandma, right?' Megan said. 'She'll take us out to dinner after church, right? So what's the prob?'

'Bess, I have to agree with Megs. And I don't want to cook, and I certainly don't want to eat anything Megan cooks—'

'Hey!' Megan interjected.

'Or you for that matter. I'm not in the mood for tofu and kale,' Alicia said.

'Second that!' Megan said.

'I do not only eat tofu and kale!' Bess said. 'There's a lovely spaghetti squash in the vegetable bin.'

Megan stuck her finger down her throat and Alicia said, 'Spare me.'

Bess turned on her heels and left the kitchen, heading back upstairs. Once in her room, she threw herself on the bed and pulled her new yearbook out from under the pillow where she'd hidden it. Without much help the book opened to a certain page. On it were pictures of seniors, like herself and her sisters. But the page wasn't in the 'P's' for Pugh. It was in the 'H's' for Harris. Logan Harris, to be exact. Blond-haired, blue-eyed Logan Harris, with the dimples and the killer smile. He was in her chemistry class this semester and sat next to her. And he smelled soooo good. Bess again read the information under the picture: 'Most likely to be running his place of employment before graduation.' And it even listed his place of employment. Bess stashed the yearbook back under her pillow and headed downstairs.

Once in the kitchen, she said, 'OK, I give up. We can go out to dinner. And I know exactly where.'

'Where's that?' Alicia asked.

'The Eyes of Texas Steak House,' Bess said.

Megan almost choked on her cold pizza. 'Are you serious? What can you eat there, Miss Vegan-two-shoes?'

'I'm thinking about red meat,' Bess said, envisioning Logan Harris bringing her a juicy steak on a sizzling platter.

*

24

We had an uneventful night. No spirits rattling chains or moaning in the hallways. Basically, no sign of 'Daddy' at all. Well, maybe not exactly uneventful. It was our anniversary, after all.

In the morning we headed downstairs, following the smell of coffee. Miss Hutchins was in the dining room, a carafe of coffee in her good hand.

'Good morning!' she said cheerfully.

I tried to be as cheerful in returning her greeting, but I really don't do cheerful – or human – until after at least my first cup of coffee.

'It's so nice to have guests again!' Miss Hutchins chirped. 'I'd been so happy here with all my guests to talk to!' The smile disappeared. 'That is, until Daddy came back, of course.' Then the smile reappeared. 'I hope you slept well.'

'Just fine,' Willis said, sitting down and reaching for a cup that he stuck out to Miss Hutchins. She filled it. I immediately followed my husband's lead.

'There is breakfast on the buffet behind you and I'll just refill the coffee and be right back!' she said with a smile, and scurried off.

After several sips of coffee I was human enough to get up and check out the buffet. Looking at the offerings thereon, I had to assume that Miss Hutchins had been up since the crack of dawn preparing it all. Obviously homemade biscuits, sausage gravy, rashers of bacon and links of sausage, scrambled eggs, hash browns and what looked like homemade preserves. I've been to my share of B&Bs, and the usual second 'B' encompassed store-bought doughnuts, a bowl of grocery store cut fruit and weak coffee. I figured,

Daddy or no Daddy, this was my kind of place. But in deference to my new body, I only had a little of everything. No, really.

After breakfast Willis and I set out to explore the little town of Peaceful. Main Street was where it was happening, so we headed in that direction. It was a beautiful day for a walk – the sun was out and not yet too hot, and the earlier spring rains had helped to make the entire town look greener. Main Street itself had large planters, one at each intersection (there were three intersections – you do the math), filled with all sorts of colorful flowers. The cisterns were artfully decorated and their small square footage was used to the best advantage possible. Some were filled with crap straight from China, others with local-made crafts, and others with antiques. The bigger antique shops were full of junk, most of which I wanted desperately. I'd given myself a budget for the weekend of two hundred dollars to spend on 'stuff.' With the cistern shops and the antique shops, I'd only hit three hundred by the time we stopped for lunch. We found a little bistro and settled in. Inevitably, the conversation turned to Miss Hutchins and her daddy.

'I think we've established that even if there are such things as ghosts, which we both doubt—' I started.

'Indubitably,' Willis said.

I rolled my eyes. 'Ghosts are not known for wielding weapons such as knives. Therefore, someone other than Miss Hutchins' father killed her mother.'

'Agreed.'

'Who?' I asked.

Willis shrugged. 'I have no idea. We don't know anything about the rest of her family, or other players that might have been around back then.'

'You think we should ask her?'

It was Willis's turn for the old eye roll. 'Here you go again, getting involved,' he said.

'What?' I said. 'I'm not doing anything!'

'Yeah, but you're intrigued. I can see it in your eyes, not to mention you're actually talking about it.'

'OK, never mind. You're right. It's our anniversary. What do we care if the old lady loses her family home because of someone playing pranks?'

'We don't know anyone's playing pranks!' Willis said. 'For all we know, she's lost customers because it's a lousy B&B.'

'When she serves breakfasts like that?' I asked, wide-eyed. 'I seriously doubt it!'

'Maybe she sleepwalks at night and the word got around.'

'Maybe you're full of it,' I suggested.

Willis sighed. 'OK. Let's ask her why people stopped coming. What it was "Daddy" did that made people run off.'

Inwardly I grinned; outwardly I just nodded my head sagely. 'I think we can do that.' Inwardly I also knew that Willis was beginning to enjoy the chase as much as I did.

When we returned to Bishop's Inn, Miss Hutchins was busy puttering around the living room, straightening things that already looked straight, fluffing pillows that were already fluffed, etc.

'May we join you?' I asked as we entered the room.

'Oh, my, yes!' she said, smiling joyfully. 'Please, sit! Mr Pugh, you take this chair,' she said, pointing to a very old barrel-shaped easy chair that had obviously been recovered at least once in its history. The latest upholstery was a tapestry of books and reading accoutrement, such as reading glasses, a fireplace and a sleeping dog. It had a matching ottoman. 'This was Daddy's chair. I'm not sure if he sits in it when he comes back, but I like to think he's grateful I kept it for him.'

Willis took the easy chair and I sank down on the camel-backed sofa. 'Speaking of your father,' I started, 'what did he do to drive away your customers?'

'Oh, this and that,' Miss Hutchins said, sitting down next to me. 'He started screaming one night, which ran off two couples who were staying here. They just packed up in the middle of the night and left. Then there was the destruction of those suitcases that time.'

'Tell me about that,' I said.

'Well, I had this lovely older couple staying with me. Gladys and Herman. Such nice people. The second day they were here, in the morning, they woke up to find their suitcases had been slashed with a knife and their belongings scattered all around – even some of Gladys's unmentionables hanging from the light fixture! Needless to say, they were very upset and I had to supply them with paper bags for their belongings so they

28

could leave immediately.' She shook her head sadly. 'I didn't dare ask them to pay for that one night. I mean, that would have just been tacky.'

I nodded my head. Tacky for sure. And a knife again. Were Willis and I wrong about spirits being unable to wield weapons? What did either of us know about ghosts and spirits and other things that go bump in the night? Not a damn thing. But I couldn't help feeling there was a live human hand at work here.

Before I could ask any more questions, the front door opened with a quick knock and two people stood in the foyer.

'Oh, goodness!' Miss Hutchins said, standing up. 'I wonder who that could be?' She moved into the foyer, with Willis and me not far behind.

'Hello!' Miss Hutchins chirped. 'May I help you?'

I realized I was staring and quickly looked down at my shoes. I always wondered about people who go out of their way to make themselves look as different as possible then get insulted when other people look too long. The man was short, maybe five foot five at the most. His hair was orange and styled in a faux-hawk, his nose, lip and ears were pierced, and there were tats covering all his exposed flesh. The woman was much taller than him, maybe my height (that's five feet and all eleven inches) or even taller, and weighed considerably more than was necessary. Her hair was jet black, shaved on one side and hanging long and loose on the other. She wore a shear chiffon dress, floating and billowing about her, over what appeared to be long johns, with a knitted poncho covering the top and more scarves than I've ever seen on one person. She had similar tats and piercings.

Ignoring Miss Hutchins' greeting, the female of the couple said, in a Minnie Mouse-ish voice, 'I feel it, Humphrey. I can feel it! It's so strong!'

Humphrey, whom I assumed was the man with her, said, 'I knew it! This is great!'

'Excuse me,' Miss Hutchins said. 'May I help you?'

'Miss Hutchins, right?' Humphrey said, grabbing her hand and shaking it like one would shake a pitcher of martinis. 'Humphrey Hammerschultz, I made the reservations.'

'You did?' Miss Hutchins asked.

'Last week. Do you have a problem with your memory? A lot of people as old as you do, you know, but it's not an issue. We made a reservation. This is my partner, Diamond Lovesy.'

'Reservation?' Miss Hutchins said, stiffening at the implied insult.

'Yes,' Humphrey said, leaning closer to her, speaking loudly and slowly. 'We made a reservation for two rooms – one for Diamond and one for myself.'

'We're not a couple,' Diamond said, looking at Willis and me and smiling.

I nodded my head, but my husband opted not to acknowledge the new people at all.

'We're psychic investigators,' Humphrey said to Willis and me. 'Or if you prefer, paranormal detectives!' He smiled widely. 'Diamond is a medium.'

Miss Hutchins turned to me. 'What are they saying?' she asked, quite anxious.

'*I called last week!*' Humphrey screamed at her. '*We were told we could come investigate the things that have been happening here!*'

Again Miss Hutchins turned to me. 'Why is he screaming at me?' she asked in a weak voice.

'You don't have to yell,' I said to Humphrey. 'She has all her faculties. Are you sure you talked to Miss Hutchins when you called?'

'No, it was her assistant. Some guy,' he said.

'A guy? A man, you mean?' Miss Hutchins asked. 'There are no men here.'

'Could it have been your helper?' I asked her.

She shook her head. 'No, she's a woman. And she doesn't have a deep voice or anything. Besides,' Miss Hutchins said, 'she hasn't been here in several weeks. She certainly wasn't here last week.'

'Well, I don't know who I talked to,' Humphrey said, 'but he took the reservation.'

Miss Hutchins walked to a small counter in the foyer, upon which sat a large, hardbound book. I moved to stand beside her. She flipped it to today's date. And there, on the right side, was Saturday, with the notation, 'Humphrey Hammerschultz and Diamond Lovesy, two rooms.' Across from it, on the left, was Friday, with information on Willis and me. It didn't take a graphologist to realize that the two entries were written by two different people.

'How did you know something was going on here at the Bishop's Inn?' I asked Humphrey.

That stopped him for a moment. 'Now that I

31

think about it, the guy I talked to here might have been the same guy who called me.'

'Someone called you? About what?' Willis asked. I was glad to see he was joining in.

'About the shit that's happening here,' he said, then, seeing the look on Miss Hutchins' face: 'Excuse my French, ma'am.'

She simply nodded.

'What did he say?' I asked. 'This man who called you?'

'He said there was definitely a spirit at the Bishop's Inn in Peaceful, Texas, and that we should get here as soon as possible before something bad happens,' Humphrey said.

Miss Hutchins grabbed my hand. 'Oh, dear,' she said.

I patted her hand.

'And you just decided to come straight here, huh?'

Humphrey puckered up. 'Of course not! I researched it. There's all sorts of paranormal activity in the Texas Hill Country,' he said. 'So Diamond and I discussed it and I called and made a reservation.'

'And didn't notice that you were talking to the same guy,' Willis said, his voice dubious.

'It had been a week since the guy called. And I *did* talk to a few thousand people in the interim!' Humphrey proclaimed.

'It was Daddy,' Miss Hutchins said in a small voice.

'Your father? He's here?' Diamond asked in her Minnie-Mouse voice.

'In a manner of speaking,' Miss Hutchins answered.

'So do we get our rooms or what?' Humphrey asked, his tone getting slightly belligerent.

'Of course,' Miss Hutchins said with a sigh. 'Just give me a minute to prepare them.'

'No,' I said, taking her arm and leading her back into the living room. 'Just tell us where the sheets and towels are and we'll all pitch in and do it.'

'And we're paying for this?' Humphrey said, indignant.

'Oh, Humphrey,' Diamond said. 'Be a sport! It'll be fun. Besides, I feel the spirits all around us and I know they want us to help this poor, beleaguered lady!' She smiled at us, one and all.

It wasn't the fun-fest the medium had proclaimed it would be. Basically it was as tedious as one would expect. The men wandered around acting as if they had no clue where one might keep linens and things (at least I know my husband was acting – there was a good possibility Humphrey Hammerschultz was really that stupid), while Diamond Lovesy and I did all the work. She kept saying, 'Isn't this fun?' By the fourth declaration I just glared at her. That was the last time she said it.

After we'd made the beds and put out the towels, the four of us headed downstairs. Miss Hutchins was setting refreshments on the coffee table in the living room. 'Oh, there you are! I was wondering what took you so long,' she said.

'Having men help us,' I said, mostly under my breath. Willis nudged me in the ribs with his elbow. It hurt. 'You didn't have to do all this,' I said, looking at the spread she'd put out. A pitcher of iced tea and five glasses, a plate of scones and a plate of finger sandwiches – pimiento cheese and what looked like liverwurst.

We all sat down, Willis nudging Humphrey away from 'his' easy chair, Miss Hutchins and me on the camel-backed sofa and the newcomers in armless stuffed chairs.

'So, Miss Hutchins,' Humphrey said, stuffing his face with scones and talking around the mess in his mouth (utterly disgusting – I was able to break my children of such antics at a fairly early age. My first inkling of the fact that this guy was raised by wolves). 'Tell us about these sightings of your father.'

'Oh, I'm the only one who's seen him,' she said. 'The first time – after his death, of course – was when I was ten and he killed my mother. Then nothing until about a year ago in the back garden late at night. And again three weeks ago, when I was walking dear Gladys and Herman out to their car, I saw him in the window of the room they had just occupied and he was smiling down at me. It wasn't exactly a friendly smile. More teasing, I guess you'd say.'

Humphrey turned to Diamond. 'Are you getting anything?' he asked her.

She closed her eyes and said, 'Ummmm.' Then, 'There *is* a presence here,' she said. 'A dark presence.' Then she started breathing hard and hugged herself. 'An evil, cold presence!'

'Oh, my goodness,' Miss Hutchins said.

I was beginning to feel chilly, but then again I'm easily susceptible.

34

Diamond, still with closed eyes, began to regulate her breathing. In through the nose, out through the mouth, slowing it down. Then she put her hands out, palms up, and said, 'Why are you here? Speak to me! I feel you, spirit! I know you're here. Why? Why are you doing these things to your wonderful daughter?'

There was a quick intake of breath and then, in a voice a million miles from the Minnie-Mouse voice of old, Diamond, or someone – possibly male – spoke. 'She's defiling my home! Letting strangers in! She has no right! She must be stopped!'

Miss Hutchins' shoulders squared and she stood up. 'This isn't your house, Daddy! You know that!' she said. 'This is *my* house! Left to me by Mama, and left to her by her mama, and back many generations! You have no right to this house! So you just get along now!'

Diamond Lovesy shuddered once and fell back in her chair. Humphrey ran to her. Looking at me, he said, 'Iced tea, STAT.' He really, really said that.

I looked at Willis and we both rolled our eyes. Diamond might have been a little more believable if she'd had any of her facts straight. Miss Hutchins had put that right, though. I poured some iced tea in a glass and handed it to Humphrey, who held it to Diamond's lips. She sipped tentatively.

Miss Hutchins sank back down next to me. 'If you people are really psychic detectives, I want to hire you to get rid of my daddy!' Then she sat up and said, 'I don't mean kill him or anything.

35

I just mean it's way past time he should be at rest.' Turning to me, she said, 'Don't you think so?'

BACK HOME
The girls got ready to go to dinner at the Eyes of Texas Steakhouse on the Black Cat Ridge side of the Texas Colorado River. It had a large patio hanging over the river, but as it was cold and damp outside, the girls thought they might eat indoors, which was just what Bess wanted to do. Megan and Alicia donned blue jeans and T-shirts, while Bess, although staying with blue jeans, opted for a gauzy top that floated around her upper body but had a deep enough V to show the little bit of cleavage she could pull up with the push-up bra she hardly ever wore. She spent way too long on her hair and make-up – long enough for Megan to notice.

'What's with you?' she asked. 'You look like you're going to a party, for crying out loud!'

'I think it's good to look your best wherever you go,' Bess shot back. 'A T-shirt with "I'm with stupid" on it is not your best look.'

'Maybe not, but it's funny when I stand to your right and the arrow points at you.'

'Hilarious,' Bess said.

'Hum,' Alicia joined in. 'Are we trying to impress someone?'

'Are we going to eat or just stand here and grill me for a couple of hours?' Bess asked, then stridently walked out the back door to the waiting minivan that was now their mode of transportation.

The other two laughed at her expense and headed for the van. 'My turn!' Megan shouted.

'No, it's not!' Alicia shouted back, running to the driver's door. 'I'm on the schedule!'

'Shotgun!' Megan shouted instead, but was less than pleased to see that Bess was already occupying that location. Griping under her breath, she crawled into the back seat. Leaning forward between the two front seats, she said, 'Y'all are both bitches, you know that?'

Alicia smiled and Bess laughed. 'And proud of it!' Bess said.

1934–1935

Edgar Hutchins hitchhiked three days after Christmas to San Antonio, where he found a Marine recruiter that was more than happy to sign him up. He brought with him the small amount of money he'd saved up since Helen had gone off to college. It had been his hope to spend it on a ring; instead, he used part of it for a good meal in a restaurant and a room for the night in a seedy hotel in a mostly Mexican part of town. The following day he began his journey to Parris Island, South Carolina.

After World War One, when the boot camp had seen more than thirteen thousand troops training there, the funding for Parris Island had all but dried up due to the severe decrease in the hectic demands of the war. By 1934 when Edgar arrived, there were fewer than three hundred men being trained. But these years before the onset of World War Two saw innovations in training. The new recruits learned how to fire automatic weapons and were among the first military personnel to see a demonstration of a trench mortar out of a combat situation. This should have excited Edgar, like it did most of the recruits then at Parris Island, but it didn't. He hated the food, hated the uncomfortable cots, hated most of the guys in his barracks, and, most of all, he hated his D.I.

Gunny Sargent Monroe Lincoln was a career Marine who had served with honors during World War One, and was determined to make sure these peace-time leathernecks were up for anything that would be coming their way. He was fair but hard. Edgar didn't see the fair, only the hard. He managed to spend the night in the brig twice for infractions and barely made it out of boot camp. But when he did, he was actually pleased to find out that he was being shipped to Shanghai, China.

Three

Willis and I went out to dinner alone that evening. Miss Hutchins recommended a nice place in Bourne, so we drove the few miles to the other town. I'd tried to talk Miss Hutchins into not hiring the, excuse the expression, 'psychic detectives,' earlier, but she was adamant.

'I love having my little inn,' she'd told me. 'And I just can't stand that Daddy is doing this! And he *did* kill my mother! Leaving me all alone for all those years.' Tears had formed in her eyes, threatening to spill over.

'I'm not convinced this is your daddy's doing,' I told her. 'It seems more likely that there is a live hand involved here.'

'You're forgetting, E.J. I saw him twice. It was definitely my daddy!'

'When was the last time you saw your father – before he died, I mean?'

She thought long and hard. 'I must have been about six. He enlisted right after Pearl Harbor.'

'So it's possible you don't really remember exactly what he looks like?' I asked, keeping my voice as gentle as possible.

Her mouth stiffened into a straight line. 'I have pictures of my father! Would you like to see them?' she said, not happy.

'Sure,' I said, and smiled, hoping to take the sting out of what I'd said. It didn't work. She got up stiffly and walked to a bookcase next to the fireplace. She grabbed two very old photo albums and brought them to the sofa. When I offered to help, she pulled the books away from me.

'I'm fine on my own!' she said with a little heat. 'I've been basically on my own since I was ten years old, you know!'

'I'm sorry—' I started, but she interrupted.

'Don't be. I'm fine.' She sat down next to me, put one book to her other side and one on her lap. 'Here we go,' she said, and opened the book to a wedding picture. The bride, the groom, parents, groomsmen, bridesmaids, flower girls – the whole shebang. Except that none of the men had faces. They had all been scratched out – not just marked out with a pen, but with enough force for it to rip through the paper to the black sheet the pictures had been glued to.

Miss Hutchins' intake of breath was audible from where I sat. 'When was the last time you looked at these?' I asked her.

She shook her head. 'I don't know. I try not to dwell in the past. It's too painful. A long time, I'd think. A very long time.'

She turned the page to reveal pictures of a honeymoon with a bride and a faceless groom. More pages, a mother holding a baby, and a faceless father standing with his arm around the woman. It was that way throughout the album. Miss Hutchins threw the book to the floor and grabbed the one sitting by her side. Again, all the male faces had been defaced. If there were two men, they were both faceless; four men, the same.

40

'Uncle Herbert has been scratched out, too,' Miss Hutchins said.

'Uncle Herbert?' I asked.

'My father's brother. He was the only family member left when my mother died, and he came to live with me. He died about five years ago.' She thought for a moment, then said: 'There were three of them – three brothers. Herbert was 4F so didn't go to war, but both Daddy and his other brother, who I believe was the youngest one – Edgar, I think his name was – did. Daddy was in Europe, but Edgar died in the Pacific. Mama didn't tell me what happened to him, so I guess it must have been pretty bad. Mama liked to gossip, and she would have told me if it was something I could hear about.'

'Should we check the other photo albums?' I asked her.

'I'm almost afraid to,' she said, dropping the second book on to the floor with the first.

I went to the bookcase and brought back three more albums. The third had no pictures scratched out, mainly because there were no men depicted. 'These were taken after Daddy left for the war,' Miss Hutchins said. 'This next one,' she said, 'should be too.' And it was. Those two books went to her other side, while she picked up the third. 'I think this book is after Mama died. There probably aren't a lot of pictures.' And there weren't. But there were some of a man – his face intact. 'That's Uncle Herbert,' she said.

The pictures of Miss Hutchins were those of a pre-teen to a late teenager, and the man in the picture looked heavy and bloated. Neither he nor

41

Miss Hutchins were smiling in any of the pictures. 'Uncle Herbert drank a lot,' Miss Hutchins said. 'I think I watched over him much more than he ever watched over me. I always had to put out his cigarettes and move his whiskey bottles after he passed out on the sofa. Then I'd cover him up with the afghan my mother knitted so many years before. But then, one year I wasn't fast enough and he dropped a lit cigarette on the afghan and burned a huge hole in it.' Her lips were pursed again and you could tell she was still hurt and angry about the loss of this possession made by her mother.

She began to cry softly. 'I don't understand!' she said. 'Why would he do that? Scratch out his own face? And his brothers' faces! Why would Daddy do that?'

I was pretty sure 'Daddy' had nothing to do with the defacing of the pictures. And I told Willis that while we partook of baked brie and white wine in Bourne.

Willis shook his head. 'I don't understand why *anyone* would do it.'

I agreed. Something was going on in Peaceful and I was bound and determined to find out what.

BACK HOME
It was a fairly typical Texas steakhouse: dead animals adorning the walls (deer heads, boar heads, whole raccoons, a bobcat sitting on a bare branch affixed to the wall), rock walls, a big fireplace going strong, hardwood tables with glossy finishes, and wait staff wearing black

42

pants, white shirts, bolo ties and cowboy boots – both males and females.

There was a girl at the reception stand they knew from high school. 'Hey, y'all,' she said, greeting them with a big smile. 'How many?'

'Hey, Tiffany. Just the three of us,' Megan said.

'Come right this way,' the girl said, and strode out in front of them.

The place wasn't all that crowded for a Friday night, which did not bode well for the restaurant's longevity. The building had been built as a seafood restaurant, which had lasted close to twenty years but changed hands when the chef/owner died. For a brief period it had been Italian – heavy on the pizza, which couldn't compete with the national pizza chains in town, and was eventually bought by someone who wanted to turn it into a high-class bar. Since the county was dry and he could never get the correct paperwork to open a private club, it was sold before it ever opened. That's when it became the Eyes of Texas Steakhouse. It had opened strong three years before, but had been on the wane ever since.

'How's this?' the receptionist said, offering them a table in the middle of the room.

Sensing Megan was about to complain, and seeing Logan only one table away, Bess figured this was his section, so quickly said, 'This is fine!' with a big smile on her face.

The receptionist left and the girls sat down. 'This is *not* fine!' Megan said. 'I'd rather have a booth! There are like a hundred empty ones! And did you notice Tiffany acted like she didn't even know us?'

'Maybe she got in trouble for being too friendly with the customers or something,' Alicia suggested. 'What are you going to get, Bess? The only vegetarian thing I see is a salad.'

'I told you, I've decided to give meat a chance,' Bess said.

'Wasn't that a Beatles' song?' Megan asked absently as she studied the steaks to try to figure out how big a one she could get without bankrupting their weekend allowance.

'It was a John Lennon song, *after* the Beatles, and it was *peace* not meat,' Alicia said with some authority.

'Why do you know so much about the— Oh, wait! Graham the retro-king,' Megan started.

But Alicia cut in. 'I think I'm going to have the fillet,' she said. 'With sweet potato fries and a Caesar salad. And maybe we can share the chocolate lava cake for dessert?'

'Share, my ass,' Megan said. 'I want a whole dessert and I'm looking at the banana split. If I have room after my sixteen-ounce porterhouse with balsamic vinegar-glazed mushrooms, risotto, and the grilled asparagus.'

'Jeez, Megan, there won't be any money left over for Alicia and me!' Bess said.

'You don't eat much,' Megan said.

'Well, I'm going to!' Bess declared. 'I'm having the six-ounce sirloin, a baked potato and a side salad. And my own dessert – that apple crisp with the Blue Bell ice cream!'

Alicia brought out her phone and turned on the calculator app. 'Hum, well, we can have the desserts or we can have the dinners, but we can't have both. Megan, if you were to get something *reasonable*, then maybe, but a sixteen-ounce porterhouse? That's like almost thirty dollars!'

'But that's what I want!'

'Well, as Daddy would say, want in one hand—' Bess started.

'Yeah, I know, and poop in the other—' Megan continued.

'And see which one fills up first!' Bess finished.

'Gross!' Alicia said. 'Can we just make this happen? With dessert? Megan?'

'Oh, fine! I'll have the fillet. But the big one—'

'Too expensive,' Alicia said.

'Fine,' Megan said, teeth clenched. 'The eight-ounce fillet. But I still want the risotto and asparagus!'

'The asparagus is extra!' Alicia said.

'Jeez!' Megan threw herself back in her chair, arms folded across her ample chest. 'OK, fine! The tossed salad! Do you think I can have a tossed salad?' she asked sarcastically, a trait learned at her mother's knee.

'Of course,' Alicia said with a big smile.

'Good choice, Megs,' Bess said, also smiling.

'Both of you – bite me!' Megan said, refusing to look at either of her sisters.

Turning to Alicia, Bess said, 'Speaking of Graham the retro-king, why aren't you out with him tonight? I mean, it *is* date night!'

'Yeah!' Megan pounced. 'Is there trouble in paradise?'

Alicia didn't answer, but her lower lip began to tremble. Quickly she got up, almost knocking over her chair, and made a fast exit to the restroom.

'What'd I say?' Megan asked, staring after her foster sister.

'What didn't you say?' Bess said with some disgust.

'You started it!' Megan said.

'Hi, Bess,' came a voice from behind her shoulder.

Bess whirled around, the smile already firmly planted on her lips. 'Well, hey, Logan!' she said. 'I didn't know you worked here!'

'Yeah, I've been here like over a year. I'm assistant manager on Sunday nights,' he said proudly.

'Wow. That's cool,' Bess said.

'Can I take y'all's drink orders?' he asked, a smile bringing out the dimples in his cheeks and the sparkle in his baby-blue eyes.

'Hey, Logan,' Megan said. 'I'm here at the table too, you know.'

He grinned. 'Hey, Megan. What do you want to drink?'

'Diet Coke.'

'Bess?'

'Real Coke, and a real Sprite for Alicia.'

'Yeah, I saw she was with y'all,' Logan said. 'Is she OK? Someone said they heard a girl crying in the ladies' room.'

'Ah, shit,' Megan said, tossing her napkin down on the table. 'I'll go. Bess, you know what we want. Just order.'

'Be nice!' Bess called to her sister's retreating back.

'When am I not nice?' Megan shot back, but noticed her sister wasn't paying a bit of attention to her. Megan sighed and headed to the restroom. Alicia was sitting at a stool by the vanity when Megan came in. 'Sorry,' Megan said. 'I didn't mean to upset you.'

Alicia nodded her head and dabbed at her eyes with a Kleenex. 'I know. It's just . . . it's just that . . .' And she burst into tears.

Megan moved to her and put an arm around her shoulders. 'It's OK, hon. Just let it out.'

'He's going back to UT in the fall,' she said between sobs.

'Graham?'

'Yes! And he thinks we should date other people—'

Megan sat down on the stool next to Alicia, her body stiff and her face turning red. 'Has that asshole been pressuring you for sex?'

'No!' Alicia said. 'Not really.' Sob, sob. 'Maybe a little.'

'You mean all the damn time?'

Alicia nodded her head.

'I'm calling Mom!' Megan announced and stood up.

Alicia stood up too, grabbing Megan's arm. 'Oh, God, no, Megs! Don't do that! I don't want Mom knowing about this! It would be awful!'

'He has no right—'

'If we're a couple I guess he does,' Alicia said, falling back down on the stool. 'If we were just a "normal" couple, this would surely be going on, right? So why is it weird that he wants to?'

'You *are* a normal couple!' Megan said. 'You *are not* related! Try to remember that.'

Alicia shook her head. 'Not in the eyes of

47

anyone who knows us. Not your parents or Grandma, but everybody at school thinks it's weird. I've tried to keep it quiet, but—'

'Yeah, I know – I told one of the twins and now it's all over school.'

'You didn't mean to,' Alicia said graciously. She sighed. 'But the thing is I think it's kinda weird, too. I mean I love him, but do I *love* him love him, or do I love him like a big brother?'

'You don't know?'

'I thought I did, but now I'm not so sure.'

'Ooo, gross.'

Alicia sighed again. 'Tell me about it.'

'So why are you so upset that he's going back to Austin for school? And that he wants y'all to date other people? I think that sounds like a good thing under the circumstances. This way you can find out if you *love* him love him, or just little-sister love him.'

Alicia swallowed a sob, then got up and went to the sink where she splashed cold water on her face and dabbed it dry with a paper towel.

'You're right, of course,' she said. 'But it's just . . . sad,' she said finally. 'Really, really sad.'

Megan sighed her own sigh and walked up to Alicia, putting her arms around her and hugging her. 'Yeah, it is. It's sad. I'm sorry.'

Meanwhile, after Megan left the table, Bess began giving Logan their food order. In the middle of it they both heard the front door of the restaurant slam open, and both turned to see what was going on. A young man, a big beefy blond wearing a serious frown, charged into the room. On seeing

48

Logan, he pointed at him and said simply, 'Outside! Now!'

Logan looked at Bess. 'Ah. I'll be . . . right back?' he said, as if not certain if he would or not. He set his order pad down on Bess's table and headed to the front door. As Logan drew close, the big beefy blond grabbed Logan's upper arm and pulled him out the door.

Not liking the look of this turn of events, Bess got up from the table and headed for the door herself.

Megan and Alicia came out of the restroom just in time to hear their sister scream and see the front door close behind her. Not missing a beat, both girls ran for the front door just in time to see their waiter, Logan, flat on the ground and their sister Bess riding the back of some guy they didn't know, flailing wildly at his head and shoulders.

Willis and I got back from dinner around eight. The house was glowing with light and looked quite welcoming, despite the 'ghost' that may or may not reside within. Unfortunately that welcome was shattered when we walked in the front door and saw Diamond Lovesy and Humphrey Hammerschultz in the living room regaling Miss Hutchins with yet another mediumesque display.

'I feel him,' Diamond whispered loudly. 'He's evil. So evil.' She was standing in the middle of the room, arms outstretched (I suppose to better feel all the evil), her eyes closed and her head tilted to the ceiling. I felt it was too bad her eyes were closed because she was missing the beauty

49

of the ornately carved metal ceiling, the crown molding and the light fixtures that had to be at least a hundred years old . . . OK, so I have a thing for old houses.

'Hello,' I said loudly, hoping to break the spell Diamond's shenanigans had produced. I got the desired result.

'Oh, hello, E.J.! And Willis. How was dinner?' Miss Hutchins asked.

'Excellent,' Willis said, walking further into the room and sitting down on the sofa next to our hostess. Humphrey already had settled himself in 'Willis's chair,' as he was wont to describe it. 'Thanks for the recommendation,' my husband said, smiling down at Miss Hutchins.

She smiled back and patted his hand – encouraging me that all had been forgiven for his earlier blunder. 'I'm so glad you enjoyed it.' She looked up at Diamond Lovesy, who still stood in the middle of the room, arms still outstretched, swaying slightly but no longer staring at the ceiling. She was looking at Willis, and that look was anything but welcoming. 'Miss Lovesy was attempting to channel my father,' she said. 'That means—'

'I've heard about it,' Willis said, and gave the medium the most insincere smile I'd ever seen cross my husband's face.

'Well, we haven't gotten much so far,' Miss Hutchins said to Willis as I found one of the armless stuffed chairs to plop into.

'We'll wait,' Willis said. 'Looking forward to it.'

Diamond's outstretched arms fell to her side,

and her head lowered as if she was studying the floor. She shook her head slowly from side to side. Then, looking up at Miss Hutchins, she said, 'I'm sorry. He's gone.'

'Oh, bother!' Miss Hutchins said. 'I really wanted to have a talk with him!' She frowned, and her lips tugged into a thin line. Pushing herself to her feet, she said, 'Well, I think it's time for a hot toddy, don't y'all?'

The 'hot toddy' consisted of the bottle of whiskey from the previous afternoon and five glasses. 'Do you have any wine?' I inquired.

'Oh, dear! Of course! I should have asked!' Miss Hutchins said, starting to push herself up from the table.

I beat her to it. 'Just tell me where it is,' I said.

'The white is in the refrigerator, of course, and the red is in the cupboard above the sink. The wine glasses—'

'That's OK,' I said. 'I'll just use the one you've already—'

'Of course not! These are high ball glasses! Let me get you a wine glass,' she said, again starting to push herself up. I, of course, was wishing I'd just drunk the damn whiskey.

'No, no, you sit. I'll find the wine glasses.'

'In the hutch in the dining room. Top right door,' she said.

And I was off in search of my goodies, leaving the four of them to devour the whiskey, which, I noticed when I returned, they'd done.

'Oh, I have another bottle! Uncle Herbert bought a whole case a week before he died. He was only able to drink about four bottles of it,' she said. 'Willis, dear, it's also in the hutch. Bottom right. You might want to bring two bottles.'

And so we sat and drank, and I noticed Humphrey Hammerschultz seemed to partake of more than his share. Diamond was limply drunk after about four glasses, while I wasn't far behind after three glasses of chilled white wine. After losing those thirty-five pounds, I find I get drunk faster. Who knew? Willis, the animal, sees that as a plus.

At around ten, both Diamond and I excused ourselves and helped each other up the stairs. An hour later, Willis woke me up when he came in the room by turning on the overhead light.

'Arugh!' I said, shielding my eyes while simultaneously staring daggers at my husband. 'Turn off that effing light!'

'God, you're a mean drunk,' he said.

'Don't make me hurt you!'

'Yeah, you and what army?' he said, crawling on the bed and attempting to kiss me. It felt more like he was licking me.

'You're drunk!' I accused.

'Hey, kettle, pot calling!' he said and grinned at me.

'So everybody's gone to bed?' I asked.

'Well, I helped Miss Hutchins to her room, but Humphrey insisted he had to stay downstairs and do some, as he put it, "recon."'

'What does that mean?' I asked.

Willis rolled off me and sat up, shrugging his shoulders. 'Hell if I know. The guy's weird. Even weirder with a little too much whiskey in his belly.'

'I bet we'll find him sound asleep on the sofa in the morning,' I said.

'Wouldn't be surprised,' Willis said and yawned. 'I'll brush my teeth in the morning.' He rolled over and began to snore.

Little did I know at the time that I was more prophetic than Diamond Lovesy. A little wrong, but closer than she'd gotten so far.

1935–1941

Edgar's deployment to Shanghai didn't start out well. He discovered seasickness, and lost the entire ten pounds he'd gained during boot camp. Although most trainees lost weight during boot camp, Edgar, who'd been forced into a habit of sporadic eating, discovered three square meals a day much to his liking. This did not continue on the long voyage to China. But once he arrived at the International Settlement outside of Shanghai, the seasickness disappeared and he was able to get back to his three squares a day. He also learned that, despite his overnight stays in the brig, and his less-than-stellar performance in boot camp, he had been assigned to the 4th Marine Regiment, one of the most sought-after assignments in the Marines. Edgar figured getting the 4th was a mistake, but one he saw no reason to rectify. Billets were converted schools, office buildings or private mansions. His platoon was housed in one of the latter, which Edgar figured was his due, after being deprived of the life he could have lived in the house on Post Oak Street back home in Peaceful.

There were other things he discovered about

53

his Shanghai duty that were even better than three meals a day and a nice billet: the U.S. dollar went a very long way, the Chinese and Russian girls were good to look at and better to bed, beer was cheap and, even as a private, Edgar could afford to hire a houseboy to take care of his gear. In fact, he was soon to learn that the Marines based in China – the China Marines – didn't have to polish their brass, mow the lawn, rake gravel or even keep their barracks clean – all this was done by servants, as were the thirty days a year they were supposed to have kitchen duty, otherwise known as KP.

The International Settlement consisted of American, British, Italian, Spanish, Portuguese and Dutch communities, with a French compound not far away. The Japanese had been part of that settlement until 1931, when they'd staged an explosion of Japan's South Manchuria Railway near Mukden. It was then that the Japanese invaded Manchuria. Edgar was regaled with stories of the war between the Chinese and Japanese that was observed by many Marines as they sat behind a three-and-a-half mile front line that had been barbwired and sandbagged with machine guns at the ready. But neither the Chinese nor the Japanese encroached on the International Settlement, and the 4th just had grandstand seats for the war.

It was an easy life for Edgar, one spent buying ivory, pearls and other extravagances he thought would sell well back in the States, seeing how many different women he could bed, and eventually finding his way into Shanghai proper for the *added spices of gambling, prostitution and his sin of choice, opium.*

But events put a damper on Edgar's blissful days in Shanghai. During his second year as a China Marine, the Chinese and Japanese were again locked in combat. A final offensive launched by the Japanese Army in October of 1937 led to China's retreat from Shanghai. This retreat left the International Settlement and the French Concession mere dots on the landscape of Japanese territory. Edgar had no choice now but to stay within the confines of the International Settlement, leading to a few problems with opium withdrawal.

Although the Allied forces within the settlement numbered at no more than 7,500 against the 300,000 Japanese now in residence in Shanghai, the settlement continued its daily routine. What was going on outside it held little interest for Edgar and his few cronies, most of whom, like Edgar, were drying out from opium abuse by becoming what was more acceptable: good old American drunks.

In 1939, during Edgar's fourth year as a China Marine, Japan's forces moved southward with the seizure of the Hainan Islands. The hostility of that attack, combined with repeated bombings and atrocities against civilian Chinese, led the U.S. Fleet to move from the American west coast to Pearl Harbor. Edgar didn't pay too much attention to this: he was more interested in something he'd heard from another jarhead stationed at the Peking Marines' summer camp at Peitaiho, which overlooked the white sand beaches and the red bluffs at the seaward end of the Great Wall of China. There was an archaeological dig going on there that produced the remains of a 500,000-year-old Peking man's bones. These remains were to be shipped back to the States in November of 1941, the same month the 4th Marines left China for the Philippines. They were never seen again. It was never proved that Private Edgar Hutchins was in any way involved.

Four

BACK HOME

Megan ran up to the big, beefy blond man who was trying desperately to remove Bess from his back, and kneed him in the privates. He grunted, doubled over, and Bess fell off him. Alicia ran up and slammed her fist into the guy's eye and he fell to the pavement, at which point Megan tried kicking him in the head, but having sandals on managed only to hurt her toes. Megan was limping, Alicia was grimacing and holding the hand she'd used to cold-cock the man, and Bess was up but rubbing the hip she fell on when the guy tossed her off his back. Meanwhile, the guy rolled over, got to his feet and ran for a white pick-up truck that had the motor still running. He jumped in and took off, laying rubber as he did so.

Bess was already kneeling by Logan when Megan and Alicia turned around.

'Is he hurt?' Alicia asked, kneeling down on the other side.

Logan carefully shook his head. 'Not really. My pride, maybe.' Then he grinned. 'But I gotta say, if I'm gonna be saved by girls, I'm glad it was you three.'

Bess helped him sit up. His lip was bleeding and his left eye was already beginning to swell.

'You need to put some ice on that eye,' Bess said.

'Come on, get up,' Megan said, extending her

57

arm. Logan took it and between the three of them they managed to get him to his feet.

Seeing that he was still slightly unsteady, Bess put one of his arms around her shoulders to help him walk, but she was so much shorter he had to lean down to accomplish this, which didn't help his dizziness.

'Oh, for heaven's sake!' Megan said, moving her smaller sister aside and instead inserting her own shoulders, which were only an inch or two below Logan's. 'Let me.'

Seeing Bess's crestfallen face, Alicia went up to Logan's other side and grabbed his arm. 'I think he'll need both of us. Where to?' she asked Logan.

'Back door,' he said. 'Do you think that putting a cold steak on the eye like you see in old movies really works? 'Cause we got plenty of beef in the kitchen.'

'Well, I should hope so,' Megan said as they moved him toward the back of the restaurant.

Bess led the way and opened the door when they got there, ushering in the trio.

'What the hell?' said a man standing at a flat top burner that held several steaks at differing temperatures. He ran up to Logan, yelling over his shoulder to a woman at another station to watch the steaks. 'What happened?' the man asked, taking Logan from the two girls and setting him down on a folding chair. 'And you girls? What happened to y'all?' he asked, studying Alicia's swollen hand, Megan's limp and swollen toes, and Bess's limp.

Bess spoke up. 'I was outside getting something from the van and this guy starting hitting on me, and Logan must have seen it from the window, because he came out and tried to talk the guy into leaving me alone, but the guy just went nuts and started whaling on him—'

'And Alicia and I saw it from the window and ran out to help.' Megan shrugged.

'But Logan was the real hero,' Bess said, smiling and clasping a hand on Logan's shoulder. He grimaced from pain and she let go.

'Where is this guy now?' the man demanded.

'Long gone, Cam,' Logan said.

'Henry,' the man named Cam called out. 'Bring three more folding chairs – quick.' Henry did, and Cam got the girls to sit down. 'I'm so sorry this happened to you,' he said to Bess, 'but I'm not surprised Logan came to your rescue.' He smiled at his waiter. 'He's one of the good guys.'

Bess smiled up at Logan. 'Yes, he is,' she said, while Alicia beamed and Megan rolled her eyes.

'Let's get a cheap steak for that eye,' Cam said.

As Cam walked off, Logan smiled at Bess. 'I guess they still do use beef,' he said. 'But I wish you hadn't told him all that. I was ready to say I fell down.'

'This sounds more like the truth,' Bess said.

Cam came back with a small steak and placed it on Logan's swollen eye. 'You need to go home, kid,' he said. 'But I don't think you should drive—'

'That's OK,' Bess said. 'We'll take him.'

Both her sisters looked at her, Megan glaring. 'No,' Logan said, 'y'all were here for dinner—'

'Give me your order,' Cam said, 'and I'll have it ready for take-out.'

Bess grinned and recited their order, complete with desserts.

'It's on the house,' Cam said. 'It's the least I can do after what happened.'

'Oh, no!' Bess started, but Megan pulled her arm.

'Thank you so much,' Megan said with a bright smile. 'But I'm afraid my sister got the order wrong. I had the porterhouse.'

I'm not sure what the time was when it woke me, but sometime in the wee hours. It was a grating sound with a plop at the end: *grrrrrrrrrr-plop, grrrrrrrrrr-plop, grrrrrrrrrr-plop.* I hit my husband in the gut, which is my emergency maneuver. He grunted, not unlike the sound in the hallway.

'What the—' he started.

'Shhhh, listen.'

The *grrrrrrrrrr-plop* was moving away from our doorway, going down the hall toward the stairs.

'Daddy?' Willis asked.

'I doubt it!' I said and threw the bedclothes off me. Unfortunately I'd only worn my underwear to bed, so it took a moment to find my robe, and even longer for Willis to find his slippers. I was willing to go barefoot, but Willis has a great fear of athlete's foot and rarely goes barefoot. I've even caught him in our shower wearing flip-flops.

Ignoring my husband and his search for adequate footwear, I ran to our bedroom door and opened it. Despite the small butterfly lamp lit on the small trestle table in the hall, I couldn't see what had been causing the noise. But I could still hear it going down the stairs: *grrrrrrrrrr-plop, grrrrrrrrrr-plop.* Willis bumped into me as we both stared into the hallway.

'It's going downstairs,' I said.

'So follow it!' he said, elbowing me in the back.

'You follow it!' I said, trying to get behind him.

He pushed me into the hall. 'Come on, Eeg, you've faced worse than this!'

Still I hung back. 'And how do you know that? We don't know what *this* is, for God's sake! You're the biggest, you go first!' I said, pulling his arm.

My husband grinned at me. 'I'm not sure I like this little-girl-lost side of you. I prefer my big, brave mama bear.'

'Shut up!' I said and shoved him toward the staircase.

When we got there, we could see nothing, despite the Tiffany lamp on the small telephone table next to the staircase. But we could still hear it, moving toward the front door.

'Go!' I whispered loudly. 'It's gonna get out!'

'*It's?*' he said. 'What's with *it*?'

'Go!'

He went – gingerly, but he went. Before we got down the stairs, we heard the front door open and close. I rushed past Willis, swung it open and stared out at the night. Nothing. Absolutely nothing. I shut the door. Willis rushed up behind me and almost knocked me over.

'Now you hurry!' I said, both hands on his chest as I pushed him back.

'Hey, me going first was your idea!' he said.

'I guess I didn't realize you were such a weenie!'

'I'll show you weenie!' he said and grabbed me in a manly hug. I know these things – I write romance novels.

I giggled and pushed him away. Miss Hutchins

certainly believed in night lights. There was another burning in the living room. On a table next to the sofa.

The sofa on which I had earlier declared we'd find Humphrey Hammerschultz asleep in the morning. Well, it was sort of morning, but he wasn't so much *on* the sofa, as half falling off, and he wasn't so much asleep as, well, dead.

BACK HOME

'Is there someplace y'all can take me other than my house? My mom will freak when she sees my face. I can call her and say I've gotta stay late and come in early. Something like that. Let this heal up,' Logan said, riding shotgun while Bess drove. Even though it was Alicia's turn, she had recognized what was going on between Bess and Logan, handed her sister the keys and quickly crawled into the back seat with Megan.

'You'll come home with us,' Bess said with some authority. 'Right, girls?'

'Sure!' Alicia said with a big smile.

'Whatever,' Megan said, sniffing the air. 'God, can you smell that porterhouse? I might die before we ever get home!'

She didn't. Bess pulled into the driveway and up to the back door, hoping Elena Luna, their cop neighbor, wasn't looking in their direction. She hustled Logan into the great room while her sisters brought in the sacks of food. There was even a little one marked 'Logan,' that his friend Cam had packed just for him.

'What do you think that is?' Bess asked as she helped unload the food.

'My nightly hamburger,' he said. 'I got burned out on steaks the second week I worked there. Now I alternate between fried chicken and a hamburger.'

Megan had unloaded her own food and was already sitting on a stool at the bar cutting into her oversized porterhouse. 'God, who could ever get tired of steak? You're obviously not a Texan!' she said.

'Am too,' Logan said. 'Born in Houston, moved here when I was two.'

Megan was no longer paying attention to anyone or anything other than her plate.

'So,' Bess started, her head bent to the task of removing food from bags – anything not to look directly at Logan. 'What was that all about tonight? Who was that guy?'

She glanced up at that point, only to see Logan looking anywhere but at her. 'Nobody,' he finally said.

Unfortunately Megan heard that. 'What nobody? Nobody comes along and beats the crap out of you?'

Logan shrugged, and Bess said, 'Megs, pay attention to your food or someone else might take a bite.'

'Not on my watch,' Megan said, and hunched over her plate to better shovel food into her face.

'I'm just glad you're OK,' Alicia said. 'Well, sort of OK.'

'Why don't we eat?' Logan suggested, a big, maybe phony, smile on his face. 'The food Cam makes is really good. But you don't want to eat it cold.'

So Bess and Alicia set the food at certain places, Alicia painstakingly placing Logan's hamburger at the far end of the bar, and Bess's sirloin right next to him. Her own fillet she placed next to Megan's spot. She couldn't help noticing the major size difference in Megan's porterhouse and her own fillet. She leaned toward Megan and speared an already cut piece of Megan's steak.

'Hey!' Megan cried, aiming her own fork at Alicia's hand. Alicia moved the hand with the fork and meat quickly to her mouth, outmaneuvering her foster sister.

'How many times has Mom told you that Miss Manners said you only cut up more than one piece of meat for children? It's your own fault.'

'I'm still a child – officially,' Megan said.

'Damn. This porterhouse is good. Can I have an—'

'Only if you want to lose a hand!'

Ignoring her sisters, Bess asked Logan, 'Are you in trouble? I mean, that guy seemed really mad. Did you do something, you know, that you shouldn't have?'

What was left of Logan's face that wasn't already a different color turned red.

'Like what?' he asked, not looking at her.

Bess sighed. 'I don't know. Like maybe took some weed or something on consignment and didn't pay him?'

Logan snorted and finally looked at Bess. 'You watch too much TV,' he said.

It was Bess's turn to blush. 'Then what?' she said, finally making full eye contact. And what eyes! The blue of the sky on a summer's day,

64

the blue of a becalmed Caribbean, the blue of a sleeping smurf . . .

Breaking eye contact, Logan looked down the line of the bar at Bess's sisters. They were busy sniping at each other, paying no attention to Logan and Bess. He sighed, then said, 'Remember Harper Benton?'

'Yes, of course. Although I haven't seen her since winter break.'

'She dropped out,' Logan said.

'You're kidding! That's so . . . so . . .'

'Trashy?' Logan supplied.

'Well, certainly ill-advised,' Bess countered. 'But what has that got to do with that guy tonight?'

'That was her brother, Tucker.'

Bess shook her head. 'I still don't see the connection. What do you have to do with Harper dropping out of school?'

'He thinks it's my fault,' Logan said, again looking down at his plate.

'Why?'

Logan sighed and looked up. 'Because she's pregnant.'

I went to awaken Miss Hutchins while Willis dialed 911. The old lady's room was warmer than the rest of the house – almost stifling. I saw a red light shining on her dressing table and, getting closer to it, realized it was emitting hot air. From what I could see through the open doorway, the room was well – if not old fashionably – furnished, with a huge sleigh bed, the ornately carved dressing table and a matching

65

chest of drawers, and everything was covered with tatted and crocheted doilies. Unfortunately the room smelled of rose scent and Ben-Gay. Not a pleasant mixture.

I touched Miss Hutchins lightly on the arm and she awoke instantly, not the least disoriented. 'E.J.,' she said. She glanced at the digital clock on her bedside table. It read four a.m. 'What's happened?'

'There's been an accident,' I said.

'Move,' she said, and swung her legs over the side of the bed. The bed was possibly two feet off the ground, and her bare feet didn't touch the floor. 'My stool,' she said, indicating a small tapestry-covered stool that I'd inadvertently shoved to the side. I moved it under her feet. She lowered her toes then stood up. 'My slippers,' she said. I found them where I'd shoved them under the bed. I wasn't going to win any prizes for grace tonight.

I helped her step down from the stool and into her slippers.

Squaring her shoulders, she looked up at me and said, 'Now. What is it?'

'Humphrey Hammerschultz appears to be dead,' I said.

'Oh, bother,' she said. 'I didn't like him much, but this is just uncalled for. You said accident. Was it? Or was it foul play?'

Remembering the sight of his head's unnatural bent, I would put my first bet on a broken neck. I didn't see how one could break one's neck by falling off a sofa that was less than a foot off the floor. But it wasn't my place to say. 'We'll leave that to the police,' I told her. 'Willis is calling them now.'

'Have you awakened his partner?' Miss Hutchins asked as she headed for the door.

'I thought we should let her sleep it off,' I said.

She nodded. 'Good. She'd just muck things up anyway.' With her hand on the knob of her bedroom door, she turned and looked at me. 'You know Daddy had something to do with this, don't you? Or are you still trying to deny what you don't understand?'

I just shrugged my shoulders, not able to get the sound of the *grrrrrrrrr-plop*ping that had led to our discovery out of my head.

BACK HOME

Bess realized she hadn't taken a breath since Logan's announcement. She sucked in air and looked at anything other than the boy sitting next to her, while avoiding her sisters' eyes. 'I didn't know y'all were dating,' she finally said. She felt the weight of the world on her shoulders and knew it would be a long while before she could look at another boy with affection. Maybe a really long while – like forever. At that moment, she vowed to be a terrific aunt to her nieces and nephews, and to find herself a fulfilling career. She was glad she was a good student; there could be a scholarship in her future. To a campus as far away from Black Cat Ridge as she could get. She could feel tears gathering behind her eyes and willed them to go away.

'We had two dates,' Logan said. 'And her brother met me. But I swear to God, Bess, I never touched her. Never even kissed her!'

Bess took her first long look at Logan. Those

blue eyes, so honest, so trustworthy – or were he and his eyes just very good liars? 'Then why would he think . . .'

'Because Harper must have told him so. God only knows who the real father is. On our last date, way before Christmas, she left me in the theater to go to the bathroom and never came back. I'll bet she left with whoever the real father is that night.'

'Did she say anything to you at school?' Bess asked.

'Yeah, on the Monday – the date was on Friday night – on the Monday she acted like everything was cool. Even asked where we were going the next weekend!'

'What did you say?'

'I told her there wasn't going to be a next weekend. That I didn't like the way she ditched me at the movies.'

'What did she say?' Bess asked, beginning to buy his story.

'She goes, "Oh, I'm so sorry! I got sick and had to leave!"' Logan rolled his eyes. 'As if,' he said.

'And now she says she's having your baby?'

'First I heard about it was tonight when her brother made me go outside with him. He goes, "You're gonna marry her right now!" Like that. And I go, "Huh?" 'cause I've got no idea what the hell – sorry, heck – he's talking about!'

Bess rubbed Logan's arm. 'There are paternity tests,' she said.

'You can't have that done until after the baby's born,' Alicia said.

68

Bess and Logan quickly turned toward the sound of Alicia's voice. Somehow, they'd forgotten they weren't alone.

'I know that because one of the girls at one of the foster homes I was at got pregnant and said it was the father of the house who'd done it. But nothing could be done and the social worker didn't believe her. She moved her anyway, and about six months later we all were moved out of that house. Pretty sure the paternity test was done – as was the father of the house. If you know what I mean.'

'Everyone knows what you mean,' Megan said from her end of the bar. 'So, Logan, who'd you knock up?'

NOVEMBER, 1941–DECEMBER, 1941

On Thursday, November 27, 1941, Edgar and the rest of the first element of the 4th Marines left Shanghai on a gray and gloomy morning. Edgar was not happy to be boarding yet another boat to be taken to yet another ship for yet another sea voyage – albeit a short one, although he had no way of knowing that at the time. Only high-ranking officers knew where the ship was headed.

The ship, the SS President Madison, *docked at Subic Bay, Philippines, three days later. Edgar did not make many friends aboard ship – actually, he made a few enemies. Poker was the game of choice aboard the* President Madison, *and Edgar had honed his poker-playing skills (and learned a few not so kosher tricks) after four mostly leisurely years in Shanghai. No one knew how short their trip was going to be, so it was* with some shock that the other participants watched Edgar Hutchins leave the ship with over a thousand dollars of their hard-earned money.

Edgar's accommodation once he reached the Philippines wasn't exactly the mansion he'd shared in Shanghai. No, this time his billet was a tent he shared with several other Marines on the rifle range of the Olongapo Navy Yard. Unfortunately, some of those in his tent were the same men he'd beaten at poker on the ship. Since Marines believed wholeheartedly that one good beating deserved another, Edgar emerged from his tent the second day in the Philippines with two black eyes, a busted lip and bruises in places his uniform artfully hid. Luckily for Edgar, he was moved to the First Separate Marine Battalion that was based on Cavite Navy Yard. He was one of seven hundred who were organized both as a defense and an infantry battalion, and were armed with three-inch dual purpose guns, three-inch anti-aircraft guns and fifty-caliber machine guns. Although Edgar had never done well at the gun range back on Parris Island, he found an affinity for the fifty-caliber machine gun.

Training went on for several days, but on December 8, 1941, while Edgar was walking to the mess hall, a major rode by in the side car of a motorcycle, shouting, 'War is declared! War is declared!'

Edgar couldn't help thinking now would be a good time to try to make it home, but the First Battalion was ordered to move to Mariveles, where Edgar was too busy to even think of a way to get out of what he assumed was going to become a hellish situation. He was ordered to prepare positions in the surrounding jungle, and ended up working ten to twelve hours a day unloading the many barges bringing in rations, ammunition and equipment. The next day, one of the brass ordered that the regiment be fed only twice a day, which made Edgar consider his idea of going AWOL more seriously.

Although the Japanese were bombing U.S. airfields and the capital of Manila, the Marine positions at Mariveles were not immediately attacked. Unfortunately an average of six air-raid alarms a day tended to shake up the Marines, whose commander ordered them to scatter at the sound of an air-raid siren. This order had to be rescinded as no work could be done. So Edgar and his fellows continued to work.

On the tenth of December, unbeknownst to the Marines in Cavite, two Japanese combat teams came ashore in northern Luzon, not far from the base at Cavite. They seized airfields for their army to support more landings of troops. But civilian workers continued to come into the Navy yard. The only sign of war at that time was an air-raid trench in the yard of the admiral's head-quarters. Only the anti-aircraft weapons had been revetted. There were now four three-inch anti-aircraft guns mounted at the ammunition depot in the yard, as well as numerous fifty-caliber machine guns mounted around the yard – one of which was to be manned by Edgar Hutchins.

At a little past noon on the tenth, Edgar and his company heard the droning of numerous aircraft engines, followed by the air-raid siren.

71

They all ran outside to look into the sky and watched as fifty-four aircraft in three large 'V' formations approached the camp. There was some confusion – first all Marines assumed the planes were Army Air Corps, but when they started dropping what was at first believed to be leaflets it wasn't long before the company realized the planes were Japanese and what they were in fact dropping were bombs. Since there were no completed trenches or any formal shelters available, the Marines, sailors and civilian personnel crouched under the nearest cover.

The Marines ran to their stations at the anti-aircraft positions and the fifty-caliber machine-gun stations. The anti-aircraft guns did no damage as the planes were too high, and the fifty-caliber machine guns were of little use. But even so, people were too keyed up to notice that one fifty-caliber gun was not manned. Edgar Hutchins was cowering under the veranda of the mess hall, where he remained huddled.

The barrage of bombs continued, starting fires all over the base. The Marines not on duty, still in their billets, were called to draw ammunition and to get outside to fire on the enemy aircraft. This unfortunately happened just as Edgar was attempting to sneak into the billet, so he too was back on duty. He stood in line at the quartermaster's office to receive ammunition. As the bombs continued to fall, the Marines dove for cover, then returned to the line, a procedure that continued through the afternoon. As the bombs struck close to them, Edgar could hear them coming down and hunched his shoulders, as if

72

to keep one from going down the back of his neck. But the small arms efforts proved fruitless as the buildings restricted the fields of fire. By the time the Japanese planes left, over one thousand civilians were dead and over five hundred injured. As the hospital had received a direct hit, a makeshift aid station was set up in the base library to treat the injured.

The Marines were evacuated out of the Navy yard and taken by truck to a site on the road leading to Manila, where the battalion set up camp. Edgar was one of the Marines sent back to the Navy yard the next day to bury the civilian dead. A bulldozer was used to dig a trench and Edgar was one of a working party on burial duty. Over two hundred and fifty corpses were buried in a mass grave. The only thing that bothered Edgar about this assignment – other than the hard work, which he was definitely opposed to – was the smell.

The Cavite area was hit again on the nineteenth of December. The bombers hit the radio towers and the fuel depot. Fuel drums stored in the hospital compound were hit, forcing an evacuation of the wounded.

On Christmas Eve, the Japanese again struck with a major force, their Sixteenth Division, and landed just sixty miles from Manila. It was at this point that General Douglas MacArthur knew the situation was hopeless. He withdrew all American and Philippine forces to the peninsula of Bataan, where they would make a final stand.

Five

The police chief of Peaceful, Texas, a small man named Rigsby Cotton whose cowboy hat was too big for his head, was the first to show up, along with his one police officer, a very young woman introduced as Mary Mays. There didn't seem to be a lot going on in Peaceful that night. Or maybe ever. Second to show up was the sheriff of Toledo County, Omar Gonzales, a much larger man than his townie counterpart, who wore his beige uniform and beige Stetson well. He had two deputies with him, neither of whom were introduced. They stayed stationed at the front door, as if on sentry duty.

'Miz Hutchins,' the sheriff said, elbowing past the police chief. 'What seems to be the problem?'

'As I was telling Rigsby, *Sheriff,*' she said, with a sort of sarcastic emphasis on the 'sheriff,' 'we have a dead body in the living room. He's a guest by the name of Humphrey Hammerschultz. If you two will behave, I'll lead you in there.'

'Yes, ma'am,' Rigsby Cotton said, just a split second before Omar Gonzales said the same thing.

I went with her as she led the authorities into the living room. Humphrey Hammerschultz was still in the same position, his head and arms aiming for the floor, his oversized abdomen and large ass anchoring his body on the sofa.

'Who moved the body?' Gonzales asked.

74

'My husband and I found him,' I said, speaking up for the first time.

'And who the hell are you?' Gonzales said, not the least unkindly, although the words were not particularly kind.

'Jeez, Omar,' Rigsby Cotton said.

'My husband and I are also guests,' I said. 'My name is E.J. Pugh. As I was about to say—'

'What does the E.J. stand for?' Gonzales interrupted.

'Omar, for God's sake, let the lady talk!' Cotton said, turning a mean eye on his colleague.

'I said y'all could come in if you behaved! I don't think either of you is behaving!' Miss Hutchins said with just a little heat.

'Sorry, Miz Hutchins,' Cotton said, hanging his head.

'Me, too,' Gonzales said, although his stance said he was anything but sorry.

'Ma'am,' Cotton said, addressing me, 'please go on.'

Gonzales glared at him, but Cotton didn't even look his way.

'I was just going to say,' I said after heaving a giant sigh, 'that my husband and I found him in this position when we walked in here.'

'Seeing that it's almost five o'clock in the morning, *ma'am*,' Gonzales said, and I do believe the 'ma'am' was said with some sarcasm, 'what were you and your husband doing down here?'

I looked at Miss Hutchins. I hadn't told her about the *grrrrrrrrrr-plop* as yet. Would she want me to? After a slight pause, I decided to be as honest as possible without saying too much. I'm

75

good at that – just like my neighbor, Elena Luna, police sergeant for the Codderville police department. So I said, 'I heard a sound in the hallway outside our room. It woke me up, then I woke up my husband, and we decided to see what it was. But when we got to our door, the sound was going down the stairs and, by the time we got there, it was already out the door.'

'The sound was out the door?' Gonzales repeated with a sneer.

'Ma'am, what kind of sound was it?' Police Chief Cotton asked.

I looked at Miss Hutchins, whose eyes were big. Then she narrowed them and nodded her head slightly. I sighed again and said, 'It was sort of a *grrrrrrrrrr-plop.*'

'*Grrrrrrrrrr-plop?*' Cotton repeated.

'Yes,' I said. 'Like someone dragging something down the hall.'

'And what was that something?' Gonzales asked, again with the sneer. I was beginning to think I wasn't Sheriff Gonzalez's favorite person – but then again he was rapidly heading to the top of my shit-list.

'Like I just said, *Sheriff*,' I said, using the same sarcastic emphasis Miss Hutchins had used only moments before, 'we didn't *see* anything. We just heard the noise but it was gone by the time we got there.'

'We, you say?' Gonzales said. 'And where is this mythical husband of yours?'

'I'm right here,' Willis said, coming in the room carrying a small tray with what was left of the whiskey and the white wine I'd been drinking earlier. Two shot glasses and a small wine glass also adorned the tray. 'And if you insist on my mythology, please call me Zeus. I've always wanted to be Zeus.' He set the tray down on the coffee table and said, 'Sorry, gentlemen, ma'am,' nodding at Chief Cotton's patrol officer, 'but there's not enough left for y'all to imbibe. Although you're both on duty anyway, right?'

'Nobody should be *imbibing* any alcohol right now, Mr . . .'

'Pugh,' Willis said. 'Willis Pugh.'

'What were y'all doing down here at such an ungodly hour?' Gonzales demanded.

Willis straightened his shoulders – and magnificent shoulders they were too. 'I think my wife just told you all that. But I will disagree with her on one issue – the sound was more of a *rrrrrrrrrr-thump.*'

'You're totally wrong,' I said to my husband.

'No, *you* are,' he said.

'OK, OK,' Chief Cotton asked. 'Can any of y'all tell me anything about this guy? Other than his name?'

Willis and I turned as one to Miss Hutchins. It was up to her to spill the ghostly beans, as it were.

Miss Hutchins followed Willis's lead and squared her shoulders, standing as tall as a five foot even woman of a certain age could. 'Mr Hammerschultz was a psychic detective. He and his partner—'

'Bullshit!' Gonzales said. 'What is this horse-shit?'

'Omar, there are ladies present!' Chief Cotton chastised. 'Sorry, ladies. You started to mention his partner, Miz Hutchins?'

'Yes, Diamond Lovesy, she's—'

Gonzales let out a bark of a laugh. 'You've got to be fuckin' with me!'

'Omar!'

Gonzales just shook his head and gave Cotton the floor. 'And where is this Miz Lovely?'

'No,' Miss Hutchins corrected. 'Lovesy. L-o-v-e-s-y.'

'And she's a psychic detective too?' Chief Cotton asked.

'No, she's a medium.'

'Ma'am?' Chief Cotton said, cocking his head to one side like an inquisitive bird.

'A medium,' Miss Hutchins said, speaking slowly and succinctly. 'She can feel if spirits are in the house and can sometimes contact the dead and let them speak through her.'

'Well, ain't that grand?' said Gonzales. 'And you buy this bullshit, Miz Hutchins?'

Again, the old lady stiffened her body. 'I do believe there are spirits in this house, and they're not all benign.'

Ignoring her, Gonzales turned to Rigsby Cotton. 'Well, now we have it,' he said. 'The rumors are true – she's nuttier than a fruitcake.'

'Omar, this is my jurisdiction, being as it's in the city limits and all, and I'm gonna have to ask you and your men to vacate the premises immediately,' Chief Cotton said.

Gonzales barked out another laugh. 'With pleasure. Hope you find the ghost that offed this guy!' he said, and went up to his two men at the front door, slapped them both on the back and laughed long and hard. The two men managed to laugh with him, although their hearts didn't seem to be in it.

After the door closed behind the sheriff and his men, Chief Cotton turned back to Miss Hutchins. 'Ma'am, where is this Miz Lovesy now?'

The old lady pointed up the staircase. 'Upstairs. Asleep. She drank a great deal tonight – excuse me, last night, and she's probably still passed out.'

Chief Cotton nodded his head. 'Were they – excuse me, ma'am, but I gotta ask – were Miz Lovesy and Mr Hammer . . .'

'Schultz,' all three of us said in unison.

'Mr Hammerschultz – were they staying together in the same room?'

'Oh, good heavens, no!' Miss Hutchins said with some indignation. 'They weren't married!'

'So could I get a look in Mr Hammerschultz's room?' he asked.

'Of course,' she said.

'Chief, Hammerschultz never went upstairs tonight,' Willis said. 'E.J. and I saw him getting very comfortable on the sofa as we went upstairs. He'd also had a great deal to drink.'

'Still and all,' the chief said.

'E.J., dear, would you mind taking Rigsby to Humphrey's room? I just can't face those stairs right now,' Miss Hutchins said.

'Of course,' I said, and turned to Rigsby Cotton. 'Chief?' I said, and headed for the stairs.

BACK HOME

Logan quickly tried to defend himself against Megan's question, but Bess interrupted. 'Megan! Enough! Logan didn't do anything! Harper lied!'

'Harper Benton?' Alicia inquired. 'We were on the same volleyball team last semester. She's very sweet! I just can't imagine her doing such a thing!'

'Humph,' Megan said. 'Harper's always thought she was hot stuff.'

'That's not true—' Alicia started, but Bess interrupted.

'Enough!' she said. 'Why are we arguing about Harper Benton's worthiness? She obviously lied to her brother about who . . . ah . . . you know . . .'

'Knocked her up?' Megan provided.

'Did the deed?' Alicia suggested.

'Whatever. She obviously lied,' Bess said.

'Maybe Logan's the one who's lying,' Megan suggested.

Bess stood up, hands on hips and glared at her sister. 'Megan Pugh! How dare—'

'No, no,' Logan said, also standing up. 'Megan has every right to say that. I mean, y'all don't really know me all that well. I could be an ax murderer for all you know.' He sank back down on his bar stool. 'But I'm not. And don't tell any of the guys this, but I . . . you know, I never, well . . .'

'You're a virgin?' Megan supplied.

Logan's face was defensive as he said, 'I wouldn't say that exactly! Jeez!'

'Have you ever had sexual relations with another person?' Megan demanded.

Logan's face began turning several shades of crimson. 'That depends on what you mean by sexual relations,' he said.

'Oh, for the love of God!' Megan said, then made an impolite gesture with the index finger and thumb of one hand while poking it with the index finger of the other hand.

Although it would have seemed impossible to an observer, Logan's face brightened in hue. 'Ah, no,' he finally said. 'I've done some heavy petty,' he said in his own defense, 'but never, you know, that.'

Bess, also several shades of crimson, still standing with hands on her hips said, 'Well, Megan, are you satisfied?'

Megan shrugged her shoulders. 'He could be lying now. We don't know.'

'Well, I do,' Alicia said, getting up to stand next to Logan. 'No boy would admit to that unless it were true!'

'Are you saying Graham's done the nasty with some girl we don't know about?' Megan demanded, her eyes lighting up with the chance of good gossip to come.

'Megan,' Alicia said, teeth clenched, 'I'm never speaking to you again!' With that she stormed from the room, her angry footsteps being heard as she stomped upstairs.

'What'd I say?' Megan asked.

Humphrey Hammerschultz's room was a complete mess. Clothes were strewn across it and his bedclothes were at the foot of the bed in a heap, possibly from an earlier nap since it was quite obvious he'd never gone to bed that night. Willis and I stood in the doorway of the room while Chief Cotton and Officer Mays went in. Using a pen, Chief Cotton picked up certain articles of clothing, put them back down then picked up others. Toiletries were scattered atop the dressing table, some lids not on properly. I worried about damage to the patina of the wood. I know, I know, a man was dead downstairs and I was worried about the antiques. Let's face it: I've seen a lot of dead bodies in my time, but not that many really good antiques.

'Mary, take a picture of the top of the dressing table then clean that mess up before it hurts the wood,' Chief Cotton said, making me feel less guilt over my earlier thought.

'Yes, sir,' the officer said and pulled her cell phone out of the Sam Brown belt she wore around her slender hips. She took several shots from different angles, then set about clearing away the toiletries. I went into the bathroom across the hall where I'd found cleaning supplies earlier when Diamond and I had been getting their rooms ready, and found some Pledge and some rags. I went back and handed them to Officer Mays.

'Thanks,' she said, smiling at me. She was a pretty young woman, probably in her mid-twenties, with pale, natural-looking blonde hair, saucer-like green eyes and a smile that would make any orthodontist proud.

'Can I help?' I asked.

She shook her head, although the smile remained. 'The chief doesn't like civilians in his crime scenes.'

'This isn't the crime scene,' I reminded her.

She shrugged. 'Better not,' she said and headed to the dressing table to clean up the mess.

The chief got up from where he'd been squatting, checking to see what was under the bedclothes scattered so haphazardly on the floor. By the look on his face when he stood up, I could only assume he found nothing.

''Fraid we're gonna have to wake up Miz Lovesy,' he said. 'Miz Pugh? Would you do the honors? I don't wanna scare the woman.'

'Certainly, Chief,' I said, and headed across the hall to Diamond Lovesy's room, which was next to the bathroom. I knocked then tried the door, but it was locked. I looked back at the chief.

'Just keep on knocking,' he said.

So I did. I knocked four times before I heard a bleary reply. 'What! Humphrey, if that's you, I'm gonna kill you!' came a gravelly voice as the door was flung open.

Seeing me standing there, she looked surprised, then frowned. Looking beyond me to Willis then the chief, who was clad in civilian clothes, appeared to tell her nothing, but seeing Mary Mays in her uniform brought her up short. Her hand shot to her throat and she said, 'What's wrong?' I couldn't help noticing the Minnie-Mouse voice was totally absent.

The chief stepped forward. 'Miz Lovesy, ma'am, my name is Rigsby Cotton, and I'm the police chief of Peaceful. May we come in for a moment, ma'am?'

'I haven't done anything!' she said, her eyes going slightly wild. I had to wonder if she was still somewhat drunk. Or if she was afraid her con was coming to a bad end.

'No, ma'am, it's nothing like that,' the chief said. He stepped into the room as Diamond opened the door further.

Willis and I started to step through, but Officer

Mays smiled at us kindly, held up a hand and shut the door in our faces. All I could think was: how rude!

BACK HOME

Bess just shook her head. 'Megan . . .' she started, but couldn't really find the words. Finally she said, 'Just eat your food.'

'Jeez, that's what I've been trying to do! But then all this drama started!' she said.

'She's right,' Logan said, smiling down at Bess. 'No more drama. I'm starved.'

Megan, who'd been eating a lot longer than the others, finished first. She got up and stretched. 'I think I'll save my dessert for breakfast,' she said and turned, heading up the stairs.

Bess started to call out to remind her sister to take her plate into the kitchen, but realizing she was soon to be totally alone with Logan, she decided she could do it herself. When she and Logan finished their dinner, he helped her clean off the bar and put Alicia's food, still only half-eaten, in foil and into the refrigerator.

'Hope you don't mind sleeping on the sofa,' Bess said when they finished in the kitchen. 'The one in the living room is more comfortable to sleep on than this one,' she said, indicating the sofa in the large family room that was part of what they called 'the great room,' which included the kitchen and breakfast room. She knew she could easily put him in her brother Graham's room upstairs, now unoccupied as Graham was living with their grandmother in the neighboring town of Codderville to give a little distance

84

between him and Alicia – their parents using the distance as a new-fangled chastity belt. Bess thought having Logan in the downstairs living room would cause the same problems for her. She had an uneasy feeling that Logan being only a room away would be too much temptation. 'And that way you can sleep in. We tend to make a racket in the kitchen in the mornings.'

'Oh, I'm used to waking up early,' he said with a smile. 'And the sofa's fine. Either one. I'll go where you put me.'

'Well, let me get a pillow and a blanket.'

He took her hand and led her to the great room sofa. 'Can we just sit and talk for a minute?' he asked her.

'Sure,' Bess said, feeling her face getting hot and wishing she had the ability to control such things.

They sat side by side on the sofa, both looking straight ahead. He had let go of her hand when they reached their destination. For a long moment, no one said anything, then Logan spoke.

'I want you to know I was telling the truth earlier,' he said. 'I'll swear on a stack of Bibles, or my mother's head, or whatever you want me to.' He looked at her earnestly. 'I'll even take a lie-detector test!'

'I believe you,' Bess said, staring into those sky-blue eyes.

Logan's head moved forward and his lips pressed against hers. They were warm and tasted of the dill pickles from his hamburger. Bess could feel heat rising from her toes and engulfing her entire being. Her hand, as if with a mind of its own, touched his arm, then went to his neck. His arms encircled her, pulling her close. She could feel his heartbeat through his white waiter's shirt, pumping hard, combining with her own heartbeat, as if they were just one heart . . . It was Bess's real first kiss. And it was way better than she'd ever imagined it could be.

'Elizabeth!' The voice came from behind them, and they both broke away quickly and whirled around to find Alicia standing there with blanket and pillow in hand. 'I thought I'd bring these down for Logan. It's way past your bedtime,' she said primly.

'Of course!' Bess said, jumping up from the sofa, as did Logan. They almost collided then moved quickly apart. 'Ah, just let me fix his bed . . .'

'No need,' Alicia said. 'I'll do it. You run on upstairs.'

Never one to take orders from her sisters, Bess started to object, but then decided against it. 'Goodnight,' she said to Logan, not looking into those blue eyes, afraid she wouldn't be able to drag herself upstairs if she did.

''Night,' he said, with what sounded to Bess's ears like longing.

Once upstairs and in her room, nightly cleansing rituals completed, Bess lay in her bed and thought about that kiss. And eventually fell asleep, a smile on her face.

JANUARY, 1942–APRIL, 1942
Edgar did what he was told, went where he was assigned, and mostly kept his head down. He had

no beef with the Japanese personally, and wanted nothing more than to get the hell out of the Philippines. He performed guard duty for the army on Bataan, then on the sixteenth his battery received new orders to join the naval battalion at the Quarantine Station at Mariveles. For the next month or so, Edgar and the rest of Marine Batteries A and C were a part of this battalion engaged in constant combat with a Japanese landing force that had made it behind American lines.

Edgar was moved inland later that first month of 1942 to an area nicknamed 'Little Baguio,' after the elite summer resort in northern Luzon. Edgar and his fellow Marines were billeted in a tent camp situated on a flat arm of an extinct volcano southeast of the Mariveles Mountains. Edgar couldn't help wondering which would be the easier death: the Japanese or a volcano eruption. Edgar's creature comforts were sorely tested at Little Baguio. Although he could smell frying bacon in the commanding general's cook tent, he and the rest of the enlisted men feasted on unappetizing and unsalted boiled rice.

Edgar, miserable and still planning his AWOL escape, paid little attention to the political shenanigans going on around him. First and foremost, General MacArthur was relieved as commander in the Philippines and sent to Australia. A General Wainwright took over from MacArthur, only to be replaced eight days later by a General King. During all these political moves, a major counterattack to capture Japanese supplies at Olongapo was foiled by the Japanese attacking with fresh troops. The enemy struck the hospital and bombed *it without mercy. The Japanese Easter offensive broke through the Marines' front lines and on Good Friday armed barges struck the rear flanks from Manila Bay. By April, the eastern front had become chaos and General King was determined to surrender Bataan's battered remnants. Edgar and a few other Marines became aware of this plan when they saw officers in a staff car with a white flag depart the camp and head north through streams of troops retreating south.*

On April 8, 1942, a severe earthquake shook Bataan and the Marines retreated to their prepared tunnel. An hour later they heard explosions as Navy personnel blew up the USS Canopus, *the dry dock and its other installations at Mariveles, followed by army demolition of ammo dumps and supply stores, to keep them out of the hands of the Japanese.*

In preparation for their surrender, officers were told to remove their insignias of rank and rid themselves of any Japanese souvenirs or currency. Enlisted men threw their rifle bolts into the jungle and destroyed the remainder of their small arms. All remaining rations were issued. Edgar grabbed what he could, eating some of it while stashing more in his clothing for later. No one noticed as Edgar went to the jungle with a small shovel and buried his poker winnings and booty bought in Shanghai. Then, knowing his fellows had been ordered to just sit and await the arrival of the Japanese, Edgar kept walking, straight into the jungle with three handguns and a rifle he had grabbed before all were destroyed, and the few rations he had stashed in his clothing.

Six

Willis wanted to go back to bed, but I was wide awake and itching to know what was being discussed in Diamond Lovesy's room. Did she have something to do with Hammerschultz's death? How could she if she was as drunk as she seemed when she went upstairs? But people killed other people all the time when they were inebriated – probably more so than when sober. And she was a big woman, bigger than Humphrey Hammerschultz. She could have easily overpowered him. But why? Why would she want to kill him? They seemed to be on the same page since I'd met them. Out to fleece the kind old lady who'd allowed them into her home. Scenario: Diamond came downstairs, an argument ensued and, with one thing leading to another, she managed to break Humphrey's neck.

But what about the *grrrrrrrrr-plop*? Or, as Willis insisted, the *rrrrrrrrr-thump*? Was it Diamond? If so, doing what? And if she went out the front door as the sound indicated, how did she get back in her room just minutes later? We were all in the living room to be sure, but we could see the staircase from there. And the back staircase led from the kitchen to the first landing of the main staircase, and could also be seen from the living room. If we didn't see her, chances were she'd never left her room and had nothing to do with the *grrrrrrrrrr-plop*. Could the murder and the dragging noise really be unrelated? Somehow I doubted it.

So if Diamond didn't do in Humphrey, who did? Daddy? I *do not* believe in ghosts – mostly. So scratch Daddy. But something was going on in this house. Someone had been scaring off Miss Hutchins' guests, and someone (*not* something!) had made that dragging sound tonight. And someone had killed Humphrey Hammerschultz, not to mention Miss Hutchins' mother those many years ago. And since Daddy had already died on D-Day, the chances were good that he hadn't committed either murder. But who had?

Could a random stranger have killed Humphrey? OK, a bum (it's always the proverbial bum, right?) sneaks into the house to steal something, Humphrey catches him (the proverbial bum's never a woman, right?), they scuffle and Humphrey lands half on the sofa with a broken neck. Was anything missing? I'd have to check that with Miss Hutchins. But what would a random stranger have to do with the *grrrrrrrrrr-plop*ping going on upstairs?

I told Willis to go to bed and that I'd be up in a minute after making sure Miss Hutchins was all right. It wasn't a total lie. I try never to totally lie to my husband. It was one of my vows at our wedding – one of the ones I never said out loud.

I found Miss Hutchins in the dining room, sitting at the long trestle table, the small glass in her hand as it rested atop the table, staring at the apparently empty whiskey bottle. I sat down next to her. Covering her free hand with mine, I asked, 'Are you OK?'

She looked at me and smiled. 'As well as can be expected,' she said. She upended the glass to drain the last drop of the whiskey.

'Do you want me to get you another bottle?' I asked, wondering why I was so willing to assist such behavior.

She shook her head. 'You know, until Uncle Herbert died five years ago, I'd never allowed alcohol to touch my lips. But he left those four cases. I just couldn't allow them to go to waste.' She looked longingly at the empty bottle. 'I've grown to enjoy a sip or two,' she said. She shook herself and pushed the glass and the bottle away. 'So, how was Mr Hammerschultz's room?'

'A mess,' I said. 'But the police chief didn't seem to find anything of substance. He had me wake up Miss Lovesy, then he and his officer went in to talk to her.'

'And he didn't let you go with?' she asked. She patted my arm. 'That was unfair. After all, you found the body!'

'Exactly!' I said.

'And knowing Rigsby Cotton as well as I do, he won't tell us squat.' She stopped for a moment, then a smile spread across her face. 'Unless I shame him into it,' she said.

'Ma'am?'

'I was Rigsby's Sunday school teacher at the First Baptist Church for many years. And I know where a few bodies are buried – figuratively speaking, of course.'

BACK HOME

Alicia lay in bed the next morning, worried about her little sister. Actually, Bess was ten days older than she, but because of Bess's miniature size, she always considered her to be her smaller sibling. Bess had never even really liked a boy, and Alicia could tell that what had gone on the night before between Bess and Logan was much more than *like*. Knowing how her own heart had reacted to finding out that Graham cared for her as much as she cared for him, she was more than a little worried – she was downright scared. She didn't know if Bess could handle this. Granted, she'd handled a lot in her seventeen years – the loss of her entire birth family, being stalked and kidnapped, among other things. But Alicia knew how tentatively she herself held on to her sanity knowing that her relationship with Graham was on the skids, and she'd only lost her family through abandonment. Not murder. Well, abandonment was pretty bad, she supposed. At least Bess had the certain knowledge that her birth family had loved her fiercely, whereas Alicia's family . . .

She threw her feet over the side of the bed. No use dwelling on that, she told herself. She was loved now, of that she was certain. Mom and Dad Pugh loved her, and her sisters loved her – even Megan – no matter what the status with her foster brother/boyfriend might be.

When Bess arrived downstairs that morning – having arisen early, fixed her hair, put on make-up and donned casual yet elegant clothing – Logan was already up, bedding carefully folded and set on the ottoman. Bess was surprised at the scent of coffee coming from the kitchen.

'You made coffee?' she said with a smile.

'Yep!' he said, smiling back. 'And good morning.'

Bess laughed. 'Good morning to you, too.'

'I also put out the desserts for breakfast, along with some bread for toasting, for those who prefer something savory for breakfast.'

'You're going to make someone a very good husband!' Bess said, then hearing her own words, blushed.

Logan's smile disappeared and he sighed. 'If I'm not careful, that could be Harper Benton in the not-too-distant future.'

Bess touched his arm to reassure him, but could feel the heat emitting from that touch. She removed her hand quickly. 'We're going to find out what's going on – why she's lying. If she's even pregnant!' she said.

Logan sank down on the sofa. 'Oh, she's pregnant all right. She was in the car – must have gotten out when Tucker came in to get me. He yelled at her to get back in, but not before I saw the distinct baby bump.'

Bess sat on the sofa next to him. 'We'll find out who did this and why she's lying. I promise you.'

Logan shook his head. 'How can you find out anything? There's no way.'

'Yes there is,' said a voice behind them.

'You bet your ass there is!' came another.

Bess and Logan turned to see both of Bess's sisters coming down the stairs. 'We're not E.J.

Pugh's daughters for nothing!' Megan said, grinning wide.

I waited with Miss Hutchins while the coroner examined the body and the crime scene investigator (one middle-aged woman with a small kit) took pictures and left behind little numbered plaques. At one point I got up and made a strong pot of coffee, which was gone in a flash, what with the police chief and his crew to serve, not to mention Miss Hutchins and myself. I was making my second pot when Diamond Lovesy's heavy tread could be heard on the stairs. I left the kitchen to meet her. She looked bad – her hair uncombed, her eyes bloodshot, and she was wearing a mu-mu that had seen better days. I said, 'Miss Hutchins and I are in the dining room. I'll bring coffee in.'

'Lots of it,' she said, her voice harsh.

I set up a tray, found Miss Hutchins' coffee thermos and filled it with the second pot, then started a third. I took the tray, laden with all the necessary paraphernalia, into the dining room. Miss Hutchins was holding Diamond's hand, stroking it gently. They didn't appear to be talking.

'Here we go,' I said, not as perkily as the words might imply. 'Diamond, how do you take yours?'

'Sweet and almost white – the way I like my men,' she said, then burst into tears.

Miss Hutchins put her arm around Diamond's shoulders, patting her madly and saying, 'There, there,' a lot.

I fixed the coffee for Diamond and found a box

94

of Kleenex in the kitchen, which I brought to her. 'Here, clean up and try the coffee.'

'I'm sorry,' she said between sniffles. 'This is just so terrible! Terrible!' She sobbed again, clutching a wad of the Kleenex tightly in her hand. She turned toward sounds emitting from the living room. 'Is he still in there?' she asked.

'They haven't moved the body yet,' I said. 'The coroner is still doing his thing.'

Diamond got up and moved into the foyer. I quickly followed her. 'Diamond, you really shouldn't—'

'He was my partner and friend,' she said. 'I want to see him. I'll need to tell his mother that I saw him. That I tried to help!'

I took hold of her arm. 'There's nothing you can do now to help him, Diamond. There's nothing you could have done, period.'

'If I hadn't gone to bed—'

'Just don't go there,' I told her.

She pulled away from my grasp. 'I have to see him.'

I could do nothing more than follow her into the living room. The coroner had the body on a gurney supplied by – I could see the name on the side of it – Leeman's Funeral Home: We Care. A young man stood yawning to one side, obviously the driver of the hearse I could see through the open door parked in front of the house.

Diamond went up to the body and started to touch it, but Chief Cotton was on her – as my mother-in-law would say – like a snake on a June bug.

'Now Miz Lovesy, can't have you touching the corpse,' he said. 'Not until he's been autopsied and released.'

'I just wanted—'

The chief shook his head. 'No, ma'am, I can't let ya do it. Procedure, ma'am. Nothing personal.'

Diamond nodded and stared at the body of her partner for a long moment, then turned to me. 'I guess I'll have that coffee now,' she said.

Seems like my husband was the only one who got any sleep that morning. Willis is very good at compartmentalizing. Why get worked up over the dead body of someone we barely knew when there was sleep to be had? Why, indeed. I wasn't so much concerned about Humphrey Hammerschultz – although I didn't like the fact that someone had come into the place we were staying and killed him (unless, of course, it was Diamond) – as I was about the entirety of the situation. I had come to like Miss Hutchins a great deal in the short time I'd known her, and thought what was happening to her and her little inn was thoroughly unjustified. And I like to solve puzzles – not the kind they put in newspapers or game shows on TV, but the kind where people do ungodly things for no apparent reason. There is always a reason – mostly a stupid one – and I want to know what it is. This penchant of mine had gotten our marriage in trouble the year before, with Willis demanding that I cease and desist in finding dead bodies. As I was knee-deep in something I couldn't let go of at the time, he ended up leaving me and moving in with his mother. We reconciled eventually with a compromise of 'let's see what happens next time,' but when our foster daughter Alicia was kidnapped he was the one pushing me to get involved – not that I really needed a push.

So here we were again. He hadn't said anything yet, but I was afraid his first words in the morning would be, 'Pack up, we're leaving.'

Chief Cotton followed Diamond Lovesy and me back into the dining room where Miss Hutchins awaited us. 'Ladies,' he said, 'until we figure out what's going on here, I need everybody to stay in place. I know that you, Miz Lovesy, and you, Miz Pugh, don't live here in Peaceful and are gonna wanna get home, but I need y'all to stay in town until this is cleared up. And your mister, too, Miz Pugh.'

I nodded my head, knowing I had the perfect counter-attack to Willis's possible 'pack up' scenario. 'No problem, Chief,' I said.

BACK HOME
'Yeah, I've heard rumors about your mom,' Logan said. 'But I still don't see what y'all can do.'

'First thing,' Megan said, flopping down on the loveseat, her long legs draped over one arm, 'we confront Harper – without her brother around! If all four of us ponce on her, we're more likely to get a true response.'

'Gawd, Megan,' Alicia said. 'If she *is* pregnant, that would be kind of harsh, don't you think? I mean, from what little I know, pregnant people are pretty sensitive emotionally.'

'To hell with her!' Megan responded. 'She

97

started this! And, Logan,' she said, staring daggers at the boy sitting next to Bess, 'if you're lying to us, you're dead meat. Understand?'

Bess jumped to her feet. 'Megan, how dare you—'

Logan stood up and put his hand on Bess's shoulder. 'She's right, Bess,' he said. 'You're really sweet to believe in me so thoroughly, but Megan doesn't, and she shouldn't. All I can tell you, Megan, is that I didn't do it. I never touched her, ever. I'm not saying I didn't want to, but she was, like, real stand-offish. I always got the feeling I'd be shut out if I even tried to kiss her. So I never did. And I can swear to that on a stack of Bibles if it would help.'

'It won't,' Megan said. 'If you'd lie about knocking up somebody, then you'd be stupid enough to lie on a stack of Bibles, too.'

'Megan!' Bess started.

'But!' Megan said, raising her voice to drown out Bess, 'I don't think you're stupid. And I *do* think Harper is up to something. So we'll help you.'

'Gee, Megs, that's so *good* of you!' Bess said sarcastically.

Logan pulled Bess back down to the sofa. 'It *is* good of you,' he said. He glanced at Alicia. 'And you?' he asked.

'Yes, I'm on board,' Alicia said, although she still had her misgivings about any relationship building between this boy and her sister. She wouldn't be able to handle Bess being hurt the way she was hurting now. Shaking herself mentally, she asked, 'So how do we get Harper alone?'

98

'You said y'all were on the same volleyball team?' Bess asked.

'Yeah, last semester,' Alicia confirmed.

'Would she be suspicious if you reached out to her?' Bess asked.

Alicia shrugged. 'Could she see that well from the car last night? I mean, I was one of the ones jumping her brother.'

'It was pretty dark in the parking lot. One of the lights burned out and Cam hasn't gotten around to having it changed yet. You gotta call an electrician to do it because—' Logan started.

'We really don't care,' Megan said. To Alicia, she said, 'I think we can take the chance. There was so much going on, and she never got out of the car while we were beating on her brother, so chances are she wasn't paying that much attention.'

'So what would I say?' Alicia asked. '"Hey, Harper, I hear you got knocked up. Anything I can do to help?"'

Megan rolled her eyes. 'Hardly. You know, just say how you've noticed she hasn't been back since winter break and you wonder if she needs you to bring her some schoolwork or whatever. Ask her, you know, if she's sick or something.' Megan grinned. 'That might even get a confession out of her.'

'So I go over there or what? I don't even know where she lives,' Alicia said, not overly keen on Megan's plan.

'I'm sure Logan knows where, but I think a phone call first.'

'Just call her up out of the blue?' Alicia asked.

99

Megan swung her legs off the arm of the love-seat, straightening herself. 'Alicia, *dear*,' she said, 'it's not that big a woop, OK? You just call her up and say what I *just* told you to say! She responds. Put it on speakerphone and I'll get paper and pen and write down the correct response to whatever she says, if you're afraid you can't do it!'

'Don't get all huffy with me!' Alicia said. 'I think I can handle it! It's just that I don't *want* to!'

'Then don't,' Logan said, standing up. 'Y'all have been great, and I appreciate the attempt, but there's nothing that can be done until Harper's baby is born. I'll just try to put off marrying her until then.'

Bess jumped to her feet. 'No! We can help! I swear we can, Logan!'

'I need to get home—'

'Your face is still a mess,' Megan said. 'Your mother will see it for sure.'

'Then I'll just tell her the same story we told Cam at the restaurant—'

'Oh, for gawd's sake, give me the damn phone!' Alicia said.

I helped Miss Hutchins fix breakfast while Diamond Lovesy sat in the dining room drinking another full pot of coffee. The body had gone, as had Chief Cotton and his entourage. Willis wandered down-stairs about a half an hour after they left. I would say he was upstairs staring out the window waiting for them to leave, but that would seem spiteful – true, probably, but still spiteful.

While I was helping Miss Hutchins with breakfast, I said, 'I've been thinking about who could have done this to Humphrey, and I thought maybe a stranger came in to steal something. Have you noticed if anything's missing?'

She flipped over great slabs of ham she had frying in a cast iron skillet and said, 'Well, I haven't really looked, of course. Maybe we can do that after breakfast?'

I continued cutting up a melon. 'Sounds like a plan,' I said.

Willis stuck his head in the kitchen door. 'Something smells great,' he said.

'It's called breakfast,' I said.

He came all the way into the kitchen. 'So what did the chief say? About Humphrey?'

'He's dead,' I said.

'The chief?' he asked, eyebrows raised but a grin tickling his lips.

I poked him in the gut with the hand that wasn't wielding the knife. 'He doesn't know anything as of this moment. Diamond's in the dining room and appears grief-stricken, and we know she's not that good an actress,' I said, remembering her performance 'channeling' Miss Hutchins' father, 'so maybe she really is. And as far as I can tell, she didn't have anything to add about Humphrey's passing.'

'Should I go in there and question her?' Willis asked.

I shrugged. 'Knock yourself out,' I said. I went to the coffee machine and handed him the fresh carafe – the fifth one, and it wasn't even eight o'clock in the morning. 'Take this in and fill up the thermos. Oh, and here's a mug for you,' I said, taking one down from the cabinet. He gave a quick nod and was out the door to the dining room.

Breakfast was a relatively quiet affair. Personally, I was starving and set about stuffing my face as quickly as possible. As usual, the food was amazing: thick ham slices were layered over chunky homemade bread, a poached egg sat on the ham, and Hollandaise sauce covered it all. Not exactly eggs Benedict, but even better with the addition of her hearty homemade bread. There was also my offering of cubes of cantaloupe and honeydew melon. And more coffee, of course. By the time we'd finished I was ready to go back to bed, but knew that wasn't in my near future.

'So, Diamond,' I said when I'd finally finished stuffing my pie-hole, 'what did the chief want when he talked to you earlier?'

'Your husband has already drilled me,' she said, her face stony. 'Why don't you ask him?'

'Willis!' I said. 'I'm so sorry, Diamond. You know men. Like bulls in the proverbial china shop.'

'Absolutely no finesse,' she said.

'The grace of a gorilla,' I offered.

'The compassion of a brown recluse,' she said.

'The—' I started, but Willis interrupted.

Pointing at me, he said, 'She made me do it!'

'Did not!' I said.

Diamond began to laugh. Unfortunately, it got out of control, the laughter turning into hysterics. I got up quickly and moved to her side. 'Come on, Diamond, let's get you upstairs. You need to rest.'

'What I need is to get the hell out of here!' she said, pulling away from me. 'Away from you and your crazy husband! And away from this batty old broad! It's all her fault, you know!' I couldn't help looking at Miss Hutchins, who appeared to have shriveled up before my very eyes. 'If she'd been a better daughter, her father wouldn't be doing this! You know he killed Humphrey! We all know he did it!'

I moved away from the banshee act now in full swing from the so-called medium.

'I really think you need to go to your room, Diamond,' I said, in the same voice I use when chastising my children for various wrong-doings. 'You know you can't leave,' I added. 'Chief Cotton said we had to stay here until—'

Diamond jumped to her feet. 'I can do whatever I want! And I want to get out of here!' With that she ran for the stairs.

No one said anything for a moment, then I walked to the phone stand by the staircase, picked up the phone and dialed 911.

'Who are you calling?' Willis asked.

'The chief,' I said. 'He needs to know what Diamond is up to.'

Miss Hutchins spoke for the first time. 'Please tell him I'm ready to turn myself in. Miss Lovesy is right. This is all my fault.'

APRIL, 1942

Once he started running, he couldn't really stop. He was now beginning to take the Japanese

103

personally. Talk about loss of creature comforts!
The food he'd stashed in his clothing hardly lasted
beyond noon. Luckily the forest was impenetrable,
and he was pretty sure no one – like the Japanese,
or the Marines, for that matter – could see him
or hear him. It was also quite noisy, what with
all the birds, and got even noisier when he found
the spot where he decided to stop at least for the
night if not longer. He might have noticed it was
a pretty spot, if Edgar had been into such things,
but the main reason for stopping was the very
noisy waterfall that poured into a pool at the
bottom. His thought process was more concerned
with fresh water than beauty. He did check out
the flora, like the cacti-looking plant with pink
bulb-like blooms, wondering if it was edible. This
first night he didn't dare try eating anything.
There were beautiful vines hanging off trees with
six-petal purple flowers, and a reddish brown
flower growing on the bark of a tree, and trumpet-
like orange flowers that, when opened, contained
fruit, berries and seeds.

He built a small fire as it got dark and huddled
next to it, not so much for warmth as for the
security of it. He could hear animals rummaging
through the forest and wasn't keen on meeting
one in the dark. He slept fitfully that first night,
only to wake up the next morning starving.

As the days and weeks moved along, Edgar
found his rhythm. Early on he'd caught what
looked like a rat and had fed it some of the fruit,
berries and seeds he'd found. He kept the rat in
a bamboo cage he'd made, and watched him for
several hours after each trial. The rat lived. So

those became a part of Edgar's diet, as did a creature he found that looked like a pig, with a crest and mane and a snout closer to that of an anteater than a pig. He roasted him whole on a spit he made of the available bamboo and fed off him for almost a week.

The armaments he'd brought with him had come in handy for killing the pig-like creature, and other creatures of the forest like deer, turkey-like wildfowl, and an animal he shot before realizing he had no idea what it was. It was spotted and striped, with a long nose, teeth like a cat and a bushy tail like a mongoose. He roasted that, too, and other than tasting a little gamy – like everything else he'd shot and cooked – it wasn't too bad.

He explored his environs, venturing out a little further week by week. At one point he found a pool that appeared to have steam coming off it. Touching the water, he discovered a hot spring. At least once a week after this discovery he would venture out at night with a torch to soak himself in the warm waters.

Edgar had been on his own in the forest for three weeks when he spotted his first human – a young woman, clad in native garb, walking into the hot spring fully clothed.

Seven

BACK HOME

Before Alicia could dial the phone, it rang. She dropped it like it had just exploded in her hand. Megan picked it up, rolling her eyes at her foster sister. 'Hello?' she said.

She listened for a moment, then covered the mouthpiece and half-whispered, 'It's Grandma! Are we going to church or what?'

The girls looked at each other. Megan said into the phone, 'Just a minute, Grandma, I'm trying to find Bess.' She raised her eyebrows at her sister. 'Well?'

'I don't think we have time for that,' Bess said.

'Well, what about lunch?' Megan said. 'We were counting on Grandma taking us out—'

'But we didn't spend any money last night,' Alicia said. 'So we're OK.'

'So what excuse do I give?' Megan asked.

Bess coughed dramatically. 'I'm sick,' she said in a weak voice.

Again Megan rolled her eyes. Into the phone she said, 'Grandma, I found Bess but she's sick—' Grandma obviously said something, because Megan's next line was 'Oh, no! It's OK. She'll be fine. I think it's just a headache. She just needs to rest. But I don't want to leave her alone, ya know?' She listened for a moment, then said:

106

'That's OK, Alicia and I will fix her some lunch, but thanks, Grandma. Really. 'Bye.' And she hung up the phone and handed it back to Alicia. 'Now call!' she said.

Sighing, Alicia dialed the number Logan had given her. A youngish male voice answered the phone and she panicked, immediately hanging up.

'Gawd, Alicia! What did you go and do that for?' Megan demanded.

'It was her brother!' Alicia said.

'Yeah, like maybe he lives there?' Megan said, sarcasm dripping off her tongue.

'So now what?' Bess said, throwing herself back on the sofa where she sat next to Logan, her arms tightly crossed over her chest.

'So now we do it again! Alicia?' Megan looked at her foster sister, one eyebrow raised.

'But—' Alicia started, until Logan interrupted.

'This isn't going to work,' he said, starting to get to his feet.

'OK, OK!' Alicia said. She picked up the phone once again, and dialed the number Logan had given her earlier, putting it on speakerphone.

An older woman answered the phone. 'Hello?'

Alicia took a deep breath and said, 'May I speak to Harper, please?'

'May I say who's calling?' the woman, presumably Harper's mother, asked.

'My name is Alicia. From school?'

'Codderville High?' the woman asked.

All four looked at each other. Then Megan waved her hand for Alicia to continue. 'No, Black

Cat Ridge High. We were on the same volleyball team last semester?'

'Ah, maybe she can call you ba—' Her voice faded as she said, 'Harper! No!'

Then the kids could hear Harper's voice. 'Who is this?' she demanded.

'Ah, hi, Harper,' Alicia said. 'It's Alicia, from volleyball? I just wondered if you needed me to bring you some schoolwork over, but your mom says you're going to Codderville?'

'That's right,' she said.

'Gosh, I didn't realize you'd changed schools. Did y'all move?'

'No,' Harper said, the word clipped.

'Well, OK, then. Well, maybe we could get together—' Alicia started.

'Why?' Harper demanded.

'Ah, well, no real reason, I guess. I just thought we got along OK as teammates, and, well—'

'You're living with the Pughes, right? Like in Megan and Bess?'

'Ah, yes,' Alicia said.

'So they put you up to this, right? Megan's one of the biggest gossips at BCR and I'm sure she wants to know *everything*, right? Well, tell her to go play with herself!' Harper said and hung up.

'Well!' Megan said, crossing her arms over her ample chest. 'I am not a gossip! I tell the twins and I can't help it if they spread it everywhere!'

'So maybe you should stop telling the twins things?' Alicia suggested.

'They're my best friends!' Megan said.

Logan rose to his feet. 'Well, thanks, ladies, but that got us nowhere. And, really, she was pretty rude. Sorry about that, Alicia.'

'No way was it your fault,' Alicia said. She looked a little crestfallen. 'I thought we got along great on the team.' She shrugged. 'I guess I was wrong.'

'Maybe she did recognize us from last night,' Bess said.

Looking at his watch, Logan said, 'I need to get to work. We start prep in half an hour for the after church crowd. Both of them,' he said, and sighed.

'Yeah, y'all didn't look all that busy last night, and Saturday night *is* date night! What's up with that?' Megan demanded.

Logan shrugged. 'I think we need to do more advertising, but Cam said he can't afford it.'

'Wow, a real *Catch-22* situation, huh?' Bess said.

'Huh?' Logan looked at her, his eyes big.

'Never mind,' she said, standing up. 'Let me get my purse and I'll drive you.'

Logan smiled at her. 'That would be great,' he said.

Alicia jumped up. 'I'll go with you!' she said, a big smile plastered on her face.

Walking past her foster sister to get to her purse, Bess patted Alicia on the arm. 'That's OK, I've got this covered.'

I slammed the phone down before anyone answered. 'This is not your fault!' I said with some heat. 'And stop taking it on! You haven't done anything – things are being done *to* you! You're the victim here, but you need to stop acting like one and start fighting back! Diamond is a complete and total bitch and she had no right to talk to you like that! And – I know I'm going out on a limb here – but it is my semi-professional opinion that none of these things have been done by the ghost of your father! Someone very much alive is doing this and we're going to find out who it is!'

I finally paused for breath and Willis stepped in. 'She gets worked up,' he said, patting Miss Hutchins on the hand. 'But she's right. This isn't your fault. This is the fault of whoever killed Humphrey and whoever killed your mother. I doubt it could be the same person, and I doubt in either case it was your father. Even if you believe in ghosts, from everything I've read and seen on TV—'

'You really need to stop watching those ghost hunter shows,' I interjected.

'—they can't do physical damage. They can't touch or anything, so how could this be your dad? Unless he's talking people into killing themselves – and I'm not even sure how one would break one's own neck,' he finished up.

Miss Hutchins sighed and wiped a leaky tear from her eye. 'I suppose you're right. But, E.J., dear, what are we going to do about Diamond leaving?'

'I'm going to finish my call, then you and I are going to search the house for any missing treasures. Sound good?'

Miss Hutchins nodded her head and gave me

a small smile, and I went back to the phone and called Chief Cotton. When I told him what Diamond had said about leaving, he said, 'Not on my watch. I'm sending Mary over there now to stop her. I'd say she could move to another B&B or motel or something if she's uncomfortable there, but that bike ride has got every place in town booked solid.'

So Willis and I cleaned up the breakfast dishes and the three of us waited for Officer Mays to show up. It took less than half an hour for the knock on the door. Luckily we hadn't seen hide nor hair of Diamond Lovesy. As far as I could tell, she was still upstairs being a bitch.

'Where is she?' Officer Mays asked as she entered the foyer.

'Upstairs,' I said, as I'd been the one to open the door.

'Thanks,' she said and headed for the staircase, one hand resting on her Sam Brown belt while the other worked the banister.

Miss Hutchins, Willis and I ended up at the foot of the staircase, our heads raised toward the second floor. We were rewarded with a bellow of 'You can't stop me!'

We heard Officer Mays saying something, but couldn't make out the words.

'Yeah? You and what army?' Diamond demanded loudly.

There was another unintelligible response from the officer, then, 'You can't do that! I have rights!'

Then we heard Diamond's heavy tread on the upper landing. All three of us scooted back into the dining room, still standing and staring at the staircase, but not quite as obvious as being right there in the foyer.

Diamond rounded the landing and we could see her, dressed in the same clothes she'd worn on her first night here and carrying a suitcase. Officer Mary Mays wasn't far behind. Officer Mays jumped down two steps and caught Diamond by her long-fringed poncho, stopping her in her tracks.

Officer Mays grabbed one of Diamond's wrists and said, 'Ma'am, you have the right to remain silent—'

Diamond tugged at her bound wrist but the younger woman seemed to have more upper body strength than one would imagine by her size. She grabbed Diamond's other wrist and threw on cuffs.

'If you don't, anything you say may be used against—'

'OK, OK!' Diamond said. 'I surrender! I'll go back upstairs! I'll stay, I'll stay!'

'Only if you give me your car keys,' Officer Mays said.

'Shit!' Diamond said, tearing up. 'I don't even have them! I don't know what I was thinking! It's Humphrey's car. Maybe they're in his pocket or something?' she said, turning her head to see the officer.

Mary Mays pushed Diamond into the dining room and pulled out a chair. 'Sit!' she commanded. Diamond sat and Mary went to the telephone, dialed a number and asked, 'Did you find car keys with the remains?'

A voice answered and she said, 'OK,' and hung

up. Coming back into the dining room, she moved to Diamond's back and unfastened the handcuffs. 'They were with Mr Hammerschultz's body. I'll go get them from the funeral home and keep them in custody until the chief decides to let you people go.' She glared at Willis and me. 'How about you two?' she said. 'Any ideas about skipping town?'

'No, ma'am,' Willis said. 'We'll be here to help Miss Hutchins in any way we can.'

I smiled up at my man, glad he was taking that attitude – for once.

She looked back down at Diamond Lovesy. 'You settled, now? No more funny stuff?'

Diamond nodded, her head down, tears falling on her bejeweled and bejangled poncho. 'Whatever,' she said.

Mary Mays stood looking at Diamond for a long moment, finally turning to Miss Hutchins. 'Ma'am, you doing OK with these people?'

'Yes, they're fine,' she said, not able to look anywhere near Diamond.

'Then I'll take my leave. You call me, ma'am, if they get up to anything, you hear?'

'Of course, Mary,' Miss Hutchins said, getting up and walking the officer to the front door. 'And please tell your grandmother thank you for the preserves she sent over.'

I could see Mary Mays smile. 'Yeah, Nana makes some mean peach preserves, huh?'

'The best!' Miss Hutchins said, holding the door open while the officer slipped out to her patrol car.

Once she was gone, Diamond Lovesy stood

up and headed for the stairs. I stopped her. 'I think you owe Miss Hutchins an apology,' I said.

'No, no,' Miss Hutchins said. 'She's upset. It's excusable.'

'It most certainly isn't!' I said.

Diamond stiffened. 'I meant what I said. Every word of it. I'm afraid to eat or drink anything here – afraid I'll be poisoned. I'm afraid to go to sleep, lest my own neck be broken!' she said, her voice growing louder and turning into a high falsetto.

'You are such a bitch!' I said.

'Did you just lose your best friend?' she yelled at me. 'No? Well, I did! And it's because of this house, this evil, evil house! If I were you, I'd take my worthless husband and go sleep in the car! One of you may be next!' With that, she lurched up the stairs to her room.

'I am *not* worthless!' Willis said. 'On paper, I'm worth plenty!'

I patted his arm and kissed his cheek. 'Yes, you are, honey. Even off paper, you're worth more than a dozen phony psychics.'

'Thank you,' he said, mustering up some dignity. 'You're right. She's a bitch.'

'All right, you two,' Miss Hutchins said, heading back into the dining room toward the thermos of hopefully still warm coffee. 'Like she said, we didn't just lose our best friend. She's distraught.'

We all sat at the dining table and poured ourselves the last bit of coffee in the thermos. When we'd consumed that, I said, 'Well, nothing to it but to do it, Miss Hutchins. You ready to see what's missing, if anything?'

She sighed and stood up. 'You're right. Besides, what else do we have to do?'

Personally, I could think of several things – all the reasons I'd booked this B&B and driven over one hundred miles to this little town for – like going antique shopping, checking out the galleries and boutiques, or just heading upstairs and jumping my husband. Looking out the windows I could see a lovely day beginning. Spring flowers were blooming, the sun was brightening the sky and the land, and I could see people walking to church and children dancing around their parents, all in their Sunday best. It was like a scene painted by Norman Rockwell, except the men wore bolo ties and the little boys had cowboy boots on their feet.

'So what do you need me to do?' Willis asked.

'Nothing, I guess,' I said.

He looked at Miss Hutchins. 'Where's your TV?' he asked.

'Oh, dear,' she said. 'I don't have one. It broke back in the late seventies and I just never replaced it. Is that going to be a problem?' she asked, wringing her hands.

I glared at Willis. He smiled at Miss Hutchins and said, 'No, of course not. I think I'll take a walk outside. It's a lovely morning.'

Miss Hutchins smiled widely. 'It certainly is!' She moved closer to Willis and I could hear her semi-whisper in his ear, 'And there's a bar about a block down that plays all the football on

Sundays.' She giggled. 'If you're interested.'

Willis looked up and smiled at me. 'See ya,' he said, and headed out the door.

BACK HOME

Once alone in the minivan, Logan said, 'I'm so sorry I got y'all mixed up in this.'

'Don't be,' Bess said, touching his arm. She didn't seem able to help herself. She loved touching him. Loved the way it made her feel. 'That's sort of a family tradition – getting mixed up in things that are basically none of our business.'

He sighed. 'See? That's what I'm saying. It's not your business, it's mine, and I don't want you to get hurt, Bess. I really, really don't!'

'I don't want you hurt either,' Bess said, eyes glued to the road. 'And I'm going to do every-thing I can to see that doesn't happen. Me and my sisters, too.'

'Look, y'all tried, I'll give you that. But I just don't see that there's anything more you can do. I'm in deep shit and I know it. Maybe I should tell my folks what's going on.'

'Can you wait?' Bess asked. 'Just let me talk to my sisters and see if we can come up with something.'

Logan sighed again. 'We close at nine on Sundays. Then I'm going home and telling them.'

'I'll get back to you before then. Give me your cell phone.' They punched in each other's numbers once they'd reached the restaurant, then Logan opened the door of the minivan to get out. He

116

hesitated, then turned and leaned in to Bess, who met him halfway. The kiss was hot and sweet and took her breath away. She wanted to keep on doing exactly that for the next hundred years or so. He broke away and smiled. 'I'll see you tomorrow,' he said.

'If not sooner,' she said, and blushed.

Meanwhile, back at the Pugh home, Megan was working on a plan. 'So when Bess gets back—'

'If she gets back,' Alicia said, despondent.

'What?' Megan asked.

'Nothing,' Alicia said.

Megan, who was rarely interested in anything that didn't directly involve her, took Alicia at face value and continued. 'Anyway, when she gets back, we get in the minivan and head to Harper's house, park a couple of houses down and wait until we see the mother and brother leave so we can get Harper on her own—'

'What makes you think they're gonna leave?'

'It's Sunday! They'll go to church, surely.'

'We're not going! And even if they do go,' Alicia said, 'wouldn't Harper go with them?'

'Not necessarily. She *is* pregnant, and Logan said there was a baby bump, so maybe her mom doesn't want the people at church to know.'

'They may not even be religious,' Alicia said. 'Lots of people aren't.'

'They'll leave for some reason,' Megan said.

'Not necessarily—'

'Jeez, Alicia! Could you *be* more of a wet blanket? Let's just go surveil, see what we see.'

Alicia shrugged. 'I don't think you can use that as a verb.'

'What?' Megan asked, frowning.

'Surveil.'

'Of course you can!'

Alicia sighed. *'Anyway,* this sounds like a big old waste of time, but whatever.'

'You can always stay here!' Megan said.

Alicia thought about what she might do alone in the house with nothing but her thoughts to occupy her. Maybe she'd call Graham. Maybe that wouldn't be a very good idea. 'No, no,' she said. 'I'm coming.' She sighed. Anything was better than being alone right now.

They heard the minivan pull into the driveway and Megan jumped up. 'Come on then!' she said, grabbed her imitation Gucci purse and headed for the back door.

'Jeez, all right already!' Alicia said, and followed her foster sister out the door.

Bess had just turned the van off when her two sisters piled in, Megan riding shotgun and Alicia relegated to the back seat. 'What?' Bess said, frowning at Megan.

'We have a plan!' Megan announced.

Bess sighed. 'I'm almost afraid to ask.'

'We're going to surveil Harper's house and wait for her brother and mother to leave,' Megan said.

'Can you use that as a verb?' Bess asked.

'Shut up. I have a plan!' Megan said.

'And what if they don't leave?' Bess asked.

'Gawd! You and Alicia both! Jeez, have some faith, you two! Drive, woman.'

And so Bess started the van again, backed down the driveway and headed out.

Our search of the house showed there were several things missing that could have been taken the night before by whoever had made the dragging noise: a Wedgwood vase Miss Hutchins' mother had gotten in England on her honeymoon, which had adorned one of the built-in bookcases in the living room; a small lithograph that had hung on the wall next to the fireplace for several generations; an antique pitcher and basin that had been in the first bedroom upstairs, the one that had been occupied by Humphrey Hammerschultz; and several spoons from Miss Hutchins' mother's spoon rack that occupied a place of honor on the ornate hutch in the dining room. We found the missing spoons in one of the drawers of the hutch; she remembered Uncle Herbert bumping into the bookcase during one of his many drunken stupors and knocking over the Wedgwood vase, which fell to the hardwood floor and shattered into a million pieces. The lithograph, she finally remembered, had been sold to pay for some groceries when her mother was still alive. The pitcher and basin were the only things missing that Miss Hutchins couldn't explain.

'Was the set worth much?' I asked her.

She shrugged. 'I really don't know. Oh, we could ask Verdeen Babcock,' she said. 'She's always coming over to' – and here the old lady used air quotes – '"visit," when in reality she's checking out my antiques. She's got one of the stores on Main Street, and I think she thinks I'm going to leave her everything in my will! Ha!' she said. 'I'd rather leave it to Diamond Lovesy!'

'Verdeen is pretty obvious about what she's doing?' I asked with a grin.

'I'm afraid obvious isn't the word. Downright rude would be more accurate.'

'So you think she'd be able to put a price on the pitcher and basin?' I asked.

'More than likely,' Miss Hutchins said, then sighed. 'I suppose that means I should call her.'

'That's totally up to you, ma'am,' I said.

She smiled and touched my hand. 'Aren't you the sweetest thing? I know you can't wait to find out, but you're going to let me think this is all my idea, right?'

'The decision is totally up to you,' I said, then grinned.

'Well, I sorta want to find out, too. Maybe I should have her come over some day and give me an estimate on all of it.' She sighed. 'I might be underinsured.'

She walked to the phone by the staircase and punched in a number, waited for a moment then said, 'Verdeen? It's Carrie Marie. Yes, dear, I'm fine. How are you?' Then, 'Oh, I'm sorry to hear it. Arthritis can be dreadful, can't it? Your knees? Oh, that *is* a shame!' She listened for a long moment, then said, 'Well, I'm sorry to hear that, but why I'm calling is to see whether you recall that rose-patterned pitcher and basin set that I had in the front bedroom?' Then, 'Uh huh, that's right. Can you give me an idea how much it was worth? It's missing and I'm wondering if I should turn it in to the insurance.' Then, 'Uh huh . . . uh huh, well, thank you, dear, and I do hope you get to feeling better.' Then, 'Yes . . . uh huh . . .

OK . . . well . . .' Miss Hutchins looked up at me with desperation in her eyes.

So I called out, 'Oh, Miss Hutchins! I need help!'

The old lady favored me with a very bright smile. 'Oh, dear,' she said into the phone. 'One of my guests needs me, Verdeen. I'd better get off the phone. Yes . . . well . . . goodbye,' she said and hung up, although I could still hear a voice coming from the other end of the phone.

'A real talker, huh?' I said.

She sighed. '*And* a hypochondriac,' she said. 'Although these days she may really have some of the problems she's been complaining about since her twenties.' She stood up from the seat of the telephone table. 'Anyway, she knew exactly what item I was talking about – of course. She said anywhere from one hundred to five hundred dollars, depending on the shape it's in and finding a buyer willing to pay.'

'Hum,' I said. 'Would someone come in just to steal that? I mean, that's not a lot, not in a house with all these beautiful antiques!'

'Maybe he was too rushed to take any of the furniture?' she said.

The *grrrrrrrrr-plop* from the night before certainly had nothing to do with the pitcher and wash basin – those could have easily been carried out by hand. But a piece of furniture? A large piece of furniture could certainly have made that sound.

APRIL 1942–JULY 1942

Edgar watched the young woman as she walked out in the water, waist deep. He couldn't help noticing she was quite a looker – young, maybe a teenager, but still quite a looker. 'Hey!' he called out. The girl whirled around and said something in another language. 'You speak English?' he asked.

She cocked her head and said, 'Little bit,' using her thumb and index finger to indicate just how little.

'Any Japs around here?' he asked.

She frowned and cocked her head again. 'Japs?' she asked.

'You know, Jap-an-ese,' Edgar said in a sing-song voice. 'Like soldiers.'

'Soldiers all gone,' she said.

'No Japs?' he asked.

She shrugged and repeated, 'Soldiers all gone.'

Edgar nodded and relaxed a trifle. 'How come you're going in the water with your clothes on?'

Again the cocked head and frown. He moved closer and patted the water of the hot spring and then pulled at his own tattered shirt.

She nodded and pantomimed washing herself. Edgar grinned and nodded back. Hell, he thought. 'This ain't so bad.'

Then she let off with a stream of what Edgar perceived as gobbledygook, and looked at him inquiringly. He shook his head and shrugged.

The girl took a breath, then said, 'You want me—' Then she pantomimed washing again and then pointed at him.

'You wanna wash me?' he asked, incredulous. She nodded and he grinned.

'No problem!' he said, and began to strip.

He kept his pants on and waded out to where

she was. She took a sliver of homemade soap out of the depths of the garment she was wearing, and began to wet then soap his upper body. Edgar felt that what she was doing was ten times sexier than his time with any of the Chinese or Russian girls in Shanghai, which was the last time he'd been laid. If this was a prelude to the deed, he was gonna be one happy cowboy in a few minutes. And then she stopped and pantomimed that he lower himself in the hot spring to rinse off. She then used the soap on herself. Seeing him still in the water, she pointed toward the bank and said, 'Sun, dry.'

'Right,' he said, slowly walked up to the bank of the hot spring and got out, took a seat on the grassy surround and waited for her to start the next part of her obvious seduction. But instead of that, she climbed up the bank, too, but kept going, with a little backward wave at Edgar. He jumped up. 'Hey!' he called out. She turned but didn't stop walking. 'What's your name?' he asked.

She stopped and cocked her head. 'My name,' Edgar said, pointing at his chest, 'is Edgar. Your name is?' he asked, pointing at her.

She grinned and nodded her head. 'Lupita,' she said. 'Me Lupita, you Ed-gur.'

He grinned back. 'Right! You Lupita, me Edgar.'

She started once more into the forest and he shouted after her, 'When can I see you again?'

She shrugged and waved her fingers at him. He didn't know if that meant she didn't know when, or if she had no idea what he was saying.

He sat on the bank of the hot spring for a while,

thinking about the pretty little Filipino girl he'd just met. Then, as the water of the hot springs settled, he saw his reflection in its smooth, mirror-like surface. Damn, he thought, I wonder why she didn't run screaming when she saw me. He'd not shaved since the morning his unit had surrendered to the Japanese, and the months he'd been stuck in the forest showed on his face. His beard grew from just under his eyes down to the nape of his neck. His hair was almost as long, his eyes were bloodshot and his clothes were a wreck. What could be seen of his face was blotched from too much sun and possibly the wrong types of food. And he'd lost so much weight he looked like a skeleton.

He got up and found his shirt where he'd dropped it. It was so dirty it could stand on its own, as could his pants had they been dry. He'd removed his boots and his socks before entering the water, and just looking at the socks made him nauseous. They were brown with dirt and grime and dried blood. He sat down on the ground and removed his pants and skivvies. Time to do some laundry, he decided.

Eight

Seeing where Harper Benton lived, the girls understood how she could so easily transfer out of Black Cat Ridge High and over to Codderville High: the street they'd turned on to paralleled the Texas Colorado River, which was the boundary line that separated the two school districts. Although this street was on the BCR side of the river, it wouldn't take too much red tape to move to Codderville High.

There was a small community lining the river, mostly single-wide trailers with a few shacks thrown in. The address for the Bentons showed a double-wide trailer in better condition than the rest, sitting on a lot of at least a couple of acres, with well-tended flower beds just coming into bloom. There was a carport that housed an ancient but well-kept Toyota Celica. The pick-up from the night before was missing.

'So the brother's gone! We know that for sure!' Megan said, bouncing up and down in her seat as Bess drove past the double wide.

The non-river side of the street was empty, save for a boat repair shop that appeared to be closed on Sunday. There were a couple of cars in the lot, but judging by the four flattened tires on one and the open hood exposing an empty interior on the other, the girls figured nobody was home. Bess pulled in and parked next to the tire-challenged car.

'Good thinking,' Megan said, patting her sister on the arm. 'We can surveil to our heart's content!'

'Surveil—' both her sisters said at once.

'Is not a verb!' Megan said, cutting them off and glaring at her sisters. 'Well, if it isn't, it should be! And that's not the point! The point is—'

'The point is,' Bess interrupted, 'we still don't know if the mother's home. I would assume that's her car . . .' She stopped abruptly and turned around in her seat to face Alicia. 'Does Harper have her own car?'

Alicia shrugged. 'As you may have gleaned from our earlier telephone conversation, we were never that close.'

'Well, we still have to err on the side of caution and assume that *is* the mother's car. So we also have to assume that the mother is still home.'

'You know what they say about "assume," don't you?' Megan said.

Both her sisters sighed. 'Yes, Megan, we know.'

Not one to give an inch, Megan said, 'Assume makes an "ass" out of "u" and "me"!'

Bess turned to Alicia and rolled her eyes. Turning back to Megan, she said, 'OK, E.J., Junior., what do you propose we do now? Barge into the house, guns blazing? Use our non-existent glass cutter to cut our way through the back door? Oh, I know, hire a helicopter with a rope and a big hook and tear the roof off, then we can repel inside!'

'You are getting on my last nerve!' Megan said, teeth clenched.

'OK, you two,' Alicia, who had become used to playing referee with her foster sisters, said from the back seat. 'Why don't we just "surveil" for a little while. See if we can see the mother. See if anyone goes in or out.'

'Works for me,' Bess said.

'Whatever!' Megan said, folding her arms over her chest and staring out the side window. Unfortunately for her, it was the side away from the Bentons' double wide.

They sat in silence for close to twenty minutes before they saw a side door open and Harper Benton come out.

'OMG, she really *is* pregnant!' Megan said, staring at the girl as she headed to the Celica under the carport.

'She looks so cute!' Alicia said, grinning.

And she did. Barely five foot two, her curly blonde tresses reaching her hips, Harper carried her pregnancy all in the front, no extra girth in her buttocks or legs or chest. Just a cute round mound covered by a gauzy hip-length top over blue jeans. She got in the driver's side of the Celica, started the car and peeled out of the driveway at an alarming rate of speed, before Bess had even turned the key in the ignition of the minivan.

'Hurry!' Megan said, pounding Bess on the arm. 'We're gonna lose her!'

'Ouch!' Bess said, hitting Megan back.

'Really, Bess,' Alicia said from the back seat. 'Hurry!'

'I *am* hurrying!' she said as she slammed the gearshift into reverse, backed up and headed out of the parking lot of the boat repair shop.

They caught up to Harper as she turned onto the highway, heading across the river into Codderville.

'Where's she going?' Megan demanded.

'How in the world would I know?' Bess demanded back. 'I'm following her, for gawd's sake! She appears to be going to Codderville!'

'Well, that's pretty obvious!' Megan shot back as Harper's car took the main exit into the town they were very familiar with – their grandmother and now their brother lived there.

'When we're through following her, maybe we can go by Grandma's. I bet she's got dinner almost—' Megan started.

But Alicia answered with a resounding 'No!'

Bess used the rearview mirror to look at her foster sister. 'What's going on?' she asked. She turned to look at Megan. 'What do you know that I don't know?'

'Just watch the road! Look, she's turning!' Megan said.

Harper turned into a strip shopping center about two miles from the interstate. Bess passed the entrance and turned on to the next street, which ran by the side of the strip mall. She stopped the minivan and the three watched as Harper got out of the Celica and headed into a dress shop.

They sat there for what seemed a very long time, before Bess brought them back to an earlier issue. 'So what's going on?' she said, turning from one sister to the next and giving them both the evil eye.

'What?' Megan said. 'Jeez, Bess, what's got your panties in a twist?'

Bess stared at Alicia. 'Why don't you want to go by Grandma's house?' she asked.

'Oh, that!' Megan said. 'Graham's pissed Alicia won't do the nasty with him so he's saying he's going back to UT and that they should date other people.'

'Megan!' Alicia yelled.

'What?' Megan asked, innocence personified. 'You wanted me to keep this from Bess? I can't do that! We're sisters!'

'Whatever,' Alicia said, sinking back into the second row of seating.

'And,' Megan said, again facing Bess, 'Alicia's afraid it's a good idea, that maybe she doesn't *love*-love Graham, but maybe she brother-loves him, ya know?'

'I'm dying here,' Alicia mumbled from the back seat.

Bess turned around in her seat. 'Is this true? Has he been sexually harassing you?'

'We're supposed to be boyfriend and girlfriend, right?' Alicia said. 'I don't know a boyfriend in school who isn't either already getting some or trying like mad to. And even the boys who don't have girlfriends only think about one thing.'

Megan nodded her head. 'You're right. All teenage boys are sex fiends. It's something to do with hormones.'

Bess's shoulders straightened and she said with some dignity, 'Logan's not like that!'

'The hell he isn't!' Alicia, who never, ever cursed, said from the back seat. 'After what I saw last night, that's *all* he's thinking about!'

Megan looked wide-eyed at Alicia, then turned

her gaze on Bess, her eyes turning into slits. 'So what happened last night? Are you still a virgin or not?'

Bess turned blood red and stared straight out the front window. 'We kissed. That's all! Jeez, you two! Can't a girl get kissed without all this drama?'

'Well, you know what kissing leads to!' Alicia said, then burst into tears.

Both her sisters were on her in a heartbeat. 'Oh, Alicia, I'm so sorry!' Bess said. 'This thing with Graham must be awful for you! Should we call Mom?'

'She doesn't want to bother Mom,' Megan said, patting Alicia's arm. 'But I bet if we tell Grandma, she'd put the fear of God into him!'

'Or poison his food!' Alicia said, still wailing.

'Maybe a little laxative in a brownie, but nothing fatal, I'm sure,' Megan said.

'It's bad enough that you two know my shame! I don't want anyone else to!' Alicia got out between sobs.

'Shame?' Bess said. 'What shame? Your boyfriend's an asshole and somehow that's your fault? You're not sure if this is the right relationship for you, and you're to blame for what? Being smart?'

'What's that line in that movie *Speed*?' Megan asked. 'Where Keanu Reaves says something about relationships that start out with bad stuff happening don't do well.'

'It was Sandra Bullock. And it's not "bad stuff happening" – it's something like relationships happening in "intense circumstances,"' Bess said.

'Whatever,' Megan retorted. 'All I'm saying is you both got real *intense*' – she glared at Bess – 'when you got kidnapped, and it was like a false foundation for a relationship.'

Bess nodded and slapped Megan on the arm. 'Good one, Megs.' Turning to Alicia, she said, 'She's right. Maybe someday y'all will find a way back to each other, when *he's* more mature, but right now, I think him going back to UT and both of you seeing other people might be a good idea.'

Alicia sighed and dried her eyes and wiped her nose on the hem of her T-shirt. 'All I know is *I'm* not going to be doing any dating! I've had it with guys!'

'You gonna go lesbo?' Megan asked.

'Jeez, Megan!' Bess said. 'You say one sensitive thing and it's just too much for you, huh? You have to go crass! And it's not "lesbo," it's lesbian. I doubt they like being called "lesbos," any more than gay men like being called . . . well, you know, those other bad words. Not to mention it's not a choice, or haven't you heard?'

'Lordy, I didn't know you were the politically correct police!' Megan said.

Bess made a face and frowned at her sister. 'Tell you what, let's ask Mom when they get back.'

'Oh, gawd no! Don't turn me in to the pinkoliberal police! You're bad enough!'

'I'm gonna tell Mom—'

Alicia sighed. 'Stop it, y'all. Why do you think she's still in there?' she asked, staring at the store Harper had disappeared into.

'You think she knew we were following her so she went in there and went out the back door?' Megan asked.

'And leave her car?' Bess asked.

'Could have,' Megan said.

'Maybe we should go in and check,' Alicia said.

Both Megan and Bess turned to look at their foster sister. 'And we know who that has to be,' Bess said.

'Yup,' Megan agreed and grinned.

Willis didn't stay long on his so-called walk. He came back disgusted that the bar was showing the 1947 Army–Navy game. The living room was still cordoned off with official yellow police tape, so Willis and I headed upstairs, leaving Miss Hutchins in the kitchen, puttering around. Once in our room, I told him about the possible theft of the pitcher and basin, and my idea that the person who took it may have also been the person making the *grrrrrrrrr-plop*ping sound in the hall.

'*Rrrrrrrrrr-thump*,' he corrected.

'No! Definitely *grrrrrrrrr-plop*.'

He sighed. 'There's just no arguing with you. You always think you're right!'

'Because I usually am!' I said. 'Anyway, I have an idea.'

'Another one?' he said, his tone implying that my ideas were less than stellar. An opinion I begged to differ with.

'You go out in the hall and drag a piece of furniture toward the staircase and I'll see if it's the same sound.'

132

My dutiful husband sank down on the bed, hands behind his head. 'I've got a better idea. You do it,' he said.

I laid down next to him on the bed, put an arm across his chest, smiled up at him and began tickling him. Willis hates to be tickled. He says it hurts. I think it only hurts his manly pride. A big guy like him giggling and squirming makes him feel less than masculine. Again, I begged to differ. I thought it was just plain cute, but still, knowing his hatred of tickling, I knew doing it would get me the desired result.

He jumped off the bed. 'Stop that!' he said.

'While you're up,' I said, stretching languidly, 'go drag a piece of furniture down the hall.'

'If you promise never to tickle me again! Ever!'

I thought about it for a moment. 'I can't promise not ever, but I can promise not while we're here in Peaceful. And I also promise to make you very happy later tonight.'

He didn't think about it nearly as long as I had. 'Deal!' he said and headed out the door, shutting it behind him.

I snuggled into the bed, laying on the side that I usually used to fall asleep, trying to as accurately as possible recreate the scene from the night before. Then I heard a sound. *Scritch, scritch, scritch.*

I got up and went to the door. He was pulling a medium-sized table down the hall. Behind him I could see a lamp and several knick-knacks on the floor. 'That's not it,' I said. 'Put that back – and the stuff back on it! – and grab something else.'

133

I could hear him sigh as I went back in the bedroom and shut the door. I hopped back on the bed and turned on my side. A few minutes later I heard: *bump, bump, bump*. My turn to sigh. I got up and opened the door. It was a large chest of drawers and Willis was moving it by walking it down the hall. 'Not that way!' I said.

'Jeez Louise!' he said. 'I can't even drag furniture right?'

'But you're not *dragging* it! You're *walking* it! Try dragging it!' I said and hurried back into the room. I wasn't even in bed yet when I heard the sound from the hall. More *scritch, scritch, scritch*. I sighed and opened the door. 'Not it,' I said.

'I'm through with this!' Willis said and walked past me into our room.

'You're just going to leave that there?' I accused, looking at the large chest of drawers right in front of our doorway.

Flopping down on the bed, Willis said, 'If you want it moved I suggest *you* do it!'

I glared at his back as he'd turned away from me and curled into a loose fetal position. Sighing as loudly as possible, I went into the hall and began to wrestle the huge piece of furniture back to where it came from. Willis had been right in the first place: walking it was much easier than dragging. I saw a darker shade of wallpaper in the right size to fit the chest, and walked it into place.

Diamond Lovesy's door burst open. 'What in the hell is going on here?' she demanded. 'I'm trying to rest! I've been through an ordeal!'

134

I just looked at her. There was a smidge of white powder by her nostrils, her eyes were bloodshot and she was talking fast. Back in my college days I had a roommate who was a big fan of cocaine. Looked to me like Diamond might be a fan herself.

'You high?' I asked her.

'What?' she said, too loudly. 'No! Of course not! I'm grieving!'

'That doesn't mean you didn't take something to ease the pain.' I walked up to her and touched the powder under her nostril. She reared back and slapped my hand.

'Don't you dare touch me!' she screamed, which brought my husband out of our room in a flash.

'What's going on?' he demanded, staring daggers at Diamond. He's very protective of me and the kids. Sometimes it's annoying. But sometimes it makes me feel all warm and fuzzy. This was one of those warm and fuzzy times.

'Your wife was making so much noise I couldn't rest!' Diamond yelled.

'I think it might be the cocaine that stopped you from resting,' I said. 'It's a stimulant, you know. Not what I would recommend for resting or even grief. I think a nice-sized doobie would do the trick.'

'You brought cocaine into this house?' Willis demanded.

'No! Of course not!' Diamond said, backing up to her door.

'Maybe we should look inside—' Willis started. But before he could finish his sentence, Diamond

Lovesy was back in her room, her door slammed in our faces.

Willis grinned at me. 'If there was any coke left, I think it will be flushed soon.'

I fitted my arm into the crook of his. 'You're just wasteful!' I said, grinning back.

BACK HOME

'But she already knows we're up to something!' Alicia said, holding on tight to the door handle of the minivan, lest one of her sisters – Megan – were to jerk it open and pull her out.

'Alicia, don't be an idiot!' Megan said. 'You just happened to go into the same store she's in! What's the big deal? Just apologize for your earlier call, say you didn't mean to offend and start looking at clothes.'

'Did y'all not notice this is a plus-size store? Why would I be going to a plus-size store?'

Alicia, who couldn't weigh more than one hundred and ten pounds, said to Megan, 'You should go in! At least you're closer to plus size than I am!'

'Am not!' retorted Megan.

'Yes, you are!' Bess said. 'What are you now? Like a fourteen? They have fourteens at plus-size stores, I betcha!'

'I'm a twelve!' Megan all but shouted.

'Ha!' Bess said. 'In your dreams!'

'Can you wear a fourteen?' Alicia asked. 'I know it would be loose on you, but could you do it?' Having started the great plus-size debate, she was attempting to mollify Megan and get her to go inside.

136

'I suppose,' Megan grudgingly admitted.

'Then I really think you should go in,' Alicia said, patting Megan on the shoulder. 'Besides, this whole thing is your production. You know what needs to be done more than Bess or me!'

Taking the cue from her foster sister, and knowing that Megan thrived on argument but was a glutton for flattery, Bess said, 'I really think you could do this better than Alicia. Remember how she botched the phone call?'

Megan sighed. 'I suppose you're both right. I'm the only one who could do this justice.' Sighing again, she exited the vehicle. 'Y'all stay here. I'll be right back.'

The two remaining sisters sat ramrod stiff until Megan had entered the store, then they turned and fist-bumped each other. 'Bess,' Alicia said, 'you are truly the great manipulator!'

Bess bowed her head. 'Thank you, awards and flowers will be gladly accepted. But you're the one!' she said, pointing at Alicia. 'I never would have gone that way without your lead!'

'Well, Megan does like a bit of flattery,' Alicia admitted.

'I know, and I forget that sometimes. It's just so much more fun to piss her off.'

Inside the store, Megan headed for a sale rack and began shuffling through the clothes. She didn't see Harper. In fact, she didn't see anybody. Then a door behind the check-out counter opened and Harper came out, carrying several pairs of pants over her arm. Seeing Megan, she said, 'Oh, hi! Can I help you?'

'You work here?' Megan asked.

Looking closer at her new 'customer,' Harper said, 'Oh, great, it's you! I'm being ganged up on by the Pughes today!'

'How would I know you worked here?' Megan demanded. 'I was told this was a good place. I don't usually wear plus sizes, but I thought I'd give it a shot. Do you have anything smaller than a fourteen?'

'No, we don't. And you're not a fourteen! You're in here after me, and I don't know why! What do you bitches want?'

Preening just a bit by Harper's declaration that she, Megan, wasn't a size fourteen, she said, 'Don't be so rude!' She tried to hide the smile of satisfaction that threatened to overtake her face. 'I'm not *after* you for any reason! I'm just doing some window shopping!'

'Bullshit!' Harper said.

'Are you pregnant?' Megan blurted out, pointing at Harper's belly. 'Or just trying to get into some of these clothes?'

'Fuck off, Pugh! And get out of my store!'

'Is this *your* store? Or do you work for someone? Do you think the owner would be happy knowing her clerk was shooing customers away?' Megan said.

Harper walked up to Megan and grabbed her arm, twisting it. Megan jerked away. 'Jeez! You and your brother! Definitely violent types!'

Harper stopped in her tracks. 'So that *was* you last night! I knew it! There aren't many three-somes that look like you and your so-called sisters! A midget, a scarecrow, and you – Godzilla!'

'Again, you are being very rude. And it's not nice to talk that way around your baby. It'll come out mean-spirited.'

Harper shook her head and moved back behind the counter where she managed to get onto a high stool by the cash register. 'Whatever. My feet are killing me! And I don't need this shit! Are you going back to BCR and telling everybody I'm preggers?'

'Not if you don't want me to,' Megan said, moving to the counter and resting her elbows on it. 'But accusing Logan Harris might get the word moving around.'

'Yeah, well, if Logan says anything, my brother's going to kill him.'

'Before or after he marries you?' Megan said.

Harper sighed. 'I'm not marrying Logan! Geez. Would that be a boring life or what?'

'You say he's the father—' Megan started.

Harper jumped up from her stool. 'Yeah. He is. Now get the hell out of here. Like now! Or I'll—'

'You'll what?' Megan said, sneering at her adversary.

Harper grinned. 'I'll call the cops and tell them I caught you shoplifting.'

Megan thought about it. Heading for the door, she said, 'We'll finish this conversation later.'

As she passed through the doorway, Megan heard Harper's parting shot: 'I doubt it!'

We heard Miss Hutchins calling from the foot of the staircase. 'Soup's on!' And by the smell wafting up the stairs it was a soup I could surely get my tongue around. I went to Diamond Lovesy's door and knocked.

'Diamond, it's time for lunch,' I said.

'Not hungry!' came the shouted reply. I wondered if her way of getting rid of the cocaine was to stuff the rest of it up her nose. I would say that normally Diamond had a healthy if not abundant appetite.

'Suit yourself,' I said. 'But something smells wonderful!'

'Leave me alone!' she screamed.

So I did. Willis and I went downstairs to see the dining table set for four. 'Miss Lovesy won't be joining us,' I said as Willis pulled out a chair for Miss Hutchins. He never pulled a chair out for *me* – ever. I opted to say nothing.

There was a soup tureen in the middle of the table and a platter of cold-cut meats next to it, with a basket of assorted breads on the other side of the tureen. There was also a platter of cut vegetables and fruits. I was thinking seriously of moving in here permanently. Miss Hutchins lifted the lid off the tureen and the smell of the soup was almost overpowering. 'Beef barley,' she said. 'Homemade.'

'Will you marry me, Miss Hutchins?' Willis asked reverently.

She giggled. 'I think E.J. might have something to say about that!' she said.

'No, no! It's OK. As long as I get to live with the both of you!' I said, ladling out half as much soup as I actually wanted. I know, I'm a slave to my body image. I also grabbed one slice of sourdough bread (a little on the large size), ham, roast beef and turkey (for the protein, OK?), two kinds of cheese (more protein!) and just a little mayonnaise, and made myself half a sandwich. I grabbed more fruit and veggies than I should have, but hey, they're good for me, right? I figured, all in all, I would only gain maybe five pounds from this lunch. I could go for a walk after.

'Miss Lovesy really should eat something,' Miss Hutchins said.

Willis laughed. 'With what she's stuffed up her—'

I coughed loudly. 'I'm sure she's just grieving. I understand that takes your appetite away.'

'Oh, yes, it does!' Miss Hutchins said with some fervor. 'When Daddy died – the first time – Mama was just inconsolable. She wouldn't eat anything! All she ever did was sleep for the longest time, then she just stayed in her room. I brought her up soup and such, but she never ate much. And when I lost Mama, I didn't eat for a week.' She stopped for a moment, staring off into space. 'Funny thing, though. When Uncle Herbert died, I didn't lose my appetite at all. Quite the opposite,' she said.

'I think we can give Miss Lovesy some slack,' I said.

'Of course,' she said, daintily sipping her soup. I wish I could do that daintily, but I tend to slurp with my intent to get everything in my mouth as quickly as possible. I know, not healthy. But at least it's efficient.

I caught my husband's eye over Miss Hutchins' bowed head. He winked. I winked back. Best

Miss Hutchins didn't know about the drugs that might still be in Diamond Lovesy's room. After lunch, before my possibly imaginary walk, I was going up there and making sure there was nothing left of the coke.

But immediately after lunch I found myself helping Miss Hutchins clear the table and wash the dishes. So I got Willis aside for a moment and asked him to go check out the cocaine situation in Diamond's room.

'She's going to yell at me,' he said, sounding somewhat distraught.

'You've been yelled at by women before,' I said, reassuringly patting him on the arm.

'Only by you!' he said.

I continued patting. 'There you go!' I said with a big smile. 'After me, Diamond Lovesy should be a cinch!'

My poor, beaten-down husband sighed and headed for the stairs while I headed into the kitchen to help Miss Hutchins.

1942–1943

Edgar tried shaving his thick beard with a sharpened flat rock, but all he ended up doing was irritating his sunburned skin. If he saw the girl again, he thought, he'd follow her, to see where she went. If the soldiers were really gone, then maybe he could stay with her – and her family, of course – and maybe find a razor or at least some scissors! But then he had to wonder . . . When she'd said, 'Soldiers gone,' had she meant the Japanese soldiers or the Americans? Because he already knew the Americans were long gone.

He was too selfish a person to wonder where they might be or how they might be faring. It would be years before he would hear about the Bataan death march or the inhumanities of the POW camps run by the Japanese. When he did hear about it, his only reaction would be pride in himself that he'd had the wherewithal to run away.

Ten days after seeing the Filipino girl for the first time, he saw her again, wearing the same garment and heading for the hot springs. But this time she wasn't alone – there was an older woman with her. He hid in the trees for a while, wondering what he should do. Would the older woman be as friendly as the girl had been, or would she immediately turn him over to the Japanese? He was pretty sure the 'soldiers gone' comment the girl had made referred to the Americans and not the Japanese. But he was hungry, and itched from all the hair on both his head and face. And he was lonely. And then, of course, he was horny. If he couldn't have the girl then hell, he thought, he'd take the old lady. So he came out from behind the trees.

The girl saw him first and broke into a smile. 'Ed-gur!' she said.

'Hi, Lupita,' Edgar said, smiling at her.

The woman had whirled around when the girl spoke and was staring at Edgar. She rapidly shot off some of that gobbledygook to Lupita, who gave a rapid-fire response. Then to Edgar she said, 'My mother.'

'Nice to meet you, ma'am,' Edgar said, smiling

and nodding at the older woman. She continued to glare at him.

Deciding to treat the woman like he would a wild animal, he sat down on the grass surround of the hot spring, crossing his legs and putting his hands on his knees, palms up. The woman's glare dimmed a slight bit. To the girl, Edgar said, 'Lupita, I need a shave and a haircut.'

Lupita cocked her head but said nothing. Edgar knew this meant she didn't understand him. So he put his hands to his face and scraped at his beard, then put his hands to his hair and mimed cutting it. The old woman smiled and got excited, rapidly saying something to Lupita in their language. Lupita smiled and mimed cutting her hair, repeating the words her mother had used.

Touching his face, Edgar said, 'Shave . . .'

Lupita copied him and said, 'Shave . . .'

Then touching his hair, Edgar said, 'Haircut.'

Lupita repeated what he'd done.

They smiled at each other, then Lupita turned to her mother and spoke. The mother smiled and nodded at Edgar, then said, 'Shave. Hair cut.' Edgar nodded and smiled back.

Then Lupita held up her sliver of soap and mimed washing and pointed at him. 'Yes, ma'am!' he said at once, and took off his raggedy shirt.

After he was sufficiently dry and Lupita and her mother had talked at length, the two women rose from the grassy surround and Lupita said, 'Stay!' and pointed at him.

He nodded and the two women headed into the forest.

Twenty minutes later Lupita was back, hauling

a Marine-green blanket being used as a sack. She lowered it to the ground and dropped the sides. She sat on the ground and handed things to him. First an old straight-razor with a blade so thin it was almost translucent. She cocked her head as she handed it to him, and he said, 'Razor.'

'Razor,' she repeated, then handed him a knife with a very sharp blade. She motioned to his hair. No scissors, he thought. So he said, 'Knife,' and she repeated it after him. Then she handed him a shirt. It was a man's shirt and looked a little small for him – at least it would have been before he'd started starving to death. It might fit him now, he realized. He smiled his thanks and said, 'Shirt.' She repeated it and handed him a pair of pants, which he named and she repeated. They continued this throughout the contents of the blanket sack, which included a bowl of rice wrapped in a cloth, a small sack of beans that he discovered from the smell were coffee beans, some fruit he'd never seen before and a silver cross on a chain. He tried to hand that back but she wouldn't let him. Instead, she leaned forward and clasped it around his neck. 'Jesus save,' she said. Then she jumped up and handed Edgar the blanket. 'Keep,' she said, then ran back into the forest.

This went on for the next several months. Every week or ten days, Lupita and her mother would come to the hot springs, bringing with them small gifts of bowls of cooked rice, pinto beans, already cooked, and an occasional new fruit. These were a great addition to the stash of game he had at his campsite. One day, finally realizing that they never brought him meat, which could mean they didn't have any, Edgar went to the hot spring with a large leg of pork and presented it to Lupita's mother. He saw tears come to her eyes when she accepted it. The next time Lupita came to the clearing, she was alone. Edgar, of course, thought if he'd known that would happen, he'd have brought the old lady meat the first day!

And so he was alone with the girl. He could tell she was smitten with him, and it didn't take too long for him to bed her. She appeared willing, if a little unwise as to the procedures.

This went on well into 1943, and by the middle of that year it was pretty obvious that Lupita was with child. Her mother came with her to the clearing to emphasize that point. She pointed at her daughter's enlarged stomach and spat out a stream of her language, in no uncertain terms accusing him of causing this problem. He couldn't very well deny it. He'd followed Lupita home one night, unbeknownst to her, and found her little village to be all women. There were no men anywhere. He'd had a bad feeling that they'd either all been subscribed by the Japanese, or just killed. So there didn't appear to be anyone else to point a finger at. Two days later Lupita, her mother and another woman met him at the clearing. The mother handed him another set of clothes. This time the shirt was white with white embroidery around the hem, and the pants were also white, with embroidery on the hems of the legs. She also brought him shoes, like beach shoes at home. They were sandals made of bamboo with thongs between the toes that came up the sides

146

and were covered in brightly colored silk. The mother washed his feet then slid the sandals on him. Then pointed at where he should stand. He stood, with Lupita at his side, while the woman he didn't know spoke their gobbledygook at him, made a few gestures that he didn't understand, then turned and left.

Edgar looked from Lupita to her mother and back again. Now what? he thought. Something told him he might have just gotten married, but he doubted it would transfer back to the States.

Nine

BACK HOME

'He is not boring!' Bess said with some authority after Megan recounted her conversation with Harper Benton.

'Well, he *is* cute,' Alicia said, 'but not exactly the brightest bulb in the box.'

'How can you say that?' Bess demanded.

'He totally flaked on your reference to *Catch-22*,' Alicia said.

'Well, it's an old book,' Bess countered.

'No, it's a classic. Anyone with any smarts has read it by our age!' Alicia said.

'I haven't read it!' came from Megan.

Her sisters looked at each other, and in almost perfect unison, said, 'Exactly!'

Megan waved her hands as if to erase the earlier conversation, and said, 'I think we should stay on topic. The topic being Harper and her baby bump. I don't know much about pregnancy, but I'd say she's into her second trimester, at least.'

'No, more than second,' Alicia said with some authority. Bess and Megan looked at each other then at her.

'So tell all!' Megan said.

Alicia humphed and rolled her eyes. 'How many foster homes do you think I've been in, huh? Enough. I had three so-called "moms" who

148

got pregnant while I lived there, and two other foster "sisters" who got pregnant.'

'You mean another one besides the one who got knocked up by the foster dad?' Bess said, eyes wide. 'Was she diddled by a foster dad, too?'

'No, it was the birth son of the foster family. They, of course, threw her out immediately.'

Bess and Megan looked at each other, both with sorrowful faces. 'I'm so sorry you had such a terrible life,' Bess said, tears stinging her eyes.

'Thank God you got us as a family, huh?' Megan said with a big grin. 'Like what's that old saying? Your boat finally came in?'

'Ship,' Bess said with a sigh.

'Whatever,' Megan said. 'But don't worry, if Graham were to knock you up, Mom and Dad would more likely throw him out than you.' She snapped her fingers. 'Hey! They already have, right? So you're OK!'

Alicia sighed. 'As you mentioned, let's get back on topic. Harper definitely claimed Logan was the father of her baby?'

'Yep,' Megan said. 'But she said she wouldn't marry him because that would be boring—'

'Yes, you mentioned that!' Bess said with some heat.

'I'm just trying to make sure I got the whole conversation out there!' Megan said.

'So now what?' Alicia asked.

'Logan said he's going to tell his folks if we don't come up with something by nine tonight,' Bess said.

'Maybe that's for the best,' Megan said.

'Will his folks believe him?' Alicia asked Bess.

Bess shrugged. 'I have no idea. I've never met them. I think Mom and Dad would believe us if we told them something like this—'

'Oh, Mom!' Megan said in a high falsetto. 'This girl says I knocked her up!' In her regular voice, she said, 'Yeah, I think they'd believe me over the girl.'

'I meant – oh, jeez, just never mind!' Bess said.

Alicia reached forward from the second row of seating and patted Bess on the arm. 'I know what you're trying to say.'

'Well, that makes one of you,' Bess mumbled.

'Do you think Harper's mom is still at home?' Alicia asked.

'I don't know. Don't know how many cars they have. Why?' asked Megan.

'I just wonder if we might get further with her than Harper?'

'Hum,' Bess said, starting the engine of the minivan. 'What harm could it do?' she said, pulling out and turning around to head back over the river.

'Her room stinks,' Willis said when we met up in our bedroom. 'She says she flushed away the rest of the coke, and I couldn't see anything just lying around. But I wasn't about to go messing around in her drawers.' He stopped, then said, 'So to speak.'

'How was her demeanor?' I asked.

'Hostile over grief-stricken.'

'I wonder why she's so hostile toward us?'

Willis shrugged. ''Cause she knows we don't buy her "medium" act?'

I shrugged back. 'Possible.' Thinking for a moment, I then added: 'Do you think it's possible she had anything to do with Humphrey's death?'

'I think that depends on whether his death and the sounds we heard that got us downstairs in the first place are connected,' he said.

I tried not to grin. It's been a slippery slope at best for the last few years regarding my penchant to get involved in murders, but he seemed to be into this one. Of course, this was the first time he was directly involved in finding a dead body. Kind of gets your juices flowing. So to speak. 'I don't see how they aren't connected,' I said, sitting down on the bed beside him. 'But does that connection automatically rule out Diamond?'

'We heard the dragger go out the front door, right? We were downstairs and never saw Diamond go back up. But she was there when the chief went looking.'

I sighed. 'Yeah, I sort of figured the same thing. So Diamond's out.'

'Not necessarily,' he said. 'If she really is a medium, maybe she had help getting whatever was being dragged out of the house.'

I looked at my husband like he'd lost his mind. He grinned at me. 'Or we can forget this horseshit and get frisky.'

I stood up, grabbed his hand, and pulled. 'Or we could go take a walk,' I suggested.

'Maybe we should call the girls first,' he said – proving he was a better parent than I. 'Looks like we won't be getting home today.'

151

Megan's phone rang and she looked at the screen. 'Oh, shit! It's Mom!'

'You think they're home already?' Bess asked, automatically stepping on the brake, which elicited a honk from the car behind them.

'I don't know,' Megan said, still staring at the screen. The phone rang for a third time.

'Answer it, for God's sake!' Alicia said. 'She'll really be suspicious if no one answers!'

Megan nodded, took a deep breath, forced her lips into a smile and clicked the phone on. 'Hi, Mom!'

'Hey, sweetie,' her mother said. 'How are y'all doing?'

'We're just fine! Are y'all home already?'

'No, that's why—'

'Because we're headed to the movies!' Megan said.

'You're not driving, are you?'

'And talking on the phone at the same time?' Megan said, widening her eyes in hopes that would show in her voice. 'Of course not!'

'Put me on speaker,' her mother said.

'OK,' Megan said and did.

'Hey, girls!' E.J. called out.

'Hey, Mom!' both Bess and Alicia said in unison.

'Look, something's come up here and we won't be able to get home tonight. Hopefully tomorrow, but even that's iffy.'

'What's going on, Mom?' Alicia asked, while Megan shot her a look.

'Nothing for y'all to worry about,' E.J. said. 'I just wanted to let you know. Do you have any money left?'

'Sure do,' Bess said proudly.

'Well, if we get stuck here any longer than tomorrow, Bess, you know the new hiding place for that credit card, right?'

'Yes, ma'am,' Bess said.

'I don't know why you think you can't trust me with that knowledge!' Megan said.

'I do!' both Bess and Alicia said in unison.

'Alicia! Do you know?' Megan demanded.

'I didn't tell Alicia because I didn't want you totally alone in your ignorance,' E.J. said. '*Anyway,*' she said, emphasizing the word, 'use it for groceries only. I know the three of you will have been eating out all weekend! So it's time to get healthy. And, by the way, go to school tomorrow, OK?'

'Gawd, Mom!' Bess said. 'You know I'd never skip school!'

Megan sat back in her seat, arms across her chest as she stared out the windshield. 'She's talking to me, y'all.'

'Of course not, sweetie,' her mother said. 'Just to the group in general. Y'all be good and I'll keep you posted on when we'll be leaving here.'

'OK, Mom,' Bess said. 'Y'all be careful. I take it somebody got murdered?'

'Goodbye girls,' E.J. said and disconnected.

'Somebody got murdered,' Alicia said.

'More than likely,' Bess agreed.

'I don't know why she always thinks the worst of me!' Megan wailed. 'I'm a good kid!'

Bess patted her hand while Alicia patted her shoulder. 'Of course you are,' Alicia said. 'Right, Bess?'

'The best,' Bess said, attempting not to roll her eyes.

'Y'all are just trying to humor me!' Megan said. 'And it's not working! What have I ever done to deserve this?' she said, a tear spilling down her cheek.

Just as Bess opened her mouth to enumerate the many things her sister had done to weaken parental trust, Alicia said, 'Absolutely nothing. And Mom loves you! Whose phone did she call? Bess's? No! Mine? No! She called yours. And who does she always call sweetie? You!'

Bess considered all that for a moment, then said, 'Yeah, her *real* child.'

Alicia threw herself back on the second row of seats. 'I give up! You're both out of your minds! You know what I'd give to have had the upbringing you two have had? An arm? A leg? Both? You bet! Try being abandoned by your parents! Then see how that grabs you!' Alicia said, then burst into tears.

Bess pulled the minivan over to the side of the road, as she wasn't able to see much because of the tears that had started streaming down her cheeks. Megan was hunched over in her seat, hands over her face, tears leaking through her fingers.

The three of them continued like this till they heard a chirping sound behind them, and Bess looked in the rearview mirror. 'Oh, great! A cop!' Still watching, she heaved a heavy sigh. 'Even greater, it's Luna!'

'Oh, shit!' Megan said, wiping her tear-streamed face on her T-shirt. The other two did the same

and Bess buzzed open her window as the lieutenant for the Codderville police department, who
lived next door and was as close as their mom
got to a best friend, sidled up to the van.

'Hey,' Luna said, smiling, 'I thought I recognized that minivan. Y'all having car trouble?'

'No! Everything's OK,' Megan said. 'There
was a bee in the van but we got him out.'

'Well, that's not fun!' Luna said. 'Anybody get
stung?'

'No,' Megan said, while her sisters vehemently
shook their heads.

'When are your mom and dad coming home?'
she asked.

'Maybe tomorrow,' Megan said.

'Something came up,' Bess added.

'Probably another dead body,' Alicia said.

'What makes you think that?' Elena Luna said
with a frown.

All three girls looked at her with wide eyes.

Luna shrugged. 'You're right,' she said, tapped
the side of the minivan with her palm, and headed
back to her unmarked car.

'Y'all still on for Harper's mom?' Bess asked,
putting the van in gear and checking her mirrors
for oncoming cars.

'Yes,' Alicia said.

'You bet your ass!' Megan said.

There was an opening in the light Sunday traffic
and Bess took it.

We strolled down Main Street hand in hand. It
was a beautiful spring day, the sun bright but not
yet killer. That was a few weeks off – hopefully.

The streets of Peaceful were clean, no litter, and the windows of the storefronts gleamed from recent wars with a bottle of Windex. Some stores had merchandise on the sidewalk in front, most artfully displayed to attract attention. We stopped at a bookstore that had shelves on the sidewalk filled with used books and unused knick-knacks. Willis grabbed a history book on the building of the state capitol – it's always been his dream to discover how Texas's Lady Liberty originally reached the top of the rotunda. There were no pictures taken at that time to show how it was done. It's a mystery. I found several real mysteries and trinkets for the kids.

We walked on, admiring this and that. I saw a dress at a sidewalk sale that screamed my name. OK, it screamed Diamond's name a little louder than mine, as it was gauzy, drapey, bejeweled and bejangled, but I loved it just the same. So I bought it – without trying it on. It was the right size. I hoped.

Moving on, I noticed a concrete building one block up unlike the lovely Texas Gothic buildings we'd been passing. There were police cars outside and a not-so-discreet sign saying, 'Peaceful Municipal Building,' and underneath that, in smaller lettering, 'City Court, City Manager, Mayor, Police, Fire Marshall.' All in one building.

I pointed at it. 'I wonder if Chief Cotton works on Sundays?' I asked Willis.

He stopped and stared at the sign, then at me. 'Was that the plan this whole time?' he asked, for some reason suspiciously.

This time I *was* innocent. 'No! I had no idea

where the police station was! How would I know?' I sighed at his lack of trust in me. 'Let's go back. He's probably not even there,' I said, letting go of his hand and turning back the way we'd come.

'Really? You didn't plan this?' he said, one eyebrow raised.

'Really.'

'On the heads of our children?'

'Jesus, Willis! I wouldn't claim the sun was shining on the heads of my children! For God's sake, what's wrong with you? No, I didn't know this was the way to the police station. No, I am not lying. No, I don't like you very much at this moment.' And with that I started walking back to Miss Hutchins' B&B.

Willis grabbed my arm. 'Sorry,' he said, smiling. 'That was unfair.'

'No shit, Sherlock,' I muttered.

He pulled me to him, his arms around my back, my head on his shoulder. 'You know there's baggage,' he said.

'I know,' I said.

'I'm trying to be more open-minded,' he said.

'I know,' I said.

He sighed. 'OK, let's go talk to Chief Cotton.'

I really hadn't thought about going to see the chief, but I still thank God Willis didn't see me smile.

BACK HOME

They were once again parked in the lot of the boat repair shop, down the road from the Bentons' double-wide trailer. There were no cars under the

157

carport or parked anywhere nearer their place than next door.

'So we just go up and ring the bell?' Bess ventured.

'All three of us!' Alicia said with some heat. 'I'm not doing this alone!'

'You didn't do the last one alone!' Megan shot back. 'I'm the one who went in the dress shop.'

'All three of us,' Bess said.

'Whatever,' Megan said.

'So what do we say?' Alicia asked. 'Megan, what's our approach?'

Megan shrugged. 'I dunno. Maybe, like, we know Harper's preggers and we also know it's not Logan's?' she suggested.

'Sounds good,' Bess said.

'And when she runs us off with a broom, then what?' Alicia asked.

'Why, we run, of course!' Bess said with a grin.

Alicia sighed and opened the side door of the minivan. 'Sorry, but that doesn't sound like fun to me.'

'Give it some time,' Megan said, patting her on the shoulder. 'This stuff is, like, addictive.'

'Pretty much,' Bess agreed, grinning at Megan.

They walked across the street and up to the threshold of the Bentons' front path. An oversized white mailbox rested atop a filigreed cast iron pole that appeared to be cemented into a half-sized barrel filled with impatiens. All three stopped as if on cue.

They looked at each other, then at the front door of the trailer. Megan squared her shoulders and took a step forward. Her sisters waited a beat, but then moved forward behind her. 'Nothing to it but to do it,' Megan muttered under her breath.

'Amen,' Alicia said quietly, taking Bess's hand in her own.

While other trailers on the street appeared to have warped and rotting wood steps leading to the front door, or cement block steps that left several inches between the top step and the actual door, the Bentons' front steps were stone and were squarely attached to the threshold of the front door. And although it was as high off the ground as the others, flowering shrubs hid the pipes and undercarriage of the Bentons' trailer, unlike the ones that were apparent all up and down the street. The front yard was newly mown, and there were a couple of trees in the front with flower beds surrounding them. From the front they could see a heavily treed backyard.

Megan stepped up to the front door and rang the bell. Her sisters stood on the steps behind her. And they waited. And waited.

Finally they heard a woman's voice say, 'May I help you?'

They whirled around to see an older woman who appeared from around the side of the double-wide.

'Mrs Benton?' Megan asked.

'Yes?' she replied. She had a floppy hat on her head, garden gloves on her hands, and was armed with a spade.

'We need to talk to you,' Megan said, her voice a little belligerent.

Mrs Benton stiffened. 'Who are you?' she asked.

'I'm sorry, Mrs Benton,' Bess said, hopping down from the steps and walking over to her. She smiled brightly and offered her hand. The older woman held up her gloved hands away from Bess's outstretched one.

'Dirty,' she said.

Bess continued to smile. 'My name is Bess Pugh, and these are my sisters, Megan and Alicia.'

'OK. To what do I owe the pleasure?' she asked.

'Could we go inside and talk?' Bess asked.

'Absolutely not,' she said. 'You gave me names, but that means nothing. In fact, I claim to be Mrs Benton, but there's no proof at the moment that I am, is there?' She looked from one girl to the next. 'Why don't you just tell me what you want?'

'I'm not sure you want us talking about this where your neighbors can hear,' Megan said.

Mrs Benton laughed. 'You could murder me in the front yard and nobody around here would notice. Well, they might notice, but they wouldn't do anything about it.'

'Rough neighborhood?' Bess asked.

'It used to be nice. Not anymore. It's horrible,' the woman said. 'Now what is this all about?'

'We know about Harper!' Megan said, coming down from the steps and moving into Mrs Benton's space. The woman used her spade to move Megan back.

'And just what do you think you know about my daughter?' she said, her eyes slits.

'That she's pregnant!' Megan said. 'And that she's claiming it's Logan Harris's and it's not!'

Mrs Benton's eyes opened wide. 'She's what?'

'Pregnant!' Megan said.

160

The woman gave Megan a blistering look. 'I know that! But what makes you think she's claiming it's Logan's?' she demanded.

All three girls looked at each other. Finally, Bess spoke up. 'We were at the place where Logan Harris works last night, and your son came in and grabbed him and took him outside and was beating the crap out of him! I jumped on his back—'

'Then we came out and began hitting on him—' Megan supplied.

'You were beating on my son?' Mrs Benton asked, her eyes wide.

'Well, ma'am, he was beating on Logan,' Bess said.

'Then after Alicia kicked him in the nuts, he ran back to his truck.'

'You kicked Tucker in the nuts?' Mrs Benton asked, looking at Alicia.

Alicia shrugged. 'Seemed like a good idea at the time.'

Mrs Benton shook herself. 'And what does any of this have to do with Harper?' she asked.

'She was there,' Bess said. 'We didn't see her, but Logan did—'

'And I talked with her less than an hour ago at her work, and she said it was Logan's. But that's not true!' Megan said.

Mrs Benton took a deep breath and stared off into space. Finally, she looked back at the girls. 'I'll handle this,' she said. 'You need to leave before Tucker gets home. Which should be any minute.'

All three girls exchanged glances, said, 'Yes, ma'am,' and made a beeline to the minivan.

1943–1946

The baby was born at the end of summer. A dark-haired, dark-eyed little girl. Lupita's mother had delivered the baby in her hut in the village. Edgar had stayed in the forest, as it was still viewed as unsafe to venture outside its confines. Lupita came to him the next day, carrying the swaddled newborn in her arms, and presented her prize to her husband.

Edgar looked at the baby then up at Lupita. To him the kid looked like a dark-haired Winston Churchill. All she needed, he thought, was a cigar. 'Nice,' he finally said.

Lupita cocked her head and he said, 'Good. You done good.'

She smiled. 'You name?' she asked.

'Me?' he said, pointing at his chest.

She nodded her head vigorously.

His first thought was to name the baby after his mother, then he came up with a brainstorm. How funny would it be to let his old man know that he, Edgar, had a child and it was named after dear old dad? And then tell him it was a girl! His old man would shit a brick! And so Clayton Marie Hutchins came to be.

With the meat Edgar brought to the clearing for the village his daughter thrived, and by the time she was three, Lupita was pregnant yet again. Edgar hoped for a son, but wasn't sure what he would do with one. He was still living in the forest while his so-called wife and child lived in the village. Everybody – all the women of the village – knew he was there, but they all kept silent when the Japanese raided the village.

162

And for this, Edgar, who really didn't understand the concept of gratitude, did know you paid for what you got. And an occasional warty pig or civet cat was a small price to pay for his life. He saw Lupita a couple of nights a week, and Clayton Marie one day a week. Even with so little time together, she was certainly picking up English, as was her mother. One night, when she'd become more fluent speaking English, Lupita mentioned a fear. 'What if Clayton Marie speaks your English when the Japs are around?'

He'd taught her to say Japs and was quite happy she'd picked it up. He hoped it would catch on throughout the village. 'I dunno,' he said, in answer to her question. 'So what?'

'They might kill her.'

He just looked at her. 'Why?' he finally asked.

'Because she speak your English! No one of us speak your English! At least, not around the Japs!'

'Well, tell her not to talk English to the Japs!' Edgar said, irritated that this was taking time away from him getting laid.

'She do, Japs burn whole village,' Lupita said. 'Then they come look for you.'

'How would they know about me?'

She shrugged. 'She learn your English somewhere, huh?'

Edgar sighed. 'Well, what in the hell do you want me to do about it?'

Lupita bowed her head. 'You take Clayton Marie with you here. She stay with you, not in village. All mothers say so.'

'What the fuck?' Edgar all but yelled. 'Those

163

old witches are throwing my baby girl out of the village?'

A tear rolled down Lupita's cheek. 'They scared,' she said.

'Yeah, well how about no more meat, huh? How'd they like them apples?' he shouted.

She looked up at him, tears streaming down her face. 'They tell Japs, if no meat. They come get you. And Clayton Marie too.'

Edgar was pacing now, back and forth around the hot springs. 'How in the hell am I supposed to take care of that girl? She's practically a baby.'

'I know!' Lupita said, her eyes big with surprise. 'I come too. We live here in forest with daddy.' She grinned big. And Edgar realized he'd just been had. She'd been bucking to move to the forest with him for over a year, and he'd said no. Now she'd mixed lies with a little bit of truth, or maybe truth with a little bit of lies, but he didn't dare test to see which. So Lupita and Clayton Marie moved into his camp site, bringing her mother along. Just until the new baby was born, Lupita promised him.

It would be another year before Edgar learned that the Japanese had surrendered almost two years before.

Ten

The inside of the Peaceful municipal building was as generic as its outside. Signs in the small lobby indicated which way to the various offices. The second floor appeared to house the offices of the city manager, the mayor, the fire marshal and the judges' chambers (or maybe just judge's chambers. Would they need more than one judge in a town this small? I had no idea). An arrow pointed to the court itself down a hall toward the back of the building. The police department was right up front. You couldn't miss it.

Willis and I went in. Mary Mays was in a bullpen behind a counter cordoned off with what appeared to be bulletproof glass. Another woman sat at the small window that had a speaker system and a small hole at the bottom to receive, I suppose, payments for tickets and such. This woman was much older than Mary, probably in her late fifties or early sixties, wearing the same uniform as Mary. Her hair was a tightly permed gray helmet, and her lack of a smile didn't bode well.

'Yes?' she said.

'We'd like to speak to Chief Cotton, please,' Willis said.

'Regarding what?' the woman asked.

'The murder at the Bishop's Inn,' he said.

'I'm sure he has nothing more to report at this

time,' the woman said and reached over to shut off the mic.

I got in quickly and hollered, 'Mary! Remember us?'

Since she'd already checked us out and ignored us, I was afraid of what response I was going to get. The response from the woman manning the counter wasn't good. She glared at me and off went the mic. But then I saw Mary Mays heave a great sigh and get up from her desk. She walked to the counter, leaned over the woman seated there and turned the mic back on. 'What do you want?' she asked.

'We'd like to talk to the chief,' I said.

'He's busy,' she said.

'Then how about you? Could we talk to you for just a moment?'

She sighed again, said, 'I guess,' turned off the mic and buzzed the door to the side of the counter open and came out into the waiting area. There were several chairs, but the entire waiting area was empty of any humanity other than the three of us.

'Sit,' she said, indicating the chairs. Willis and I sat. She loomed over us, her arms tightly crossed over her chest. 'What do you want?'

'Ah, we just wondered if there was any progress on the case? We have children at home we need to get back to,' I said and smiled.

'We don't discuss ongoing investigations,' she said. 'We'll let you know when you can leave town.' And with that she turned, flipped the other woman a hand signal of some kind and I heard the door click open.

So maybe it wasn't my smartest move. Maybe she'd pissed me off. Maybe I'm a complete idiot. Any of those things, and many more, may have been the cause of what happened next. Officer Mays pushed the door open, not knowing I was directly behind her. In a flash, I was inside the inner sanctum.

'What the hell?' Mary said as she twirled around.

'I really need to talk to the chief,' I said. Through the small window at the counter, I could see my husband, still sitting in his chair, his hands over his eyes, his body shaking. He was either crying or laughing. I'm not sure which.

'I told you he's busy! I should arrest your ass right now!' she said. Her voice had risen, which was probably the reason a door opened and Chief Cotton's form appeared.

'Mary, what's going on?' he asked. Seeing me, he nodded and said, 'Miz Pugh, right?'

'Yes, sir,' I said. 'I just wanted—'

'I was talking to her and her husband in the waiting room, and told her we didn't discuss open cases! And then she just pushed in behind me!' Mary said in what I deemed to be an overly agitated voice.

'Miz Pugh, why don't you wait in my office. Mary, go get Mr Pugh, if he's still in the waitin' room.'

'But—' she started.

The chief sighed. 'Just do it, Officer!' he said.

I smiled to myself as I headed into the office the chief had so recently exited. He entered shortly after me and took a seat behind his desk, indicating that I sit in the visitor's chair. The room was small, with a fifties-style crank-out window, a desk too large for the space, two filing cabinets and a credenza. There was barely room in there to breathe. Mary Mays knocked on the door frame, with Willis behind her. 'Mr Pugh, sir,' she said, and was not particularly happy about it.

'Bring in another chair for Mr Pugh, please, Officer.'

'Yes, sir,' she said, did a militaristic about-face and headed out of the room.

The chief stood and shook hands with Willis. 'Nice to see you again, Mr Pugh, Miz Pugh,' he said.

Then Officer Mays was back with a straight-back chair, which she set down in front of the chief's desk. I wasn't sure if my husband's long legs would find any room in this tiny space.

'Shut the door on your way out,' the chief said to his officer. She grudgingly did so.

'Now, Miz Pugh, you shouldn't have done that,' the chief said.

'Sir?' I asked, playing innocent.

He just stared at me, then said, 'You know, she coulda shot you and gotten away with it. You barging in here like that.'

'I'm just happy your officer showed some restraint,' Willis said.

The chief laughed. 'I don't know if I'd call it that, Mr Pugh.'

'Please, call me Willis,' my husband said with a big smile.

'Fine. Please continue to call me Chief Cotton.'

'Of course,' Willis said.

Feeling I'd lost the thread of why we were here, I stepped in. 'So, Chief, we were just wondering if there's been any progress—'

'Can't discuss an open case,' he said.

'Oh, it's OK,' I said, giving him my own big smile. 'I work with the police back home all the time.'

'You ain't back home, ma'am,' he said.

'You can call Lieutenant Elena Luna with the Codderville police department. She'll verify that I've worked on—'

'Ma'am, that makes no difference. We don't allow civilians to dick around in our cases in Peaceful. It's just a rule we have. Ya know?'

'My wife and I need to get home, Chief,' Willis said. 'We have four children that are on their own at the moment.'

'Well, three,' I said. 'Graham—'

My husband gave me a look. I closed my mouth.

'Sorry, can't let y'all leave until we have a handle on this thing,' the chief said.

'What do you consider a handle?' I asked.

'Well, knowing who done it would be a nice thing to hold on to,' he said.

'Do you have any leads?' I persisted.

He was quiet for a long moment, then said, 'Ma'am, what part of I ain't talking did you not understand?'

'I really can help—'

The chief stood up. 'Mr and Miz Pugh, I thank y'all for coming in, but I got work to do and a murder to solve, and I like to do those things without the help of civilians.'

He walked around his desk, opened the door and called out, 'Mary! Come walk these people out.' He turned to us. 'You'll be the first to know when you can go home.' He thought for a moment, then said, 'Well, maybe not the first. But you'll be right up there, promise.' And with that he shut the door basically on our butts.

BACK HOME

Once back at the house, Bess called Logan on his cell phone. 'We talked to Harper and her mom,' she said. 'If you can, you might want to hold off on telling your folks about all this. Harper told Megan that you're the father, but her mom seemed totally confused by her saying that.' Bess had told him all this without taking a breath. She did so now, a big one. 'Here's the thing: we girls have decided that whoever knocked her up was someone her brother knows and he would, like, kill him or something if he found out. He probably pressured Harper to tell her who did it and she just picked you at random.'

'She just decided to ruin my life for shits and giggles, huh?' Logan said.

'Well, she did tell Megan that she wasn't going to marry you.'

'Why not?' Logan asked defensively.

Bess was silent. She didn't dare tell him Harper said it would be boring married to him. That would hurt his feelings. Finally she said, 'She didn't really say why.'

170

'Well, good, I guess. I don't want to marry her either, obviously.'

'I think now that Harper's mom knows what she's saying about you, and the fact that Tucker tried to beat you up, I think her mom's going to get this all straightened out.'

'Why would she care?' Logan asked, his voice dejected.

'Because she's a mom!' Bess said, as if that explained everything, and in Bess's world it did.

'I don't know, Bess. I think I really need to talk to my folks.'

'OK, and their best reaction would be what?' she asked.

He was quiet for a moment, then said, 'I dunno. I guess they'd believe me and be really pissed, mostly about Tucker beating on me, but by Harper lying, too. Then my dad would confront Tucker and my mom would call her mom . . .'

'Worst case scenario?'

Again, Logan was quiet. Then he said, 'My dad goes ballistic, threatens to disown me, my mom cries, and somehow this gets all over the school.'

'Which do you think is most likely?' she asked.

Bess could almost hear his shrug over the phone. 'Probably something in the middle.'

'And?'

He sighed. 'I'm not going to tell them, all right? You've convinced me!'

'No, you convinced yourself, Logan,' Bess said in a quiet voice.

'I'm sorry,' he said. 'I'm not blaming you. This

isn't your fault! This is my fault for ever asking that bitch out in the first place!'

'No, it's Harper's fault. She's the one telling lies.'

'So what do I do now?' he asked.

Bess squared her shoulders. 'Well, my mom and dad aren't coming home tonight after all. What time do you get off?' she asked, and squeezed her eyes shut while she waited for a response.

'We close at eight on Sunday,' he said. 'I can tell my mom I'm doing inventory or something and come over there. Maybe we can watch a movie?'

'Sure, that sounds good,' Bess said, barely able to contain her grin.

'And, hey, I'll bring some food so y'all hold dinner, OK?'

'Will do.'

The two hung up, and Bess threw herself down on the couch and hugged herself, letting the grin spread far and wide.

The first thing I did when we got back to the Bishop's Inn was call my friend and neighbor, Elena Luna, at her office in the Codderville Crime Prevention building. It used to just be called the police department, but a new mayor thought this sounded more officious and spent one hundred grand on changing signs, stationery and other items that used the more mundane previous name. He didn't get re-elected but the newer mayor thought it would be unwise to spend more money turning everything back. I presume it will remain the Codderville Crime Prevention building for the foreseeable future, even though everyone still calls it the police department.

'Lieutenant Luna,' she said.

'Hey, it's me,' I said.

'Y'all home?' she asked.

'No, not exactly. We're still in Peaceful—'

'Still say that's a dumb name for a town.'

'You've been proven right,' I said, then went on to explain the goings-on in not-so-peaceful Peaceful.

'Not my jurisdiction,' she said.

'Of course it isn't. The police chief here is named Rigsby Cotton and he's not being very cooperative—' I started but was cut short by her hoot of laughter.

When she'd stopped laughing, she said, 'By that I suppose you mean he doesn't seem to want your input? Like I ever did! So why don't you just do what you always do to me? Jump in anyway and gum up the works any way you can!'

'I've never gummed up the works, as you so eloquently put it,' I said stiffly. 'I've helped you in innumerable ways!'

'Yeah? Name seven,' she said. 'And why exactly have you called me?'

I sighed. I was beginning to think my idea wasn't going to work. 'I was hoping you'd call Chief Cotton and explain what a help I've been—'

Again, I was stopped by yet another hoot of laughter. The woman had some serious lung power. 'Why in the hell would I do that?'

'To get me off your back and onto his?' I ventured.

173

She was silent for a moment. I crossed my fingers in hopes that she was actually considering it. Finally, she said, 'Nope. Can't do it. I can't intentionally inflict that kind of pain on another peace officer. I think I took an oath not to sic you on anyone else.' Then she giggled – a sound I'd never heard coming from her until recently. The return of her husband from a twenty-year stint in Leavenworth had led to many changes in Luna's attitude and behavior – most of them good.

'Luna, Willis and I are stuck here until he solves this thing, and believe me, that's not going to happen. The guy doesn't have a clue. I think this may be his first murder.'

'Huh,' she said.

'Are you listening to me?'

'What? Yeah, more or less.'

'Let's try more!' I said. 'We can't leave the girls unattended much longer! Children's services will come and take them away!'

'I won't let that happen. They can move in with me. I've always wanted a girl! It'll be fun fixing their hair for graduation, oh, and picking out wedding dresses—'

'Can it!' I said with a little heat. No one was picking out wedding dresses but me! 'Luna! I'm serious! We need help here.'

She sighed long and hard. Finally she said, 'OK, tell me again what's going on. Details.'

So I did.

AUGUST, 1947–NOVEMBER, 1947

He found out quite by accident. He and Lupita and Clayton Marie were at the hot spring when

174

Clayton Marie took off, as a four-year-old is wont to do. And like most fathers – including bad ones like Edgar Hutchins – he ran after her, ending at the village. Clayton Marie ran to her grandmother, but Edgar stopped short. There were men there. Old men, young men, strong men, weak men, but they were all back. Some of them looked at him strangely; others looked at him and laughed. Why were the men back? Where were the Japs? What the hell was going on? Edgar asked himself. Then he asked out loud, 'Speak English?'

The women were quiet but one man, maybe in his fifties or sixties – for Edgar it was hard to tell with Filipinos as they all looked alike to him – said, 'Yes. I speak.'

'Where are the Japs?' Edgar asked.

The man cocked his head the way Lupita used to do. 'The Japanese!' Edgar shouted. 'The fucking Japanese!'

'They gone,' the man said, while the women gathered to whisper and Lupita's mother held Clayton Marie close.

'When?' Edgar demanded.

The man shrugged. 'Before last harvest,' the man said.

He looked around him at the men gathering grains and vegetables from the fields.

'Like a year ago?' Edgar said, almost in a whisper.

The man cocked his head, but Edgar didn't really need a response. He turned and stared at the old woman who held his daughter, turned and walked back into the forest.

175

Without a word to his wife or Clayton Marie, he gathered up a few belongings, including the handguns he'd confiscated, and headed deeper into the forest, on his way to the stash he'd buried many years ago.

And it was still there. The thousand dollars in cash and the ivory, pearls and other gemstones he'd bought cheap in Shanghai. He pocketed it all and headed through the now dead and deserted Marine camp, not thinking at all, nostalgically or otherwise, about his time encamped there. He made his way to a port and hopped a freighter headed for San Francisco.

He used the name Don Winslow, after a character in his favorite series of boy stories from when he was a kid. No one gave it a second thought. And no one on the freighter asked for ID. He landed in San Francisco in September of 1947 and jumped ship. He spent a couple of months in that city, discovering that a thousand dollars didn't go far, and that hocking his pearls and other gemstones didn't bring him nearly what he had thought it would – barely more than what he'd paid for them in Shanghai.

He was almost at the point of thinking about actually getting a job, when he began to fantasize again about the treasure in the house on Post Oak Street – the house that should have been his. He'd stopped thinking about it around the same time he'd taken off from the base, the day the Japanese moved in. Trying to stay alive took up most of his thinking time. But now, broke and facing eviction from the fleabag hotel he was staying in, the fantasy came back in full force.

But he was too broke to even make it to Texas. And what if he did? He knew his brother Norris wasn't going to let him in the house. So with his last twenty bucks, he entered a poker game he'd heard about near his hotel. Two fortuitous things happened at that game: one, he won close to five hundred dollars, and two, one of the guys said, upon seeing him, 'Jeez, you're the spitting image of a guy I knew in the army.'

'Oh, yeah?' Edgar said back, only being polite to someone he intended to fleece. 'Who was that?'

'Guy named Hutchins. Good guy. Sad to see him blown to hell on D-Day. But, shit, most of 'em were. Me? I got out of it by the skin of my teeth!'

Somebody snorted and said, 'Gawd, Miller, we've heard this shit before. Let it go, fer Christ's sake!'

So he had some money and a plan. Now that his brother was dead and not about to keep him out of the house on Post Oak Street.

Eleven

BACK HOME

'I guess we need to go to the store,' Alicia said.

'Why?' asked Megan, who was lounging on the sofa, one long bare leg stretched out, the other knee bent as she inspected her calf. 'God, I need to shave!'

'Well, don't use my razor! You always ruin it!' Alicia said.

'I can't help it if your peach fuzz is no match for my womanly growth!'

'Womanly, my ass!' Alicia said. 'Let's just say manly and get it over with!'

Megan sat up and stared at her foster sister. 'Are you calling me manly?' she said, her voice menacing.

'No! I'm calling that thatch of steel wool on your legs manly.'

'Humph. Well, at least I can grow hair!' Megan shot back as she sank down on the sofa and continued her perusal of her body hair.

Alicia just shook her head. 'If we're going to go to the store for groceries, we better get it done or we won't have dinner tonight!'

'I thought there was food in the refrigerator,' Megan said.

'Yes, there is, and it's all frozen. So we either go to the store or have popcorn for dinner.'

'We could order a pizza. We still have money left—'

178

Bess walked into the room and caught the last part of her sisters' conversation. 'No pizza. Logan's coming over and he's bringing dinner.'

Megan tossed her legs on the floor and sat up. 'He remembers I like the porterhouse, right?'

Bess glared at her. 'You'll eat what he brings and you'll be happy to get it! Also, we're going to reimburse him for whatever he spends.'

'I'm sure he gets a nice discount,' Megan said. 'But he better bring something good because I'm not paying for something I don't like!'

'Even though you'll eat it?' Alicia said.

'Duh! How will I know I don't like it if I don't eat it?'

'Do you think we can straighten up in here?' Bess asked, surveying the great room. There was a size 36C bra hanging off the back of one of the bar stools, shoes dotting the floor at random, and the Sunday paper was scattered from the breakfast table to the coffee table with the funnies adorning the bar. There were also dishes in the sink and on the counter, and the dishwasher, which was only partially filled, was standing open, as were the doors of two kitchen cupboards. Someone had brought dirt in on their shoes and left scatterings from the back door into the kitchen.

Without looking, Megan said, 'Looks fine to me.'

Alicia looked around and had the decency to blush. 'Pretty much a mess, huh?' she said to Bess.

'Pretty much.' Bess turned to Megan, who appeared to be attempting to pull out one of her

179

leg hairs with her thumb and index finger. 'How much of this mess is yours, Megan?'

Not being able to get a handle on the pesky hair, Megan finally looked up. 'What mess?'

Bess just waved her arm, indicating the room in general. Megan looked at a pair of white running shoes with rainbow-colored laces. Pointing at them, she said, 'Those aren't mine.' And she traded legs to continue her inspection.

'Wow. That's great! One pair of shoes in the maelstrom of madness isn't yours!' Bess said with some scorn. 'So pick up the rest of the crap and put the dishes in the dishwasher! I already put mine in *at breakfast*! Like any normal person would!'

'Are you saying I'm not normal?' Megan asked, still staring at her other leg.

'You bypassed normal as you came out of the birth canal!' Bess said. 'Get up!'

Megan put her leg down but didn't rise. Instead she just looked at her sister with narrowed eyes. 'I believe in efficiency. Why put dishes in the dishwasher three times a day when you can just wait until bedtime and put them all in then? That's efficient! And besides, why should I have to clean up for your boyfriend?'

'What do you think Mom would say if she knew we were entertaining company in a filthy house, and that it's all your fault?'

'I think she'd say, "Who gave you permission to entertain guys in the house when we're away?"' She grinned at Bess. 'Wanna call her and see what she would consider the bigger problem?'

'I hate you,' Bess said with gritted teeth.

'No, you don't,' Megan said, going back to her inspection of things hairy, 'you love me. You're pissed, but you love me!'

Alicia stood up and went to Bess, who seemed to have tightened every muscle in her body. 'Come on, I'll help you clean up. And Megan's right about one thing: those aren't her shoes,' she said, pointing at the white sneakers. 'They're yours.'

'Bite me!' Bess said, picked up the shoes and took them upstairs.

She sat on her bed in her room for a few minutes, trying to calm down. Megan was the one person in the world who could really, really get to her. When she complained to Mom about it, she just said, 'I had three sisters. They certainly can be maddening. But you love them just the same.'

Bess wasn't all that sure about that. Sometimes she felt she could rip Megan's throat out and dance around with it on the end of a fork but, she reminded herself, if anybody else messed with her sister, there would be hell to pay. So did that mean something? Something more than the fact that Bess would prefer being the one to destroy her sister? Maybe . . . maybe not.

She sighed and laid back, her head on her pillow. She wanted things to be perfect when Logan got here. She wanted him to believe that she and her sisters were good people, that they lived in a beautiful home and had caring, doting parents. Most of which was true, except for Megan being a good person. Megan was a self-centered bitch! Bess thought. But she was funny, that she had to concede. And she had other good points, although Bess wasn't sure she could enumerate them at the moment. OK, she could be generous. She was protective of Bess – whether Bess wanted her to be or not. And she was getting that way about Alicia, too. And Alicia needed it. And she liked to read, which Bess considered a trait closer to God than cleanliness. But don't get her started on Megan and cleanliness. Hell, she thought, you could barely put the two things in the same sentence without someone gagging!

OK, she told herself, sitting up and putting her feet on the floor. There was no way Megan was going to clean her own mess. She grinned. But two could play at this game, Bess thought, and headed downstairs to get that size 36C bra and stash it in the oven.

We were just sitting down to an awesome Sunday dinner when the doorbell rang. It was just Willis, Miss Hutchins and me as Diamond Lovesy hadn't seen fit to stick her head out her door since breakfast, a meal she'd just picked at. I worried how she would be able to keep her abundant figure this way. Certainly it required at least a couple of thousand calories per meal. Or am I being catty? Having lost thirty-five pounds – and kept it off for almost a year! – I do tend to be a bit bitchy about people who haven't been as fortunate. I mean, come on! If I can do it, anybody can! Which is a statement I've always abhorred when anyone else used it. My argument has always been that we have no idea what someone else's struggle is all about, or how much help the person who made the statement had to get where they are. But then, of course, I lost thirty-five pounds and became the queen of the universe.

Willis excused himself and went to the door. I leaned back in my chair to peer down the hall to the front door, and almost lost my balance when I heard Chief Cotton's voice. I straightened the chair and looked wide-eyed at Miss Hutchins. 'It's the chief!' I stage-whispered.

'Don't worry, dear,' she said. 'I'm sure he's not here to arrest you.'

Wide-eyed turned to bug-eyed. 'What? Of course not!' I said.

She patted my hand. 'You just seemed so worried,' she said.

And I was. Not about a possible imminent arrest, but the fact that he might send us packing, and me with an unsolved murder to deal with!

Willis and the chief walked into the dining room. 'So sorry to disturb y'all at suppertime,' he said.

Miss Hutchins stood up. 'It's quite all right, Rigsby. I made a lovely pork roast with sauerkraut and boiled potatoes with butter. I'll get you a plate.'

'Oh, no, ma'am, you don't have to do that!' he protested, but I couldn't help but notice he was sniffing my plate.

'Miss Lovesy hasn't joined us, so there's more than enough to go around,' Miss Hutchins said.

'Well, ma'am, I sure do appreciate that. The wife's visiting her mother in Lubbock and I ain't had a decent meal for a week!'

Miss Hutchins laughed. 'I've had your wife's

cooking, Rigsby, and I'd say you haven't had a decent meal in thirty years!'

The chief sat down across from me where a place had been set for Diamond Lovesy. 'I'd agree with you but I'm afraid you'd tell my wife!'

'Never!' she said, putting her index finger to her lips. 'It's our secret.'

As she left the room, the chief sighed. 'Well, if it was just that one secret, it might be OK, but I hate to say Miz Hutchins knows where all my bodies are buried.'

'Figuratively speaking?' I said.

He grinned. 'Oh, yes, ma'am.'

Willis sat down beside me and squeezed my hand under the table. I think he might have noted, as I had, that the chief was being much more amiable that he'd been at the station. If I were the type of person to get scared – which I'm not – I would have been a little frightened by said amiability.

Miss Hutchins brought out a plate laden with pork roast, sauerkraut, boiled potatoes and butter, with a little bowl of brown mustard. 'If I remember right, you like a little dark mustard with your pork roast?' she said to him.

'Miz Hutchins, you are a marvel,' he said and dug in. He didn't look up again until he'd demolished half his plate. How someone as scrawny as the chief could put away that much food that fast was beyond me.

Finally, halfway through his plate – while even Willis had only consumed no more than a fourth of his, and I was still salting mine – he looked up at me and said, 'Got a call a little while ago. Wanna guess who?'

I dug my fingernails in Willis's thigh. He flinched but luckily didn't cry out. 'I have no idea,' I lied.

'That lady you mentioned. Elena Luna, that lieutenant from the Codderville PD? She called me up. Told me all about you. We had us a few laughs.'

I may have broken skin on my husband's thigh by this time. 'I'm sure you did,' I said while gritting my teeth.

'She says you're a real nuisance,' he said.

'Oh, she did, did she?' I was never speaking to my former friend again. Ever.

'Yeah, that's what she said. But she also said you'd helped on occasion. OK, more like you've helped her on a lot of occasions.' He frowned at me. 'Why do you do that?'

'Do what?' I asked in all innocence.

'Mess around in murders? You think you're Miz Marple or somebody? She was in them Agatha Christie books,' he added.

'Yes, I've heard of her,' I said. 'I just like to help when I can,' I added, and heard my husband cough rather loudly and infinitely longer than necessary. I rested my foot a little less than gently on his and pressed.

'Well, Elena says I should feel OK about keeping you in the loop, that you got what she calls "good instincts."'

I tried not to preen. It was hard, but I managed. 'I'd be happy to help you in any way I can,' I said.

'You can't be serious!' came from behind us and we all looked up to see Diamond Lovesy standing there, hands on ample hips, a frown so deep on her face that the space between her eyes had all but disappeared.

Willis and the chief both stood up. Funny, Willis never stands up for me.

'Miz Lovesy,' the chief said. 'How you doing?'

'Well, I came down to eat, but hearing that bullshit, I think I've lost my appetite!' she said.

'And what bullshit would that be, ma'am?' the chief asked.

Pointing at me but looking squarely at the chief, she said, 'Letting this . . . this . . . woman get involved with the investigation! She and her so-called husband supposedly found poor Humphrey's body! Is it such a stretch to think they're the ones who killed him?'

'Now, ma'am, why would they? You know if they got a motive?' he asked. Then pointing at a vacant chair next to him, said, 'Please come sit down.' Turning to Miss Hutchins, he said, 'Ma'am, is there enough food left for another plate?'

'Oh! Forgive me! Of course!' She jumped up and gave Diamond her one-hundred-watt smile. 'I do so hope you enjoy a good pork roast!' she said, and headed into the kitchen.

'Please sit!' the chief said again.

Diamond reluctantly came around the table and sat next to the chief. I got up – rather than sit there and have her continue to stare daggers at me – and sorted out her place setting. 'Miss Hutchins makes her own sauerkraut,' I said.

186

'And it's wonderful. And the bread is home-made, too.'

'Are you trying to bribe me with sauerkraut and bread?' Diamond said, still with that deep frown on her face.

I sighed. 'Diamond, you need to let up or you're going to get early wrinkles!' I said.

She continued to frown until Miss Hutchins came in with her plate. The smells seemed to do more to dissipate the frown than any words from me.

The chief had resumed eating the minute Diamond took her seat and was through before Diamond had cut her first bite of pork roast. 'Now, Miz Lovsey, I don't want you to be alarmed, but I wouldn't mind getting Miz Pugh's input on some of this. Turns out she's actually been involved in a lot more homicides than me.'

Diamond looked up at me. 'Are you a serial killer, E.J.?' she asked.

'No more than you're a psychic,' I said with a tight smile.

'Bitch,' she said under her breath as she leaned down to shovel food into her pie-hole. OK, I'm being catty again – but she did lean down to eat. I swear.

'Now, ladies, behave,' the chief said with a wide grin. 'Miz Pugh, what are you thinking about this here? Got any ideas? Find any clues?'

I was beginning to get a sinking feeling that he wasn't going to take my expertise – such as it was – very seriously. 'I have theories, Chief, as I'm sure you do. Are you aware of the strange

187

occurrences that have been going on here at the Bishop's Inn?'

'You mean the ghosts and goblins?' He laughed out loud. 'I heard tell.' He looked at Miss Hutchins and said, 'Ma'am, I mean no aspersions to you or yours, but I'm not a big believer in spirits and haunts.'

'That's because you've never seen my daddy walking these halls and messing with things,' Miss Hutchins said.

'You're right, ma'am, I've never had the pleasure of meeting your daddy either alive or dead. And I hope to hell I don't.' He turned to look at Diamond. 'You seen her daddy?' he asked.

'I've not seen him,' Diamond said haughtily, 'but I've felt his presence and even channeled him once, or was it twice?' she asked, looking at Miss Hutchins.

'I think only once, dear,' Miss Hutchins answered.

'What's that mean?' the chief asked. 'You "channeled" him?'

'It means his spirit entered my body and spoke through me.'

The chief hooted with laughter, but caught himself before it got out of hand. 'I'm sorry, Miz Lovesy, but that sounds like a whole bunch of hokem, if you don't mind me saying so.'

'Actually, Chief, I do mind!' Diamond said. 'If you know nothing about a subject, I would think it would behoove you to keep any opinions to yourself.'

'Well, now, you might have a point, ma'am,' the chief replied, 'except we got us this murder

188

here, and these so-called sightings of a dead man, and I can't see how the two are connected. One is reality and the other is balderdash. And as I don't believe in the existence of haunts, I gotta think there are live human beings involved here, and that you, ma'am, if you don't mind me saying so, are as full of shit as a Christmas turkey.'

'I do mind you saying so!' Diamond said, jumping to her feet. I noted she'd already cleaned her plate and doubt she had any intention of staying downstairs with us no matter what the chief said. She flung herself up the stairs, her back rigid, without another word. Not even to thank Miss Hutchins for a wonderful meal.

'You think it was something I said?' the chief asked those of us still assembled. He was grinning ear to ear, and I couldn't help thinking the man was having a great time.

BACK HOME

Logan showed up a little after eight that evening to find a clean house and two seemingly well-behaved girls and one anxious one. He was carrying two bags full of food, and the smell was duly noted by Megan. 'Do I smell a porterhouse?' she asked.

Logan grinned from ear to ear. 'You sure do!' he said.

Megan grabbed the bags and said, 'Man, I could kiss you!' Then, sensing her sister's penetrating gaze of pure hatred, said, 'But I won't.' She went to the kitchen bar and began setting out the food.

'How much do we owe you?' Bess asked him.

He shook his head. '*Nada*,' he said.

189

'Oh, no, we really need to pay you our share!' Bess said. 'It's not fair—'

'Cam said it's on the house. And anytime you wanna come eat at the restaurant, he said that would be on the house, too. Including your parents.'

'He can't do that!' Bess said. 'He'll go broke!'

Logan shrugged. 'He's closing the place in a couple of months, so it doesn't really matter.'

'No!' Megan cried, already digging into her porterhouse. 'That can't be!'

'Yeah,' Alicia said. 'Where in the world will you get your free porterhouse fix?'

'Bite me,' Megan said. 'I'm just sad for Logan and the rest of the staff.'

'B.S.,' Alicia said under her breath.

'Don't worry about us. Cam's more than fair and we'll get good severance packages, even if it's all in red meat.'

'If you get any of these,' Megan said, holding up her fork, 'you know where you can bring them.'

'Come on, y'all, let's eat before Megan takes it all,' Alicia said, grabbing plates for the three of them.

Bess set out the rest of the food, which was an exact duplicate of their first meal at the Eyes of Texas Steakhouse, right down to the burger for Logan. They didn't talk about Harper Benton or her brother, Tucker, or anything that might ruin an appetite. It wasn't until Bess and Logan were seated in the family room, while Megan and Alicia cleaned up, that the subject was broached.

'So are you still not going to tell your folks?' Bess asked.

Logan shrugged. 'No. I mean, my dad's an attorney, and he'll want to sue somebody, I'm sure. He gets like that. And that would just make matters worse. I mean, everybody would know what she's saying, right?'

'Yeah, I guess,' Bess said.

'So what's our next move?' he asked.

Bess liked that – the 'our' part. She wasn't sure what any move might consist of, but she was glad he wanted her to be part of it. 'I think maybe we need to talk to Harper's mom again.'

'She'll be at work tomorrow,' Logan said. 'But I know where she works.'

Bess lifted an eyebrow. 'You do?'

Logan grinned. 'Yeah. She's a waitress at that Denny's on the highway.'

Bess grinned back. 'So what are you doing for lunch tomorrow?' she asked.

DECEMBER, 1947

He hitched part of the way, took a bus with some of the money and made it to Peaceful, Texas in about two weeks. He disguised himself with facial hair, sunglasses and a fedora, and no one seemed to notice him, one way or another. Used to be, before the war, a strange man in town was an event – one to be looked on with favor or fear, depending on your outlook – but now the place was crowded and he saw a new mill on the outskirts that may have been the cause of that. And there were new houses, too. Little bungalows that all looked alike and practically sat on top

*of each other. This is what we fought a war for?
Edgar asked himself. Well, not him! No sad little
house with a wife and kids. And then he had to
laugh thinking of Lupita and his two half-breed
girls living side by side with the new residents
of Peaceful. Wouldn't be 'peaceful' for long! he
thought. He wasted no time heading to the house
on Post Oak Street. It looked the same, if maybe
a little rundown. He wondered if that had been
due to the war years, and maybe the death of his
brother. He felt no pangs of regret for Norris's
death. In fact, he felt nothing at all. He half
wondered about his dad and Herbert, but not
enough to do anything about it. He had one goal
in coming to Peaceful, and that was to confront
Helen and find his pot of gold. He wasn't sure
which he wanted most, and then realized that,
yeah, it was that pot of gold. Bitching out Helen
was just gravy.*

*The front door of the Bishop's house was
unlocked so he walked right in. He heard a voice
calling from upstairs, 'Carrie Marie? Is that you?
You're home early!'*

*Carrie Marie, Edgar thought. Who was that?
Maybe Norris had a kid and, just like Edgar
himself, had given his daughter the middle name
of their mother. 'Nope,' he said out loud. 'Not
Carrie Marie.' He went up the stairs and into the
bedroom he knew had been her parents', and saw
her lying on the bed, her back pressed up against
a stack of pillows, clad in a housecoat and
slippers.*

*'Who are you?' Helen asked, pressing her hands
against the bed as if ready for flight.*

'You don't know me, you cheating whore?' Edgar asked. 'Tell you what, did ol' Norris leave any of his stuff behind in the bathroom. Like a razor?'

He went into the bathroom that was connected to her parents' large bedroom. 'Like this bathroom,' he called from the open door. 'Real convenient having one right in your room, and all.' He found a straight-razor, obviously not his brother's favorite because it hadn't gone to war with him. But even as a back-up it was a lot better than the one he'd been using for the past few years. It was in a red velvet sheath with Norris's initials on it. Whatever, he thought. He lathered his face and glanced in the mirror at Helen, who appeared to be getting up off the bed.

'Whoa, now,' he said, brandishing the razor, 'stay where you are, little lady. Not gonna have you gallivanting around. Figured out yet who I am?'

He began to scrape away the beard, alternating between watching himself shave and looking at his ex-sweetheart. He smiled when he saw recognition dawn.

'But I thought you were dead!' she said.

'Not so I've noticed,' he replied, cleaned the soap off his face and came back into the room. 'Thought I'd come home and pay my respects to the widow. Now, see, if you'd married me like you were supposed to, you wouldn't be sitting up here in your room at three o'clock in the afternoon pining away for a dead husband.' He made a 'tsk-tsk' sound with his tongue. 'And still in your night clothes! You oughta be ashamed of yourself!'

'Get out,' Helen said, her voice unsteady.

'No, now, why would I want to do that? I've come to claim what's rightfully mine. Like you and this house. And whatever might be hidden in it,' he said.

'I didn't love you back then and I won't have you now!' she said, a little more heat in her voice. 'You're not worthy of the same last name as Norris! Your father was right about you – you're a wasteful piece of trash!'

Edgar didn't realize the straight-razor was still in his hand when he struck out at Helen. Not until she screamed and he saw the blood oozing out of the cut in her face. Somehow he couldn't stop. Even after she stopped screaming, and then stopped moving at all. Not until he heard a voice coming up the stairs.

'Mama! Mama? I'm home!'

Then a girl came in, maybe ten or eleven, a pretty little thing with a withered arm. She looked around at all the blood and then at Edgar. 'Daddy?' she said in a small voice.

'That's right,' Edgar said. 'I'm your daddy. Back from the dead. So you'd better be a good little girl.'

And then he left, without a backwards glance.

Twelve

After dinner that Sunday evening, the four of us – the chief, Miss Hutchins and Willis and I – sat in the living room for over an hour discussing the case. The chief himself had removed the crime scene tape so we could enter the room. There was very little agreement: Miss Hutchins insisted the killer was her father back from the dead; the chief vehemently disagreed, going with his 'no such thing as haunts' theory; while I came down somewhere in the middle. I'm not sure I gave any credence to Miss Hutchins' dead father walking among us and killing people, but I was convinced they were somehow connected. With Miss Hutchins' permission, I showed the chief the photo albums with the scratched-out faces of all the men. He still didn't see any connection. I couldn't articulate what the connection might be, but somehow I knew there was one. Insisting on this only brought doubt to the chief's eyes. I had a feeling he was not only doubting me, but Elena Luna as well.

He left around eight that evening, and Willis and I took a stroll in the cool of the night. It was close to ten p.m. before we headed back to the Bishop's Inn.

When we walked in the door we found a frantic Miss Hutchins. 'Oh, I'm so glad you're here!'

195

she cried, grabbing me by the arm. 'Miss Lovesy is missing!'

'Missing?' I repeated. 'What do you mean?'

The old woman gave me a withering look. 'I mean she's not here. I mean she's gone. G-O-N-E.'

Willis ran upstairs, coming back in a brief moment to declare, 'Her stuff's still here. Did you call the chief?' he asked Miss Hutchins.

'No,' she said, wringing her hands. 'I didn't know what to do! I mean, y'all went for a walk – maybe she did too? And if I called the chief, it could be like the little boy who cried wolf.'

I took her lightly by the elbow and guided her into the living room, sitting her down on the sofa where Humphrey Hammerschultz had met his maker. I sat down next to her.

'I wish you'd called me on my cell—' I started, but was interrupted.

'I don't hold with those things! Everybody's listening to everything you say! And besides, I hear they cause brain cancer!' she declared.

'Well,' I said, pulling out my cancer-causing but color-coordinated accessory, 'I think I'll just make a quick call to the chief.' I dialed the number of the police station and got the not-so-cooperative gray-haired lady I'd met earlier that day. 'May I speak to the chief, please?'

'This is the emergency line. We're closed. Is this an emergency?'

'Where's the chief?' I asked.

'In bed for all I know.'

'Do you have any way of contacting him?' I asked.

There was a brief moment of silence before she said, 'Maybe.'

'Well, if you are able to do so, could you please tell him E.J. Pugh called to let him know that Miss Lovesy has left the Bishop's Inn. Please tell him her things are still here, but she's not.'

'You're that woman who barged in here this morning, right?'

'I was there this morning, yes,' I said, not willing to admit I'd 'barged in' anywhere.

'And you think the chief would actually care what you have to say?' she said, her voice skeptical.

'Why not contact him and find out? You *are* a public servant, right? I'm the public, so serve me!' I said and hung up. Not exactly the best way to get positive results, I'll admit, but she was getting on my last nerve.

A couple of hours later I was in the kitchen helping Miss Hutchins with supper – her plan had been to make *carnitas* with the leftover pork roast, but due to our uninvited guest, there *was* no leftover pork roast, so we were going with canned tomato soup and grilled ham and cheese sandwiches – when my cell phone rang. It was in my pocket so I wiped my cheesy hands on the butt of my blue jeans and turned it on.

'Hello?'

'Miz Pugh? It's Chief Cotton. We found your missin' psycho—'

'Psychic,' I corrected.

'Whatever. Don't matter. She's dead either way you pronounce it.'

BACK HOME

Megan and Alicia decided to move upstairs and leave Bess and Logan on their own. Well, Megan decided and browbeat Alicia, who was still somewhat worried about Logan's intentions, into agreeing. That didn't stop her from coming out of her room as soon as she heard Megan's door shut. She sat down at the head of the stairs and waited for the conversation to stop. That's when she planned to pounce. There would be no sex of any kind on her watch, goddamit!

'What do you think Harper's mom can do for us?' Logan asked Bess.

She shrugged. 'I don't know, but maybe she can tell us who else may have had the opportunity to, you know . . .'

'Jump Harper's bones?' Logan suggested.

'Yeah, well, that.'

He put his fingers under her chin and lifted it, grinning at her. 'You're blushing,' he said, his voice a half-whisper.

'Am not,' she half-whispered back.

His index finger stroked her cheek. 'You're so pretty,' he said.

'Thanks,' Bess said, and knew for a fact that, if she hadn't been before, she was definitely blushing now.

His mouth found hers in a soft kiss that turned more heated as the seconds flew by. When Bess could feel his tongue tickling her lips she drew back. A girl at school who had gone to Catholic schools until transferring to Black Cat Ridge High her junior year had told Bess in no uncertain terms that the nuns had assured her that French kissing was the same as doing the deed. Bess figured that they'd meant symbolically, but she felt it best to err on the side of caution.

'What's the matter?' Logan asked.

'Ah, I'm not sure I'm ready—' she started, but he interrupted.

'I'm sorry—'

'No, no, it's not your fault—'

'Of course it is!' Logan said, standing up. 'I need to go home. Mom's probably worried.' He headed for the front door, Bess on his heels.

'You don't have to go!' she said.

'It's late,' he said, his back to her. He reached the door and opened it. Turning to face her, he said, 'I'm sorry for being such a . . . such a . . . prick?' he said.

'No, not at all!' Bess said, and could feel her face in flames.

'I'll see you tomorrow. Lunch, right?' Logan asked.

'Right,' Bess said to his retreating back.

She felt tears streaming down her face as she shut and locked the front door, then felt a presence behind her.

'That's what they do,' Alicia said, making Bess whirl around, her breath catching in her throat.

'What are you talking about?' Bess demanded, frowning at her younger sister.

'They try to guilt you into it. They act all sorry they did this or that, in hopes that in your guilt, you'll let them go a little farther—'

'Jeez!' Bess said, a little too loudly. 'Were you listening?'

'Damn straight!' Alicia said. 'I told you I was going to keep an eye out for you!'

Bess pushed past her. 'Just stay out of my love life!' she said.

Alicia followed her as she went through the house locking doors and checking windows. 'How do we *know* he's not the one who knocked up Harper? We only have his word for it! And he's certainly trying to get in your pants!'

Bess whirled around to stare at her. 'Listen! Just because my brother tried to guilt you into having sex with him is no reason to think all boys are like that! They're not!'

'Bullshit!' Alicia said with some heat. Hearing her cuss took Bess aback. This was not Alicia's usual choice of words. 'All boys are like that! Men, too! You think Graham was the first guy to try to get in my pants? Not by a long shot! You know that foster sister of mine who got knocked up by the foster dad? You think she was the first one he tried that on? Hardly! But I managed to jump out the bedroom window while he had his pants down around his legs! And that foster brother who made it with that other girl in the next house? He said he'd pay me for a three-way! I declined! You think just because I was like a plain Jane before y'all did that make-over on me that I was some innocent? Well, I may still be a virgin, but it's from my own due diligence and not trusting men! And that includes your – our – brother, and your new boyfriend!'

Her voice had gotten louder and louder as she spoke, to the point where the last of it was delivered at a volume that would often be called

200

screaming. She turned and ran up the stairs, almost knocking Megan over at the landing. Stopping to watch Alicia run up, with her mouth hanging open, she finally turned and finished walking down the steps.

'Did I hear that right?' she asked Bess.

'Don't,' Bess said, her voice menacing.

'Do you think it was true?' Megan insisted.

'I don't want to talk about it!' Bess said, heading for the stairs and her room.

'Jeez, I wish I knew what was going on around here!' Megan said to her sister's departing back. 'Y'all are acting all kinds of weird, you know that?'

The chief told us where he was and, rather than walk the half mile to the location, I took the Audi and got to the crime scene tape in two minutes. Willis and I jumped out of the car and walked up to where the chief was kneeling. Diamond Lovesy's body could easily be seen around the chief's scrawny one.

'What happened?' I asked as we ducked under the tape that cordoned off a small alley. The body lay in the driveway of the alley between two buildings off a side street. The business on the left was closed; the building on the right was empty.

The chief turned around and I was able to see Diamond's face. There was what could only be a bullet hole in her forehead. He stood up, shook hands with Willis and nodded to me. 'Looks to me like she's been shot, but I'm not willin' to swear to that until the coroner tells me I can. I'd

201

also be unwillin' to stipulate at this point that it was *not* self-inflicted, as there's no residue around the hole and – if she was shot – there ain't no gun lying around like she dropped it. Get my drift?'

'Sure do,' I said, staring at the lifeless body of the woman who had given me nothing but grief. I felt bad for her – as you would for anyone who dies young, or anyone whose life is taken by someone else. But I didn't feel much sorrow. I had to wonder if I was growing callous to these things – like many peace officers do. I shook myself to get back to the matter at hand.

'She was murdered,' I said.

'Well, now, I'm not willin' to say that until I know for sure she didn't die of natural causes,' the chief said.

A gargling sound came out of Willis's throat.

'How does one go about getting a hole in one's forehead *naturally*?' I asked.

'Like I been saying, I'm not gonna speculate till the coroner says I can.'

I noticed Mary Mays standing in the darkness of the alley. She was glaring at me. I smiled at her and wiggled my fingers at her in a friendly manner. It seemed to do nothing to appease her. Finally another vehicle pulled up, followed by the same hearse that had been parked outside Miss Hutchins' house after the discovery of Humphrey Hammerschultz's body. The same coroner who'd been busy with Humphrey in Miss Hutchins' living room got out of the car and the same driver got out of the hearse.

'We got us a crime spree, Rigsby?' the coroner

asked, kneeling down by the body. 'Maybe a serial killer?'

'Don't even know she was murdered yet, Bob. Up to you.'

His fingers still on the hole in Diamond's forehead, the coroner looked up and said, 'I declare this woman dead and, to be verified at autopsy, I will, at this juncture, deem this a likely homicide.'

'Well, all right then,' the chief said, looked at me, smiled, and gave me a thumbs-up. Turning to Mary Mays, he said, 'You check out the scene?' She nodded. 'Find anything?' he asked. She shook her head. 'You call Alice?' he asked.

'On it,' she said, and pulled her cell phone of her belt.

'Alice?' I asked.

'She's our forensic specialist. She took a course,' the chief said.

'Mind if I look around?' I asked. 'I promise I won't touch anything.'

The chief shrugged. 'Knock yourself out,' he said, while Mary Mays' frown deepened and, as the saying goes, if looks could kill, I'd be deader than Diamond Lovesy.

But that didn't stop me. I looked around the body then walked deeper into the alley, passing Officer Mays whose glaring stare followed me the whole way. There wasn't even any litter. Not a damn thing. As I headed back to the mouth of the alley, Mary Mays leaned toward me and said, 'Did you think I was lying?'

'No, I just thought you might have missed something,' I said.

'Oh,' she said, folding her arms across her chest. 'Not lying, just incompetent.'

I smiled. 'Yeah, something like that.'

I wasn't winning friends and influencing people in Peaceful, Texas, I can – in the chief's vernacular – *guaran-damn-tee* you that.

'Mary, wait here for forensics,' the chief said as the hearse driver and his helper managed to get Diamond's body on the gurney. 'Me and the Pughes here are going back to my office.'

We followed the chief to the municipal building where we parked in the back next to one of the squad cars. The chief was driving his, but it had been the only one at the scene. I briefly wondered how Mary Mays was going to get back to the station, but, in reality, I didn't really care. We went in a back door, bypassing the waiting room and the frowning gray-haired lady at the front desk, and straight into the chief's office. The straight-back chair that Willis had been in earlier was still there, so we both took our seats.

'So I'm wondering what kinda shenanigans those two frauds had been up to and if it followed them here to our peaceful little town.' He stopped and looked at us one at a time. 'That was on purpose,' he said, waving his hand and smiling. 'Throwing in the "peaceful little town" part.' He stared at us as we sat opposite him. I wasn't sure how to respond, or even if we were supposed to respond. 'Some people think that's funny,' he said, losing the smile.

'Oh, right!' Willis said, and issued a phony laugh. 'Because the name of the town is Peaceful!' he said and laughed yet again.

204

'If you gotta explain it, it ain't funny!' the chief said, the smile so long gone that a frown had taken its place.

'Are you implying that these two murders have nothing to do with the goings-on at the Bishop's Inn?' I asked, slightly incredulous.

'I ain't implying dog shit, excuse my French. I'm downright saying it: ain't nothin' going on at the Bishop's Inn that these two con artists didn't bring with 'em!'

I sighed. 'Chief, listen, please. This has been going on for over a year! Like noises in the night, guests' luggage tampered with and sightings of someone else in the house. And I showed you those disturbing pictures in Miss Hutchins' family albums! Not to mention that Willis and I both heard something the other night. A sound like someone dragging something down the hall. It woke us both up. By the time we got to the hall, we could hear someone going out the front door. So, I reiterate: something is going on in that house and I truly believe that Diamond's and Humphrey's deaths are somehow involved.'

The chief sighed right back at me. 'Look, I ain't saying nothin's going on. I believe y'all heard what you heard, and I certainly did see those pictures, but I just don't see how it's connected.'

'Someone *did* kill Miss Hutchins' mother,' Willis said.

'Yeah,' the chief said, frowning, 'in 1945. Anybody big enough to have done the damage I've read about had to be an adult. So let's say twenty. Miss Hutchins was ten years old. She is now seventy-something. Which would make the killer at least somewhere in his eighties. You think someone that old is running around the inn causing mischief and is quick enough to never be seen? Not to mention some eighty-year-old breaking ol' Humphrey's neck!'

Willis appeared to be sulking. 'Well, y'all never did find Miss Hutchins' mother's killer.'

'No, sir, we never did. But my point is valid, donja think?'

Willis shrugged. He was new to speculating on murders and was getting a little defensive. I patted his hand. I'd tell him later how proud I was.

1948–1952

Edgar was surprised at how calm he felt as he walked away from Peaceful, Texas. He'd never killed anyone, not even a Jap, but he now understood that it wasn't all that hard to do. Not that he had planned on killing Helen, or even knew that's what he was doing at first, but when he heard the scream and saw the blood he felt something akin to real pleasure. And it wasn't as if she didn't deserve it. He'd thought, as he'd left the house on Post Oak Street, about going the extra mile out of his way to see his father and last surviving brother. It would be a pleasure to see his dad and watch his face as he killed Herbert. Not that dear old Dad cared that much for Herbert, but it might mean something to him. Mainly, he just wanted to kill the old man, but not enough to go out of his way to do it. Killing Helen hadn't been that pleasurable.

And so he left Peaceful, hitchhiking his way

east. He ended up in Biloxi, Mississippi, where he got a job, doing the only thing he knew how to do: digging ditches. It didn't pay well, and he hated it, but it got him a room in a boarding house with three squares a day (the landlady's daughter slipped him a sack lunch when nobody else was looking), and he won a little bit now and then at poker. A black guy at work taught him how to play craps and he found he was made for this particular game. One night he managed to win over six hundred dollars, but as he was leaving the back alley where the game was held, three of the black guys from the game grabbed him and stole back the six hundred, as well as the five dollar bill he'd hidden in his wallet, and beat him bloody.

He missed several days of work due to his injuries and lost his job because of it. But one thing he did win from this ordeal was a new bed partner, namely the young daughter of his land-lady, who had started out by nursing him back to health and had ended up under the covers. Her name was Rita, and she was a pretty girl, even if she was as cross-eyed as a goose. And it didn't take too long before Rita was with child. His landlady was just about as happy with this situation as Lupita's mother had been, and he and Rita were rushed into – if not a shotgun wedding – then at least a pretty quick one.

It wasn't bad being married to Rita. She, like Lupita, was a real pleaser, but unlike Lupita, didn't seem to be bright enough to lie to him or to try to put anything over on him like Lupita had. He got sore just thinking about the way she kept him in that forest so long after the war had ended. But Rita was willing and able to do anything he wanted and never bugged him about getting another job. His life with her consisted of days waking up around two or three in the afternoon, raiding the boarding house refrigerator and pantry of anything his little heart desired, and his nights spent playing poker or shooting craps. He learned never to earn too much money when playing with black people. The baby was born and it was a boy, and they named him Chester, after her father. Edgar was pleased to have a son, someone he could pass things down to. He wasn't sure what, since he didn't play sports, or hunt or fish (other than out of necessity back in the Philippines), or use tools, other than his head. He could teach the boy how to shoot craps, how to play poker, and maybe even to shoot pool, if he got better at it than he was now.

In those years with Rita, that's where most of his gambling earnings went: back into gambling, which was slowly evolving to include pool, and onto his own back. He discovered his body type liked the zoot suits of the era, and that he looked really good in them. And women liked the way he looked. So he'd play pool, wear his high-top pants and long jackets, smoke his cigarettes, drink a lot of booze and treat strange women to a drink and a dance, and even a bauble or two, before bedding them in any nearby fleabag hotel.

His new mother-in-law hated his guts and wasn't shy about expressing her feelings. She knew, as most women did, what he was doing out *every night, and resented him for it. She put him up in her home for free, fed him for free and took care of his wife and child, and all he did was whore around all night, drinking and gambling, making poor Rita a laughing stock. Luckily, Rita didn't know this. She was a simple girl, and was quite happy to have her man and her baby boy.*

Things were going swimmingly for Edgar until the summer of 1952. That's when he won too much money at craps again and got jumped by two black guys as he was leaving. But Edgar was a fast learner, and since the first assault had been carrying his dead brother Norris's straight-razor in its red velvet monogrammed sheath in his pocket – the same razor he'd used to kill his former lady love. And when those two black boys came at him, Edgar fought back, killing one and badly maiming the other. It was the next day that he heard through the grapevine that the whole of the black sector of town was out to get him. That's when Edgar packed up a suitcase with three of his new suits, all of his money and some Rita had been saving out of the money her mother gave her as an allowance. He kissed his wife's cheek, patted his three-year-old son on the head, and left by the back door.

Thirteen

BACK HOME

Bess woke up Monday morning feeling depressed. She wasn't sure why at first, then the whole thing with Logan came rushing back, along with the things Alicia had said. She had to admit she *had* felt guilty. But did she believe that was Logan's intent? And look at Alicia and Graham – they'd thought they were in love, and still Graham had tried to make her feel guilty for not having sex with him. Bess sat up, her feet on the floor, her head in her hands. Maybe Alicia was right – maybe all guys were like that! Maybe she should become a nun. There was a problem with that, though – Methodists didn't have nuns. Maybe a lesbian? Bess thought. But how different would that be? Probably not that much.

She pushed herself up off the bed and headed to the hall bathroom. She always awoke ten to fifteen minutes before her sisters so she wouldn't be disturbed in there. She went in, took a quick shower, got out and contemplated blow-drying her hair and/or putting on make-up. Why bother? she thought. She'd go to the Denny's for lunch with Logan, see what Mrs Benton had to say, then that was it. She'd wash her hands of the whole thing. And never see Logan again.

She sighed and left the bathroom, noticing

neither of her sisters was even up yet. She didn't much care about that either.

'I understand they were both from Houston,' I said to the chief. 'Have you checked out their addresses or anything?'

'I checked with Miz Hutchins and they didn't put down their addresses in the registration book like they were supposed to.'

'Surely they had identification on them when the bodies were found?' I asked.

'Well, yeah, Humphrey did, and we checked out the address on his driver's license, but it was two years out of date. And the woman, that Diamond person, she didn't have any ID on her,' the chief said.

'I checked her room after Miss Hutchins told us Diamond was missing,' Willis said, 'and I noted that all her crap was there. She may have left without her purse and we can find ID in her room.'

I stood up. 'Willis and I will go back to the Bishop's Inn and find out,' I said.

The chief laughed. 'Well, now, ma'am, y'all can sure go back to the inn, but I'll be right behind you and I'll be doing any checkin' myself.'

'I thought you were going to allow me to help you, Chief,' I said, putting a little pout into my words.

'That's right, little lady, I did say that, didn't I?' He stood up and came around the desk to pat me condescendingly on the shoulder. 'So's how 'bout you stand out in the hall while I search?' he asked. 'You can watch!'

He grinned like the Cheshire cat and headed for the door to his office. Willis and I followed him out the back door to the parking lot. He looked at my little beauty parked next to his giant squad car.

'Now what's this little ol' thing called?' he asked.

'It's an Audi TT Roadster,' I said proudly.

'You get it as a Cracker Jack's price?' he asked. I stiffened while my husband guffawed. Then he and the chief bumped fists – I was amazed that the chief knew anything about that. Watched too much TV, I suspected.

I suggested Willis ride with the chief and I got into my beautiful car and broke a couple of speed limits getting back to the inn. The chief, thankfully, did not pull me over. I think he thought he might live longer if he didn't. He was right.

I was halfway up the stairs when Willis and Chief Cotton came in the front door.

'Now hold on, little lady!' the chief yelled from the entry hall.

I whirled around. 'Call me "little lady" one more time, and you'll realize just how little I'm *not*!' I said, gritting my teeth.

The chief turned to Willis. 'Feisty, ain't she?' he said.

Willis grinned. 'You don't know the half of it,' he said.

Locking eyes with my husband, I asked, 'Which dead person's room would you prefer to sleep in tonight?'

With that I headed back up the stairs, both men hot on my heels.

BACK HOME

'Jeez, what's with you?' Megan asked Bess when she came downstairs twenty minutes later.

Bess was at the bar, a cup of coffee in her hands, staring into space. 'What?' she said, not looking at her sister.

'You look like death warmed over!' Megan said, heading for the coffee pot. 'Did you make enough for me?'

'Of course I did. I made enough for you and Alicia and a third cup for myself.'

'That's your second cup of coffee?' Megan asked, pouring her own cup. 'Didn't Mom tell you this stuff will stunt your growth? And you don't need that!' And with that she let out a bark of laughter. 'Because you're so short, get it?'

Bess ignored her and continued staring into space.

'Seriously, what *is* your problem this morning?' Megan insisted.

'Nothing,' Bess finally said.

'Bullshit!' Megan said.

Bess finally looked at her sister. 'Since when do you care? And since when do you even notice if I'm in a bad mood?'

Megan put her cup down on the bar and climbed onto the stool next to Bess. 'Since I heard what Alicia said last night. And I figure you're thinking Logan's just another asshole trying to get in your pants, right?'

Bess looked away and stared into space – again. 'Leave it alone,' she said.

'Ain't gonna happen,' Megan said, then took a healthy sip of coffee. 'See, the thing is she's partly right. Teenage boys think about sex like every minute of every day. Even when they sleep! You've heard about wet dreams?'

'Gross. Just stop.'

'It's true. But that doesn't mean they don't genuinely care for a girl. Sure there are guys who'll pretend to like a girl just to jump her bones, but that's not Logan,' Megan said.

Bess laughed without humor. 'And what makes you think that? Because he's such a stand-up guy? Hell, for all we know he *is* the father of Harper's baby!'

Megan shook her head. 'No. I can read people. I've *always* been good at that. He didn't do the nasty with Harper, I'm one hundred percent certain of that. And I'm also one hundred percent certain that he really, really likes you. And as far as Alicia and Graham go—'

'What about Alicia and Graham?' came a voice from the stairs. The two girls turned to see their foster sister standing there.

'Nothing,' Megan said, and got up from the stool.

Alicia came down the stairs and into the great room. 'No, really, Megan. What about Alicia and Graham?'

'I said nothing!' Megan said, going into the kitchen and dumping the dregs of her coffee in the sink. 'Anybody want breakfast before we head out?'

'Just say what you have to say!' Alicia shouted.

Megan whirled around. 'You're not gonna like it!'

'Like that should make a difference to you?'

214

'Yeah, well it does!' Megan shouted back. 'I know y'all both think I'm this uncaring person, but truth be known I love you both, and I love my brother! And I don't want to cause you any more pain than he already has!' Tears were trailing down Megan's cheeks and Bess and Alicia looked at each in pure befuddlement.

Bess got up from her stool and went to her sister. 'It's OK, Megs. Come on, let's sit on the sofa. All three of us. We'll get this straightened out.'

She led Megan to the couch, sitting her in the middle between herself and Alicia. 'Now, what's this all about?' Bess asked.

Megan shook her head.

Alicia touched her arm. 'You have to tell me now, Megs. If you don't, my mind will just make up something ten times worse than reality.'

Again Megan shook her head. 'Nothing can be worse than this.'

Alicia sighed. 'Maybe I don't want to know,' she said softly.

'But maybe you *should* know,' Bess said. 'Megan, just tell it. It's best not to keep secrets. They just cause all sorts of problems.'

Megan sighed. 'Last week – when I went to the movies with the twins?' Both of her sisters nodded their heads. 'I saw Graham there. And he wasn't alone.'

'Who was he with?' Bess asked.

'Lotta,' Megan said, lowering her head.

'Lotta Esparza?' Alicia half-whispered. 'His old girlfriend?'

The other girls didn't answer. They felt no reply

215

was needed. There was only one Lotta Esparza in their world, and it was definitely Graham's ex-girlfriend.

'What were they doing?' Alicia said, her voice getting strident.

Megan didn't look up, nor did she answer.

'Megan!' Alicia said. 'What were they doing?'

Finally Megan looked up, but not at Alicia – she looked at Bess instead. 'Making out,' she told her sister.

'Oh my God!' Bess said, but Alicia said nothing. Instead she headed for the stairs. 'Where are you going?' Bess asked. 'We've got to get to school.'

'I'm taking a sick day,' Alicia said.

I got to the door of Diamond Lovesy's room before either the chief or my husband. I grabbed the knob and turned, but before I could push the door open, I felt something on my wrist. Looking down I saw that the chief had slipped one half of a set of handcuffs onto my right wrist.

'What the hell?' I said, trying to pull away. He grabbed my left wrist and finished the process, cuffing me, thankfully in front not in back. 'What do you think you're doing?' I shouted.

'Keeping you from interferin' in an ongoing investigation. Or, maybe I'm keeping you from tampering with evidence. Or possibly even keeping you from destroying evidence, if maybe you're the one who's done the deed!' he said, pulling me away from the door.

'Now you think *I'm* a suspect?' I shouted. 'God, you *are* desperate!'

216

'Eeg,' Willis said, touching my shoulder. 'Calm down—'

I whirled on him. 'You! You— Don't touch me!' I was livid. Possibly as mad as I've ever been. At least since the day I found Bess's birth family. That was horror that turned into great sadness that finally morphed into the most intense anger I've ever known. This wasn't even a close second, but it beat the third by a long shot.

'Chief, I know you don't think E.J. had—'

'If your wife was involved with this, *Mr* Pugh,' the chief said, 'then I think it's safe to say you were too—'

'Now just a goddamn minute!' It was Willis's turn to shout.

'I think it best if both of you go downstairs and wait in the living room while I check out Miz Lovesy's room. Or you think I oughta call Officer Mays in to hold the two of you?'

I turned on my heels and headed for the staircase. I would have surely taken a header to the landing if Willis hadn't grabbed my cuffed hands to steady me at that first step. Even that wasn't enough to get him out of my doghouse.

We sat in the living room and waited. Fifteen minutes later, the chief came downstairs. 'Well, now, looks like back in 2005 Miz Lovesy lived in a town called Bellaire, but that's when her driver's license expired, so it's possible she moved since then. I'll call this Bellaire town and have it checked out.'

'Bellaire is a city within the Houston city limits. There are two, actually. Bellaire and West University Place. Both surrounded by Houston.'

217

'Got their own PD?'

'Hum. I know West University does, because my family lived there when I was little, but I'm not sure about Bellaire.'

'Guess I gotta call Houston then and find out.'

I held up my wrists. 'They're chafing,' I said.

He came toward me with a key and unlocked the cuffs. 'Sorry about that, but no way were you getting in there first. Little lady, you need to show some restraint.'

I stood and rubbed my wrists. 'I *am* showing restraint, Chief. I haven't hurt you for calling me "little lady" again.'

He grinned at me. 'You wouldn't be threatening a peace officer now would you, Miz Pugh?'

'Of course not,' I said, and smiled back – although I don't think mine was as genuine as his. He seemed to be getting quite a kick out of making my life miserable. 'I was just explaining how I was already showing extreme restraint.'

'And I do appreciate that,' he said, his Cheshire grin still in place. 'But I'm gonna have to buckle under and ask you to come take a look at Miz Lovesy's room with me. Don't know if it's a lady thing or a big city thing, but there's stuff up there I don't know diddly-squat about.'

'I'd be happy to help,' I said, in what I felt was an appropriately warm and inviting manner.

'Well, you could be a little nicer about it!' he said, and headed up the stairs.

I looked at my husband. 'What?' I mouthed.

'You were a trifle patronizing and conde-scending,' he said out loud.

'A trifle?' said the chief from halfway up the

218

staircase. He shrugged. 'Maybe a little more than a trifle.'

He continued on and Willis and I followed him. Diamond Lovesy's room wasn't as big a mess as her partner Humphrey Hammerschultz's room had been, but it certainly wasn't neat. I'm not sure if this was Diamond's fault, or if it had been caused by the chief's fifteen-minute search.

It was a well-appointed room, as were all the rooms I'd seen thus far at the Bishop's Inn. An antique four-poster bed dominated, with turn of the century (nineteenth to twentieth, not twentieth to twenty-first) matching night stands, a six-drawer chest and a dressing table from the thirties, I believe, in a slightly lighter wood with a large round mirror and rounded edges to the table itself. It was in perfect condition. The comforter on the bed was white and covered in wild roses with a bed skirt of cotton eyelet and pillows with cotton eyelet edgings. The bed had been hastily made and there were items of clothing strewn across it, the stuffed chair in the corner (also covered in wild roses), and even some on the floor. Strangely enough, there were plenty of hang-ups in the closet and three of the six drawers of the chest were filled with clothing. It was as if Diamond Lovesy had planned to stay a while in Peaceful. And maybe she had. I had to wonder how she and Humphrey had found out about the 'hauntings' at the Bishop's Inn and what their real intention was in coming here. I was beginning to doubt their story of the phone call from a stranger. Did they plan on becoming so indispensable to Miss Hutchins that they'd be able to

219

just move in? Or was there something more sinister involved? How long had they actually been in Peaceful? Could they have heard about what happened to Miss Hutchins' mother all those years ago and have somehow managed to stage what had been going on of late? But how?

I shook my head. There were too many questions that were too unanswerable at the moment.

'So what is it you have questions about?' I asked the chief.

He pointed to the dressing table. 'All this crap here. Is it all just lady stuff or what?'

There were jars and tubes and bottles piled on top of the marble center of the dressing table. I sat down on the stool in front of the table and looked at it all. 'Can I touch this stuff?' I asked the chief.

He shrugged. 'If we need to print it I'll just take your prints for elimination,' he said.

I glanced at Willis, one eyebrow raised. He imitated the chief with a shrug. I wasn't sure I was all that happy with Chief Cotton having my fingerprints on file. And if they were on file here, where else would they go? Then I remembered the two or three (OK, make that four) times I'd been jailed in Codderville. I knew that on at least one of those occasions I'd been fingerprinted. The other times were just Luna's way of getting my attention.

So I picked up a bottle. The lettering on it claimed it was vanilla-scented body spray. I sprayed it – yep, smelled like cookies. There was a jar of night cream, a tube of eye cream, a bottle of shampoo and one of conditioner, a bottle of body wash and a box containing make-up. I rifled through that and discovered Diamond had preferred blue eyeshadow and black eyeliner, but I already knew that just by looking at her. There was mascara – black – and an eyelash curler, three tubes of different shades of very red lipstick, and a black eyebrow pencil. There were two side drawers. One was filled with nail paraphernalia – bottles of polish in varying shades of blues, greens and purples; a dozen or so emery boards; nail clippers and scissors; polish remover and a big bag of cotton balls. In the other drawer were papers: bank statements, unpaid bills, cancellation notices from a cell phone provider, and a plastic sleeve with pictures. My first instinct was to check the address on the bank statements and unpaid bills, but that proved to be a P.O. Box in Houston. I showed these to the chief.

'Yeah, saw that. Between the Bellaire police and the Houston post office, I might find an address for her,' he said.

'I don't know, Chief,' I said, looking at all the crap in the room, and at the bills piled in the drawer. 'I have a feeling this was now Diamond's home. I'd venture to say wherever she lived in Houston is empty now.'

I picked up the sleeve of pictures. Thumbing through them, I saw only Diamond and Humphrey, and sometimes an older woman who had Humphrey's arm around her shoulder. I decided this must be Humphrey's mother, the one Diamond had mentioned. I wondered if she'd ever had the chance to notify the woman of Humphrey's death. And then there was a photo of Diamond with a

221

very handsome man. They were arm in arm and smiling at the camera.

I heard an intake of breath behind me. Turning, I saw Miss Hutchins standing there. 'Why is Diamond in that picture with Daddy?' she asked.

1952

Edgar made his way to Savannah, Georgia – a good town, he'd heard, for a gambler. And that's what he now considered himself: a professional gambler. But Savannah had real gamblers, real pros, and Edgar was just a midnight snack for them. Within a month he'd lost all his money and was into a shark for over a thousand, with no way of paying it back. He heard of a high-stakes game going on in the rich part of town and, wearing one of his best zoot suits from Biloxi, headed that way. But the buy-in was much more than he had on him – or ever had the hopes of having on him – and they teased him about his clothes. The biggest teaser was a guy named Walker, an arrogant SOB barely out of his teens. He called Edgar a 'white nigger,' and shoved him. To Edgar this was the last straw – his dead brother's straight-razor was out and he sliced the boy named Walker long and deep.

In all truth, the Walker boy would have made it if any of his friends had stayed around to call the authorities, but none did. And neither did Edgar, who ran back to his fleabag hotel only to find part of his belongings out on the street – and not the good stuff either. So there was an altercation with the hotel manager, the straight-razor was brandished again, and the police were called.

Once they had him in the jail, it didn't take long for the truth about the Walker boy to come out. As the only son of a district judge, the boy's death was considered a major crime and, with no attorney at his side, Edgar took a plea bargain and was sent to prison for twenty years.

Fourteen

BACK HOME

'Why didn't you tell me?' Bess asked as Megan drove the minivan to school that Monday morning. Alicia was conspicuously absent.

'Tell you what?' Megan asked.

'Oh, I don't know,' Bess said sarcastically, 'like maybe seeing Graham sucking face with Lotta, for God's sake!'

'Because I figured it would just upset you. Like I knew it would upset Alicia.'

'Well duh. Her boyfriend making out with his old girlfriend? I guess so!' Bess said. She couldn't help wondering if Megan seeing them together had been the first time Graham had snuck out with Lotta. Somehow she didn't think so. Lotta had been the love of his life. And he the love of hers, until that guy Ramon had come along. He was some professional Latino muckraker and started out chastising Lotta for being with a gringo – namely Graham. He'd already turned her cousins and uncles into rebels for his cause, and it didn't take all that long to turn Lotta. She'd broken up with Graham, announcing she could no longer tolerate his white man ways. As far as Graham had known, he didn't have any 'white man ways,' so it crushed him on many levels when she walked out on him. At the time Bess had wondered if he might not give up his happy home and beg to be adopted by a Latino family. Thankfully, he hadn't.

And then there was the whole kidnapping ordeal that Alicia had gone through, and the two of them falling into each other's arms. That line from *Speed* sure seemed to be resonating now.

'You know this is killing her, don't you?' Bess said.

Megan glared at her sister. 'I didn't want to tell her! You made me!'

Bess sighed. 'I know I did. This is just so . . .'

'Fucked up?' Megan suggested.

Bess nodded. 'For want of a better word, yes.'

'What are we gonna do? She can't just skip school. We've got finals coming up,' Megan said.

'Let's give her the day,' Bess said.

Megan shrugged. 'Yeah. Well, should we tell the office, or is she gonna call in or what?'

'I don't know!' Bess said, aggravated at the thought of the bureaucracy involved. She sighed and picked up the phone, hitting the button for their home number. No one answered. 'Either she's gone or she's not picking up,' she told Megan.

'Where would she go?'

'I don't know! How would I know?' Bess demanded.

'Because she was your best friend before she came to live with us. That's why!'

'She still is one of my best friends,' Bess said quietly. 'Right next to you.'

Megan slammed on the break, almost getting rear-ended by a teenager heading for the school only a block away. He honked his horn a little

225

more insistently than necessary as he swerved around the minivan.

'How dare you call me your best friend!' Megan yelled.

Bess's eyes got big. She'd never seen Megan this angry. She hunkered in the corner, trying to make herself an even smaller target than she already was. 'I'm sorry! I thought you knew!'

Megan slammed the heel of her hand on the steering wheel. 'That's just so . . . so . . .'

'So what?' Bess asked tentatively.

'So sweet!' she said and broke into sobs. As she reached for her sister, Bess drew back, but found herself in a bear hug that was causing heart palpitations and an inability to breathe.

She patted Megan on the back and got out the words, 'I can't breathe!'

Megan lightened up her grip on her sister. 'Sorry,' she said as she wiped her eyes on the hem of her T-shirt. Then she sighed. 'I don't think anybody's going to school today, huh?'

'It's probably a good idea to stay at home,' Bess said. Then remembered her 'date' with Logan to go see Harper Benton's mother at the Denny's where she worked. 'But I'll need the minivan around noon. I've got someplace I need to be.'

'What?' I said, staring at Miss Hutchins.

She was still pointing at the photo. 'That's my daddy,' she said. 'But that can't be . . .' She frowned, her pointed finger gone, her hands at her sides. Then she brightened. 'But maybe Miss

226

Lovesy really did channel Daddy and somehow got this picture!'

I looked around the room. In the photo Diamond was wearing an intricately patterned silk kimono. I checked the closet and the clothes strewn about the room. The kimono was not there. 'This was taken before Diamond came here,' I said to one and all. The chief had grabbed the photo from my hand as I stood up to search the room, and now he, Willis, and Miss Hutchins were studying it. 'See that kimono she's wearing?' I asked the three of them. 'It's not here. She certainly wasn't wearing it when she was killed. So that picture wasn't taken here.'

'It's outdoors, though,' Willis said, his head bent toward the snapshot. 'Can you see anything to ID the location?'

The chief shook his head. 'Don't look like Peaceful to me. Don't got any sidewalk cafes in Peaceful,' he said.

It was my turn to snatch back the photo. They certainly were standing in front of a sidewalk cafe. Behind them were several occupied tables with umbrellas and behind that a plate glass window with a few words and letters visible: 'G-A-N-I-C,' 'A NATURAL,' 'BELINNIS,' 'G-R-K,' and 'S-U-N'. I found a piece of paper and pen and sat down at the dressing table, pushing aside some of the paraphernalia on top. I wrote down the letters as the three others gathered around.

Willis pointed at the first set: 'G-A-N-I-C'. 'Organic!' he said triumphantly.

I fist-bumped him. 'All natural,' Miss Hutchins said of the next. So I fist-bumped her.

'Don't know what that next one could be,' the chief said.

'Just what it says,' I told him. 'Belinnis. It's an Italian sandwich.'

'G-R-K,' Willis read. 'G-R-K?'

'Greek!' I all but shouted.

He put his hands on my shoulders and squeezed. With all the tension that had built up over the last few days, I would have been quite happy to have him continue doing that for another hour or so.

'S-U-N?' I asked, looking up at my husband.

Willis shrugged and stopped kneading my shoulders.

'Sundried tomatoes?' Miss Hutchins asked.

'Is there enough room for that?' We all bent over the photo again. 'I don't think so.'

'Maybe they sell sundaes?' the chief suggested.

I shrugged and Willis said, 'See how much bigger that S-U-N is than the rest of this?' He pointed at the plate glass window in the photo. 'Maybe it's the name of the place.'

'Good point!' I said. Turning to the chief, I asked, 'You ever heard of a place in or around Peaceful with S-U-N in the name?'

'Well, there's a place over to Boerne called Sonny's, but that's with an O and it don't have tables outside. It's just a hole-in-wall bar,' he said.

'Do you have wifi here?' I asked Miss Hutchins.

'No, dear, I don't. But the library does.'

'Is it open on Sunday?' I asked.

228

She shook her head. 'No. Only Monday through Saturday, with a half day on Thursday.'

'I know the librarian though,' the chief said. 'We can get her to open it up. What are you thinking?'

'I have my laptop. I just need to get to the internet. See if I can put in the clues we have and come up with a restaurant name.'

'You can do that?' he asked.

'I'll start with Houston. That's the most likely place this picture was taken,' I said.

We all looked at each other and then out the window. It was pitch black outside. 'What time is it?' I asked.

The chief looked at his watch. 'Damn. It's after midnight.' He looked at me and shrugged. 'I ain't waking Shirley up at this time of night. She's my wife's cousin and has a tendency to get a might uppity – her having an advanced degree and all. But I'll come get you and your machine in the morning.'

And with that we all said goodnight. I noticed Miss Hutchins pocket the snapshot of Diamond Lovesy and Miss Hutchins' 'daddy.'

BACK HOME

Bess and Megan let Alicia know they were back and also taking the day off. They did this through the closed and locked door of her bedroom. 'Whatever,' she said in reply, thus letting them know she was there, not having run off somewhere, and that she just didn't answer the phone earlier. That, of course, would have required her leaving her room, and the two sisters wondered if she ever would or if they would spend the next twenty years or so sliding skinny food under her bedroom door.

Bess and Megan went downstairs, where Megan declared she was hungry. 'Aren't you always?' Bess asked.

'Is that any way to talk to your best friend?' Megan asked.

Bess flopped down on the sofa and sighed. 'I'm never going to live that down, am I?'

'Nope,' Megan said, opening the refrigerator. Turning to Bess, she grinned her biggest grin and said, 'Bestie!'

'Bite me!' was Bess's response.

'Hum, bite me, Bestie! Sounds like a song title!'

'Bite me, Bestie, take a huge chunk—' Bess said.

'Just don't bite me, Bestie, in my trunk!' Megan finished and both girls laughed out loud.

'What's so friggin' funny?' Alicia asked as she came down the stairs.

'We wrote a song—' Megan started.

Bess said, 'Never mind. Are you OK?'

Alicia stopped in her tracks and stared at Bess. 'Why wouldn't I be OK? I mean, just because I found out that my boyfriend has been cheating on me for God only knows how long? Just because I now realize that every *fuckin'* thing he's ever said to me is a lie? Just because I almost gave it away to a lying, cheating son-of-a-bitch—'

'Yeah, ah, maybe not the last one?' Bess suggested.

'Sorry,' Alicia said, and fell down on the love-seat. 'I hate him.'

'Good,' Megan said as she came out of the kitchen, Bess's leftover steak from the night before in her hand. 'You need to hate him. It's healing.'

'Is that my steak?' Bess screeched, jumping up.

'What? Oh, is this yours?' Megan said. Bess grabbed for it, and Megan, being almost a foot taller, held it just out of her sister's reach. 'It's delish.'

'Gimme!' Bess said, jumping up to grab the meat.

'I thought you were a vegetarian?' Megan said. 'Are you condoning cow murder now?'

'Gimme, bitch!' Bess said, snarling.

'I'm saving you from yourself. You know you don't really want this nasty dead cow now, do you?'

'I'm gonna cut you!' Bess said, which made Megan laugh.

'Oh my God! You've turned into a carnivore!'

Bess grabbed the arm Megan was holding above her head and jerked it down, tearing the steak out of her sister's hand. 'What's mine is mine. If I have turned into a carnivore I'll eat it, but if I haven't, I can just throw it away! And you can't touch it because it's mine!'

'So you'd rather that poor dead cow died for nothing than to have it nourish your bestie?'

'You are no longer my bestie!' Bess declared.

'Ha! I knew it! Fairweather bestie!'

'Will you two stop it? Megs, I have some of my steak left in there. It's in the meat keeper. You can eat it. Just stop. My head can't take any more.'

231

The two sisters calmed down and Megan went back to the refrigerator. Turning quickly, she asked Alicia, 'Can I get you something while I'm in here?'

Alicia just stared at her. She'd never heard those words come from Megan's mouth. Finally, she was able to speak. 'Why, yes, Megan, thank you. A glass of ice water would be nice.'

'Coming right up,' Megan said.

After the two sisters had demolished the dead meat, Megan said, 'OK, so Saturday night you were all "I'm not sure I *love* him love him, or brother-love him," and now you hate his guts—'

'Because he's cheated on me!' Alicia said. 'He didn't know of my ambivalence! How could he? So that had nothing to do with his cheating! And how do I know when this started? Last Thursday's when he said we should start seeing other people! When did you see him sucking face at the movies?'

Megan sighed. 'The Saturday before.'

Alicia fell back on the sofa. 'That's cheating. Pure and simple.'

Megan and Bess looked at each other. They couldn't disagree with that statement.

Changing the subject, Megan asked Bess, 'So where are you going at noon? You said you needed the van?'

Bess nodded. 'Yeah, I'm meeting Logan at the Denny's where Mrs Benton works. We're hoping she'll be willing to tell us what's really going on.'

'Well, it's eleven twenty now. Don't you think you should do something about your hair and face?' Megan said and shrugged. 'I'm just saying . . .'

'That I look like shit?' Bess provided.

'I didn't use those words!' Megan said.

'You could look better,' Alicia provided.

'*Et tu?*' Bess said to Alicia, then got up and headed upstairs.

At five minutes to twelve Bess turned into the Denny's parking lot. Her hair was fixed, even curled, and her make-up was well-applied. She saw Logan's car in the lot and was able to park next to it. Logan was still sitting behind the wheel. He got out and came around to the passenger side of the minivan. Bess unlocked the door and he slid inside.

'Hi,' he said, smiling.

Bess smiled back. 'Hi,' she said.

'I like your hair,' he said.

'Thanks. Just trying something new,' she said.

'I like it,' he said.

'Thanks,' she said.

'Well,' he said, the smile slipping away.

'Yeah,' she said, her smile also slipping away.

'What do you think we should do?' he asked.

'Do we know what section is hers?' Bess asked.

He said, 'Yeah. Well, at least I know what section was hers months ago when I met Harper here for a free lunch. She had that left corner area,' he said, pointing at the location. They could see a woman in a Denny's uniform standing by a table.

'Is that her?' Bess asked.

'Yeah, I think so,' he answered.

233

'So,' she said, looking at him. 'I guess we should just go in?'

'Right,' he said.

'What if the hostess doesn't seat us in her section?' she asked.

'We can request that section. It doesn't look too full. It should be OK,' he said.

'Well, OK then,' she said.

They both sat there for another moment, staring at the left-hand section of the diner. Then they looked at each other and both sighed. Then they laughed awkwardly. 'Well, let's do it,' Bess said.

Logan nodded and they both opened their doors.

In the morning I found Miss Hutchins in the living room, the disfigured photo albums in her lap. I sat down next to her. She held the snapshot of Diamond and the handsome man in one hand and appeared to be comparing it to that of the man in the wedding picture with her mother. The face was still scratched out but the body was visible. The two men in the pictures definitely didn't have the same body type. Miss Hutchins' father was a big man, half a foot taller than his wife, whereas the man in the picture with Diamond Lovesy was slight of build, and was practically the same height as Diamond. I mentioned this to Miss Hutchins.

'But lots of men lost weight during the war,' she said. 'That means nothing.' She stared at the picture. 'And I think as a ghost you'd look the same as when you died, don't you think?' she asked me.

I shrugged. 'I have no idea. But look at the difference in height,' I said.

She looked back and forth between the two pictures. 'Well, this means nothing,' she said. 'Mother was a tiny woman, and Miss Lovesy was quite tall.'

She had me there. I was afraid this was going to take math to figure out – not my strong suit. 'How tall was your mother?' I asked her.

'I don't really know. I was just a child when she died, but everyone has always said she was a small woman. Especially in comparison to my dad.' She pointed to the wedding picture. 'See?'

'Yes, I see,' I said, wondering how tall Diamond was. I excused myself and went to the hall phone.

I heard Miss Hutchins sigh. 'I suppose I should start breakfast. Oh, dear,' she said, clasping her hands. 'I haven't even made coffee yet.'

I said, 'No problem,' while in my head I was thinking, 'So hop to it!' It was early, I'd been up late – I'm not proud of my thought, but at least I had the decency not to say it out loud. She left for the kitchen and I dialed the chief's office. The gray-haired lady answered the phone and I asked for the chief, identifying myself. She made a 'humph' sound but put me right through.

'Hey, Miz Pugh,' the chief said. 'To what do I owe this honor?'

'Can you find out how tall Diamond Lovesy was? The ME should know that, shouldn't he?'

'We ain't got an ME. What we got is a funeral director with two semesters of med school. But he does OK.'

235

'He should be able to give you her height, don't you think?'

'Oh, sure, and her weight, and her stomach contents, if you need that.'

I gagged slightly. 'Oh, no, that's not necessary. Just her height.'

'Well, I'm busier than a long-tailed cat in a room full of rockin' chairs, and then you and me got a date to go to the library, right, little lady? But I'll have him call you. His name's Ernest.'

Before I could ask first or last name, he'd hung up on me. But first name Ernest, last name Emory, called before I'd left the foyer. He told me that Diamond was five feet, eleven and a half inches tall and weighed two hundred and sixty-five pounds. When he started on stomach contents I severed the call.

OK, so she was half an inch taller than me and, well, even at my heaviest, she still out-weighed me. I hate to admit I was proud of that. It's just the whole misery loves company thing – it's always better when the company's misery is worse than yours. Human nature? Or am I just a bitch?

So what did this tell me, besides the fact that I'm not as nice a person as I'd hoped to be? If she was five feet, eleven and a half inches tall and, looking at the picture once again, the man standing next to her was equal to her height – and yes, I checked shoes: they were both wearing running shoes (and don't get me started on running shoes with a silk kimono) so any height difference would be negligible – then he too was probably around five foot eleven. But

236

everyone, including Miss Hutchins herself, claimed Norris Hutchins, her father, was a tall man. And even as early as the nineteen forties, tall was probably considered somewhere over six feet. Was this proof that the man in the picture with Diamond Lovesy was *not* the dead Norris Hutchins? Like I needed proof of that? I asked myself. Well, maybe not for the chief, my husband, or any other rational being out there, but maybe for Miss Hutchins. She was bound and determined this was her daddy, and that all the weird goings-on at the Bishop's Inn – up to and including the murder of her own mother – had somehow been at the hand of her very deceased father. And why should I challenge that? If somehow between the chief, Willis, and myself we were able to get to the truth of the matter, then confront her. But why upset her now?

I went in search of coffee. After the night I'd had, I could use a pot – or two.

BACK HOME

The Denny's was decorated in 1950s chic, with black and white tiles and jukeboxes and lots of red touches, like all the Denny's in the world. Logan got them a booth in Mrs Benton's section and she saw them almost immediately. She may not have recognized Bess from their brief encounter, but she certainly knew who Logan was. Instead of coming to their table, however, she turned and walked into the kitchen.

Bess and Logan looked at each other. 'You think she's running out on us?' Logan asked.

Bess shrugged. 'I dunno. Should we follow her? Or go outside and look for her car?'

But before they could make any decision, the woman came back in and walked up to their table, pad in hand. 'Can I get y'all something to drink?'

'Ah, a Coke,' Logan said.

'Water for me,' Bess said.

'Great!' she said, turned and left.

'Why didn't you say something?' Bess demanded, leaning forward across the booth to whisper.

'I don't know!' he said, whispering back. 'Why didn't you?'

'Because this is your fight! You've got to stand up for yourself!'

'I thought you were here to help me!'

As their whispering got progressively louder, Mrs Benton was back with their drink orders. 'Have you had a chance to look at the menu?' she asked.

'Ah, no, not yet,' Logan said, looking down at said menu.

'Ma'am, I don't know if you remember me,' Bess started, but was interrupted.

'Yes. You're one of the girls who ambushed me at my home. And I see you're here with Logan. But you need to order some food or I'll get in trouble.'

'Ah, a cheeseburger and fries,' Logan said, handing her his menu.

'A salad,' Bess said.

'We have several different salads,' Mrs Benton said. 'Which do you prefer?'

238

'Just the dinner salad with oil and vinegar, please,' Bess said.

'Certainly,' the waitress said, picking up Bess's menu and turning to leave.

'But we really want to talk to you!' Bess said.

'I'm off at four o'clock. Meet me at the library,' Mrs Benton said.

They ate their lunches, and Bess couldn't believe she was coveting Logan's cheeseburger. She'd been a vegetarian for over a year! One weekend of meat and she was back to being a carnivore? She shook her head and demolished her dinner salad.

'I noticed you weren't at school this morning,' Logan said. 'None of you were.'

'Yeah, well, we found out some bad news—'

'Is it your parents?' Logan asked, grasping her hand. 'Are they OK?'

She shook her head. 'No, it's not my parents. They're fine. It's just that one of my sisters is having trouble with her boyfriend. And it got sorta bad.'

Logan sat up straight. 'Did he hit her? I'll beat the shit out of him if he did! Which sister? Who's the guy?'

Again Bess shook her head. 'No, no, nothing like that. And I really can't talk about it. The people involved wouldn't want any outsiders knowing about it.'

He let go of her hand and slumped against the seat of the booth. 'Is that what you think I am? An outsider?'

'No, no, of course not!' Bess said, wondering

how she'd gotten herself into this mess. 'It's just that . . . well, you know . . . it's family.'

Then he nodded sagely. 'Oh. OK. That. I heard that Graham Pugh was dating his sister – Alicia, not Megan, right?'

'She's his foster sister! And yes, Alicia! Jeez, Megan? That's sick!'

'A sister's a sister, right? If you're willing to bang one, why not all of 'em? And you're like adopted, right? You best be careful!' Logan said.

Bess felt the dinner salad begin to congeal in her stomach. She could only stare at Logan. Finally, she said, 'He's not banging anyone – well, he's not banging Alicia! And you've got the check, right?' she said, throwing her napkin on the table and jumping up. 'You're going to be late getting back to school!' she said and stormed off.

'Hey, Bess, what's the matter?' Logan called after her, but she ignored him as she ran out the door.

1960–1972

Edgar hated prison. The food was lousy, people kept trying to beat him up, and one guy even tried to diddle him. Most of the assaults he was able to ward off, even without the help of his dead brother's straight-razor. He learned a lot of things you could do with a toothbrush or an illicit spoon stolen from the mess. He was eight years in when a guy finally got to him. It was a big black guy who took umbrage to something Edgar had said. By the time the guy jumped him, Edgar had totally forgotten his offense, if he had ever known it. The guy beat the crap out of him, sending him to the infirmary. Two days later Edgar was released. During yard time the day of his release Edgar had stowed his sharpened toothbrush shiv under his shirt and, in front of twenty or so big black guys, he stabbed his assailant in the neck, nicking the carotid artery and stood there, his arms pinned behind his back by a couple of the black guys while they all watched Edgar's victim bleed out. The guards took their own sweet time getting to the scene. By then Edgar was out cold from the beating he'd received from the guys holding him. When he woke up in the infirmary, he discovered he had a concussion, a broken nose, three missing teeth, a dislocated shoulder, a ruptured spleen and ten years added to his sentence. He was lucky – if his victim had been white, he would have gotten more like fifteen.

In June of 1972, Edgar was released from the Georgia State Penitentiary having done his whole time with no parole. So he was free to leave that great state, which he did, heading back to Biloxi where he thought he might still have a wife and son.

But the old boarding house had been torn down and there was a shopping center where they'd all used to live. He looked up the name 'Winslow' (the name he'd taken when he boarded the freighter that took him away from the Philippines and had given to his wife and child) in the phone book and found only one – his son, Chester. Asking at a gas station, he discovered that the street his son lived on was only a couple of blocks *from where he stood, so he walked there, dragging his small cardboard suitcase with him.*

The address was a four-unit apartment building, two up, two down, and Chester's name was on the postal slot for apartment 2A. Since the bottom floor was 1A and 1B, he surmised that 2A would be upstairs. He dragged his body and his suitcase up the stairs and knocked on the door of 2A. It was opened by a shirtless young man holding a medical device to his mouth, with a marijuana roach clasped in the device. The young man sucked on the roach and said while still breathing in, 'Yeah?'

'Chester?' Edgar asked, knowing there was no doubt he was standing in front of his son. The Hutchins' genes were more than evident: the kid had his face – or at least the face Edgar used to have.

'No. Chet. Who are you?'

'I'm your dad,' Edgar said.

'Bullshit,' the kid said.

'No really. I just got out of prison.'

'Huh. My mom always said I looked just like you. Sorry, but I don't see a resemblance. How do I know you are who you say you are?'

Edgar pulled out his old driver's license from Mississippi and showed it to the boy. 'Yeah, that's my dad,' Chet said. 'Mom showed me pictures. But that ain't you!'

'I got sorta messed up in the joint,' Edgar said.

'I'll say. So what do you want?' the kid said, taking another deep drag of the still-burning roach. He held it out to Edgar, his eyebrows raised.

Edgar shook his head. It wasn't as if he'd never smoked marijuana. He'd tried it several times when he was hanging out with the black guys here in Biloxi, but he'd never liked it much. It just didn't have the punch he'd gotten to like so much in his Shanghai opium days. 'I was hoping for a place to stay,' he said to his son.

'Huh,' the kid said. He was still blocking the door to his apartment. 'You mean like here?'

'If I could,' Edgar said. Then added, 'Please.'

Chester, or Chet, shook his head. 'Hell, I'm not sure you even are who you say you are. For all I know, you're some lowlife who stole my real dad's driver's license.'

'Your mom'll know me,' Edgar said. 'Is she here?'

Chet laughed. 'Here? Are you kidding me? Like I got the time or the inclination for that! Naw, she's in a home run by the state. Over on the other side of town.'

'What's she doing in a home? Is she sick?' Edgar asked.

Chet looked at him like he was nuts. 'I'd have thought my real dad would know my mom's a retard. Seems like she always has been. Seems he mighta noticed!' He went to slam his front door, but Edgar stuck his foot in the door.

'Your mom's name is Rita, she's a little bit cross-eyed and not real smart, but I never woulda taken her for a retard. And I can prove I know her – she's got a mole right under her navel on the right as you look at her,' Edgar said, his words delivered rapidly in his attempt to keep the door partially open.

243

'Oh, gross, man, like I'd ever look at my mom's belly button!'

'What about your grandmother? She knows me.'

'Ah, man, she's dead. Like two or three years ago. That's why mom's in a home – I sure as hell can't take care of her. Granny's the one who really raised me. Mom didn't know squat about bringing up a kid.' He sighed. 'But she still mighta done a better job than Granny. That old bitch really enjoyed beating the shit out of me every chance she got.'

Edgar felt something in or near his stomach, a pang of remorse or even guilt, but just for half a second. 'So let's go see your mom. Rita'll know me, even after all these years, even with . . .' he pointed at his scarred face, '. . . this,' he ended quietly.

'Yeah, you're butt ugly, and Mom always said how handsome you were. Doubt she'll recognize you even if you are telling the truth.'

'We can always get a nurse to check her belly button,' Edgar said.

Chet pulled the door open wide. 'Yeah, I guess. Come on in while I get a shirt on.'

Fifteen

The chief picked Willis and me up around eleven that morning and we headed to the library. There were two computers, each with internet access. I Googled 'Houston Restaurants' then punched in 'paninis' and 'Greek' and 'organic' and came up with about twelve results. Only one started with the letters s-u-n: Sunkissed Kafe, on Jett Street, which, when I looked it up on Mapquest, turned out to be a small side street of only two blocks, just to the west of Montrose Avenue, in the trendy Montrose area of Houston.

The chief sank down in the chair next to me. 'OK, great. Now what? What the hell does this tell us? We know where Diamond Lovesy was when she had a picture taken with some guy who, according to Miz Hutchins, looks just like her daddy. So what?'

I leaned back in my chair, feeling some level of defeat. 'I don't know,' I said, trying to ignore the hint of a whine in my voice.

'So maybe it's a relative?' Willis suggested.

The chief and I both just looked at him. Then we looked at each other, jumped up and headed for his squad car.

BACK HOME

Bess was devastated. She couldn't believe Logan had said those things! Like the Pughes were

245

some hillbilly family where your mama is your sister and your daddy is a cousin! Is that what the whole school thought? I'm never going back! she thought. I'll get my GED and go straight to college! she told herself. I'll let the others make up their own minds, but I'm telling them this! Then had to rethink that. How badly would it hurt Alicia to know that anyone, even just Logan, thought such a thing? And Megan? Well, maybe at first she'd find it funny, but at some point it would get to her, of that Bess was certain. Megan was no dummy. She might do stupid things on occasion – well, more like half the time, Bess amended herself – but she was not stupid!

Bess felt tears streaming down her cheeks as she drove the minivan home. Logan was such a tool to say such things! she thought. And to think she made out with him! Yuck! OK, she thought. He was a good kisser, but he's an awful person! And I'm not making out again with an awful person! Yet still the tears came. She'd liked him so much. The way his blond hair fell in his eyes when he was studying, or the way his cheeks dimpled up when he smiled. And he'd seemed so sweet, so considerate. And maybe he was a little too tall for her, but they'd fit just right when they were on the sofa. Making out on the sofa. She could feel the same heat that had filled her body from his touch fill her up at just the memory of it. 'Damn!' she said out loud. 'Get over it!'

As she pulled into her driveway, she couldn't help but notice Logan's car in her spot.

'No, it was just Daddy and Uncle Herbert and their younger brother Edgar, but he died in the Pacific. It was all very sad. My grandfather never got over it,' Miss Hutchins said. 'Uncle Herbert said it broke his daddy's heart, and then, when my daddy died too, well, he just went. Right when Mama called about the telegram.'

'What about cousins?' I asked.

'Well, now, Uncle Herbert never had any children, and Uncle Edgar died in the war, so no first cousins. And Grandpa Hutchins was an only child, and his folks were long dead by the time I came to be. I don't know if they had kin, but I've never heard of another Hutchins around here,' the old lady said. 'As for Grandma Hutchins, she had a sister, Auntie Christine, but she, well, she traveled a lot, never married, and died young.' Miss Hutchins leaned into me and whispered, 'Mama said it was a venereal disease! I had to look that up.' She straightened and said, 'But she never had any children.'

And there was a united sigh from her audience of three. 'Back to the drawing board,' the chief said.

BACK HOME

'What are you doing here?' Bess demanded as she burst in the back door to find Logan sitting on the sofa, with her sisters as bookends.

He jumped up. 'Man, I'm so sorry!' he said. 'Things just come out of my mouth sometimes and I don't even know it! That was an awful thing to say—'

'Just leave, please,' Bess said, her words measured.

247

Alicia stood up and went to Bess, putting her arm around her and hugging her. 'It's OK, Bess,' she said, holding her at arm's length and smiling at her. 'Logan told us what he said. And it's just about what I suspected was going around the school. But he's promised he'll beat the crap out of anyone he hears saying it again!'

'Alicia!' Bess said.

'I told him no,' Alicia said, 'but what's a girl to do when a guy goes all Galahad on her?'

Logan moved closer to Bess and Alicia went back to the sofa. 'I'm so sorry,' he said softly. 'That was an awful thing to say, even if I was just repeating what I'd heard—'

'That's no excuse!' Bess said.

'You're right! It isn't. I'm an asshole. You know it and I know it. It's just that I've been knowing it longer than you have. My assholeness is just new to you, and it takes some getting used to.'

'I'm not sure I can forgive you—' Bess started.

'Jeez, what's to forgive?' Megan said from the sofa. 'He said a dumb thing! Like you haven't? Shall I list the dumb things you've said this week alone? OK, one—'

'Stop!' Bess said, her hand raised like a traffic cop. Turning to Logan, she said, 'Do they know you thought the sister my brother was, excuse the word, banging, could have been Megan?'

'Oh, yuck!' Megan said from the sofa.

'Ah, no, I didn't mention that,' he said, head down.

'And that you warned me to watch out for my own brother because, and here I quote, "You're adopted"?'

'Double gross,' Megan said, and then laughed.

Bess whirled on her sister. 'Why are you laughing?'

'Because it's so stupid! Jeez, Logan, are you really that dumb?'

'Yeah, I guess,' he said, still staring at the floor.

Alicia stood up again. 'Come on, Bess, Logan's one of the good guys—'

'You were just telling me the other night there *are* no good guys! That they're all out to get in my pants!'

'Whoa, now!' Logan said, finally looking up from the floor, both arms raised in surrender. 'I never ever tried anything like that!'

'Not yet!' Bess shot at him.

'Yeah, not ever!' he shot back. 'I mean, you're cute and all, but I signed a pledge at my church to stay a virgin at least until I graduate high school, and I have every intention on signing another one after graduation that'll take me through college! That's one of the reasons why this thing with Harper is pissing me off so bad!'

Bess just looked at him. 'You could have told me that,' she finally said.

Logan's face began to infuse with color. 'I told you that I hadn't . . . Well, it's kinda embarrassing. It's not something I, like, you know, advertise.' Then his eyes got wide in panic, as he looked around at the three sisters. 'Please, y'all, don't tell any of the guys, OK? Please!'

Alicia and Bess looked at Megan. 'What?' Megan said. She sighed. 'OK, I know I blew it when I told the twins about Alicia and Graham, but I've learned my lesson.' She mimed locking

249

her lips and throwing away the key. 'Your secret is safe with me.'

'Shouldn't you be in school?' Bess asked, turning back to Logan.

'I told them I had a doctor's appointment. And I wrote a note from my mom so they believed me.'

'So,' Megan said, jumping up. 'What's the plan, Stan?'

'Who in the hell is the guy in the picture with Diamond?' I asked the room in general. There were two manly shrugs and one small voice saying, 'Daddy, of course.'

The chief, Willis and I exchanged glances. Did we argue with her? Try to set her straight? Ignore her? Then both guys were staring straight at me, as if I were the only one qualified to handle her. Personally, I didn't see where I had any qualifications for this particular job. I mean, Chief Cotton was in charge! It should be *his* responsibility. Then I remembered how he'd handled the ghostly aspect of this business earlier. Let's just say he was no Henry Kissinger or Hillary Clinton.

'Miss Hutchins, this may well be your deceased father, you're right,' I said, as tactfully as possible. 'But we have to consider the more likely possibility that it's someone who's actually living.'

'Well, of course you do!' she said. 'But don't you see? That's exactly what Daddy wants! He wants y'all traipsing around, trying to find some imaginary killer while he sits around the house waiting for his next victim!'

'You think he's in the house?' the chief asked.

'Well, of course! I don't have mice! Yet I hear scurrying going on up there day and night!' she said.

'Up where?' the chief and I asked in unison.

'Why, in the attic, of course.'

'Have you been up there?' I asked her.

She shook her head. 'I haven't been up there in years. My arthritis, you know.' The three of us exchanged quick glances again and, as one, jumped up and headed for the stairs.

BACK HOME

'Logan and I are supposed to meet Mrs Benton at the library at four o'clock,' Bess said.

'Harper's mom?' Megan asked. Bess nodded. 'So she didn't tell y'all anything at this lunch thing?'

'No, just to meet her at four,' Logan said, as he and Bess took their places on the loveseat.

'Think she'll show up?' Megan asked.

'Why would she tell us to meet her there if she's not going to show up?' Logan asked, wide-eyed.

Bess couldn't help finding his trusting nature adorable. 'To get us off her back,' she said, patting him on the hand. 'If she doesn't show up at the library, and we try to track her down at her home, then maybe Tucker will be there, and we can't very well talk to her with him around.'

'She'll show up,' Logan said. 'I betja.'

All four of them headed out in the minivan at three-thirty, on their way to the library in Codderville. When they arrived they didn't see the car they'd seen Harper in the day before, but

251

weren't sure if Mrs Benton had her own vehicle. 'Should we go in?' Alicia asked.

'Yeah, maybe she's already in there,' Megan said.

'Do you know how many cars they have?' Bess asked Logan.

'I only saw the one when I picked Harper up that night. But Tucker had that truck. So maybe two?'

'Maybe we should go in because she could already be in there,' Alicia said.

After arguing about it for a few more minutes, majority ruled and they left the minivan and went into the library.

The Codderville Library was new, and quite impressive for a small town. Four thousand square feet divided into sections: an adult fiction and non-fiction section with several sets of tables and chairs, a walled-off section for children, complete with puppet theater and lots of smaller-sized tables and chairs, meeting rooms, an audio lending library including a new section for ebooks, and a large area of desks with computers and a few printers.

Not seeing their prey, the kids decided to split up – Bess and Logan at a table closest to the front doors, and Alicia and Megan three tables back from them.

At ten minutes after four, the front doors opened and Mrs Benton came in.

We found a door on the second floor that led to the attic and Willis and I were more than happy to let Chief Cotton lead the way. He even had his gun drawn, just in case. Very little light came through two shuttered windows, but I found a switch and turned it on. Two bare bulbs hung from wires from the rafters, one on each end of the attic, and held what could only be forty-watt bulbs. The attic was huge – covering all of the house, and filled with the kinds of things that can collect after more than one hundred years. There was an old-fashioned, large-breasted dress form, trunks of different styles from different eras (boy would I love to rummage through those – another time, perhaps), old furniture – some in stable condition, other pieces broken to the point of no return (why they were still up there was anybody's guess), and lots of boxes, sealed and unsealed. But the most interesting object was a twin-sized mattress on the floor, blankets atop it, an unlit kerosene lamp on an upside-down wooden box, an open box filled with bottles of water, crackers, peanut butter, a bag of Hershey's Kisses and a bag of beef jerky. Someone was definitely living in Miss Hutchins' attic, the same person who made noises like the pitter patter of mice, the same person who dragged something down the second floor hallway in the dead of night, and the same person who, more than likely, killed Humphrey Hammerschultz and Diamond Lovesy.

BACK HOME
Mrs Benton saw Bess and Logan, nodded to them and headed their way. Alicia and Megan turned their heads away, afraid the older woman might recognize them and bolt. If she did notice them

at all, she didn't react. She sat down across from Bess and Logan and asked, 'Now what is this all about?'

'Why don't you tell us?' Bess said. 'We know the baby Harper's carrying has nothing to do with Logan, so why is she saying it's his?'

Mrs Benton glanced from Bess to Logan and back again. She smiled. 'You certainly are trusting of your boyfriend,' she said to Bess. 'I've never had that luxury.'

Bess's face turned crimson and she said, 'He's not my boyfriend.'

'Yet,' Logan said, and put his hand over Bess's. Bess looked into his eyes and the two were lost for a moment.

'Whatever!' Megan said, standing up and coming to the table. 'Mrs Benton, Logan's not the father, OK? We know it and you obviously know it. And Harper needs to take back what she said! It's not fair to Logan – or my sister.'

Megan sat down next to Mrs Benton, while Alicia pulled up a chair from the next table.

'I'm feeling a bit outnumbered here,' Mrs Benton said, still smiling.

'Do you really think this is funny?' Megan said, her voice rising. She got a stern look from the librarian and several patrons.

'Of course not,' Mrs Benton said, lowering her voice. She looked at Logan and said, 'Logan, I'm sorry. Harper said you were a nice boy, and I'm not sure why she decided to dump this on you. I know it's not fair and I'll have her retract her statement. Hopefully, it hasn't gotten much further than the four of you.'

254

'I hope not,' Logan said, still holding Bess's hand.

'So what's really going on? Who's the daddy?' Megan asked.

Mrs Benton stood up. 'That's none of your business,' she said. 'I'll take care of this, Logan. And if you see either of my children again, just stay clear of them.' With that, she turned and walked out the door.

'Do ghosts eat Hershey's Kisses?' Willis asked.

'Not that I ever heard tell,' Chief Cotton said. 'Not into peanut butter either.'

'Thank God we've got a ghost authority here,' I said sarcastically. I bent down to go through other boxes that were in close proximity to the mattress. After discarding one that held turn-of-the-century baby clothes, I found one with more modern clothing, although it could have belonged to either a man or a woman. Generic T-shirts and blue jeans. Underneath those I found some boxer briefs that led me to surmise that the person sleeping on this mattress was more than likely a man.

'Whatja got there?' the chief asked, squatting down next to me.

I showed him the clothes as I tossed them on the floor, going for the bottom of the box. There was a Dopp kit there containing the usual items one would find in such a place: deodorant, shaving cream and a bag of Bic razors, aftershave, a bar of soap and a wash cloth, fingernail clippers and a toothbrush and toothpaste. At the bottom of the kit was a red velvet sheath. The chief reached down and picked it up, lifting the flap at the top of the sheath and pulling out an old-fashioned straight-razor.

1972

Chet had a car, of sorts. An early sixties Plymouth Valiant that smoked and sputtered but still seemed to get the job done. Edgar didn't have much to say – he couldn't see himself regaling his son with tales of prison life. None of his stories ended well. Chet talked a bit. About his girlfriend who he'd just dumped because she'd caught him with her sister and said he couldn't do that. Chet broke up with her because he thought she wasn't being fair. Edgar understood completely. But then, Chet told him, the sister had decided she didn't like the way he'd treated his girlfriend, saying he cheated on her.

'Hell, man,' Chet explained to his dad, 'I'm the one who cheated? Shit, she was just my girlfriend! That bitch was her sister! She's the one who cheated, donja think?'

'Sure,' Edgar said, staring out at the streets of Biloxi, marveling at how much the town had changed.

'So I said, "Hey, bitch! I wouldn't fuck you with a ten foot pole anyways!" And she goes, "Yeah, you and what army?" And I go . . .' Chet said, while Edgar tuned him out, thinking, he might have my face, but he's got his granny's mouth! If ever there was a person who could talk your ear off it was that old bitch.

They got to the facility where Edgar's wife was housed after a fairly short twenty-minute ride. It was weird to think of her as his wife – but as far as he knew she still was. Of course, it had been hard for him to think of her as his wife when he was living with her, too.

The facility was a large, state-run place, red brick and institutional, with an unmanned gate that they easily drove through. Once inside Edgar found himself in a no-frills room filled with patients milling about, some just wandering around, some talking to themselves, others sitting in chairs and staring out the windows. A couple of men played forty-two at a table in the center of the room, and three women appeared to be putting together a jigsaw puzzle at another table.

Chet walked up to a counter, behind which stood a nurse in a starched white uniform. 'Hey, June,' he said, grinning big.

'Well, hey there, Chet!' the woman said, smiling up at Edgar's son's handsome face. Edgar couldn't help thinking, that's the way women used to look at me.

'Did your mom know you were coming?' the nurse asked.

'Nope. Surprise visit. This guy' – Chet said, pointing over his shoulder at Edgar – 'says he's my dad. I wanna see if Mama recognizes him.'

The nurse his son called June looked Edgar up and down, then shook her head. 'Rita always says you're the spitting image of your daddy. I don't see it.'

'Me neither. But he says mom's got a mole—' He turned to look at Edgar. 'Where'd you say?'

'On the right side just under her belly button as you're looking at her,' Edgar said.

The nurse nodded her head. 'Well, that's true.

257

She does have that. How come you don't look like Chet?' she asked Edgar.

He shrugged. 'Got in an accident,' he supplied.

She shrugged. 'That's a shame. The world needs more pretty men like Chet here,' she said, coming around the counter and squeezing Chet's arm. 'I'll go get your mom,' she said, heading for a door.

'You ever knock boots with that?' Edgar asked Chet.

Chet made a face. 'Jeez, are you kidding? She's gotta be like thirty! Naw, not my type. 'Sides, I like really big ta-tas.'

Edgar nodded his head. 'Always been partial to that myself.'

Chet led Edgar over to a grouping of sofa, loveseat and easy chair, no two items matching, and they sat down. It took only a few minutes for the nurse to come back. And there she was, Rita, the pretty girl with the crossed eyes that he'd cheated on every chance he'd got. She was still cross-eyed, and, Edgar had to admit, still pretty – for an old woman. At least she didn't look like her mother.

Rita saw Chet first and a grin spread across her face. 'Hi, baby-boy,' she said, moving toward him. Then she noticed the man standing next to her son and stopped short. Her mouth dropped open and she stood there for almost a full minute. Finally, she ran up to Edgar and threw her arms around him. 'You've come back!' she cried. 'I always knew you would!'

Sixteen

BACK HOME

'So it's over?' Logan asked as they all climbed back in the minivan.

'I guess so,' Alicia said.

'Who's the daddy?' Bess asked.

'What does it matter?' Megan said. 'As long as she's no longer accusing Logan, it's all good, right?'

Alicia, who was driving, said, 'Jeez, Megan, are you *not* E.J. Pugh's daughter? Don't you want to know the truth?'

'After what looking for the truth in all the wrong places has done for Mom? I don't think so! She and Dad almost got divorced over this kind of thing! Besides, there's no murder here,' Megan said. 'Just a girl lying.'

'You didn't look in Tucker Benton's eyes, did you?' Bess insisted. 'There was murder in there! He would have killed Logan if we hadn't been there!'

'No, now, Bess,' Logan started.

Bess interrupted. 'Don't you side with them! That guy was out to beat the crap out of you! If we hadn't been there—'

'I know, I know,' Logan said and heaved a great sigh. 'Three girls saved my ass. I know. But he wasn't going to kill me. And besides, I need to know *why* she lied about me. I mean, there could be a real crime going on here. What if whoever knocked Harper up was like some old guy, you know? What if she was like raped or something? I mean, why else would she lie about me?'

'Because she's a bitch and she wanted to get you into trouble?' Bess asked sarcastically.

Logan turned his head and looked out the window. Bess crossed her arms over her chest and looked out *her* window.

'Logan's right,' Alicia said. 'There could be something bad going on here! I just read online about this rapist who's suing his victim for custody of the child she had because of the rape! Can you believe it?'

Megan shook her head. 'That's seriously gross.'

'I know!' Alicia said. 'First time I was alone with that guy, I'd gut him like a chicken!'

'Alicia!' Bess said from the back seat.

'Well, wouldn't you?' Alicia demanded, turning in her seat to look at her sister.

Bess appeared to think about it for a moment, then said, 'Then pour rubbing alcohol all over him so it would burn.'

Megan laughed out loud. 'Damn straight!' she said.

Logan stared open-mouthed at the three girls, then said, 'Back in the olden days, armies used to throw their prisoners to the women. Now I understand why.'

Looking at the straight-razor in front of him, Chief Cotton said, 'Too bad neither Hammerschultz or Lovesy died from a cut throat.' He turned the razor around in his hand, seeing

260

the glint of the forty-watt bulb reflect off its sheen. 'Then we'd have us a murder weapon.'

'That would make a good one,' Willis said. 'Even as old as it is. Look how worn the steel is.'

'Wait!' I said, staring at it. 'There was someone with a slit throat, remember?'

'Who?' Chief Cotton said, raising an eyebrow at me.

Willis looked at me, grinned, and said, 'Miss Hutchins' mama.'

'Oh, fer Christ's sake!' the chief said. Then he stared at the razor. 'And I just got my fingerprints all over it.'

'Look!' I said, pointing at the barely discernable initials on the heft of the straight-razor. 'NMH,' I said. 'Norris Hutchins?'

Gingerly he put the razor back in its sheath. 'If we find Norris Hutchins' fingerprints on this thing, I'm quittin' and movin' to Florida,' he said.

BACK HOME

As they turned on to the main road out of the library, Megan noticed Mrs Benton coming out of the library. She had her cell phone to her ear and was walking rapidly toward her car, the one they'd seen Harper driving the day before. On a pretty, sunny day in April, the windows of the minivan were down and they distinctly heard the woman say, 'Call nine-one-one! I'm on my way!'

Alicia put her foot on the brake, stopping the van in the middle of the road, alienating the cars behind her. 'Nine-one-one?' she said, turning to the rest.

'Could it be the baby?' Bess asked.

Alicia pulled the van to the side of the road and they watched as Mrs Benton got in her car and rushed out of the parking lot. 'Follow her!' Megan said.

Alicia did. Mrs Benton led them straight to Codder County Memorial Hospital where she pulled up under the emergency portico – reserved for ambulances – and bailed out of her car. Alicia let everyone out of the minivan and went to park in a proper spot.

Walking back, she noticed Mrs Benton had left the driver's side door standing open and the keys in the ignition. Being the person she was, Alicia hopped in the car, started it up and drove it to a proper parking spot, right next to the minivan. She pocketed the keys and headed into the emergency room.

After being dropped off, Megan, Bess and Logan followed Mrs Benton inside the ER waiting room. She went straight to the counter housing the ER nurse, said something they couldn't hear, and was immediately taken back behind closed doors.

The three looked at each other then back at the locked doors that led to the bowels of the emergency room. 'What now?' Bess asked the other two.

Logan shrugged and Megan said, 'We wait?'

'For what?' Bess demanded.

Megan's turn to shrug. 'I dunno. Alicia?'

'You rang?' Alicia said, coming in the door behind them. 'What's going on?'

'Harper's mother went in and we don't know what's going on,' Bess said.

'We don't even know if it *was* Harper the call was about!' Logan said. 'For all we know, Tucker could have been in a car wreck or something.'

At that point the ER doors swung open and a man came running inside and up to the counter. Megan elbowed Bess in the ribs. 'That's Coach Robbins!' she stage-whispered.

The coach yelled at the ER nurse, 'Harper Benton! Where is she? Is she OK?'

'Oh my God,' Bess whispered.

'Daddy's here,' Megan said.

'How long will it take to get DNA?' Willis asked the chief as they took their booty downstairs.

'Weeks,' he said.

Willis and I looked at each other. Part of me was thinking, weeks in this bucolic little town? Sleeping late and eating Miss Hutchins' food? Wandering the antique shops and lazing in the Bishop's Inn's garden? Then the practical part of me remembered that my husband was self-employed and we were already losing money on this Monday morning. He'd had to cancel three appointments with potential clients. And I had a deadline approaching on my latest bodice ripper.

And then, of course, there were the kids. I figured they were doing OK though without us. They sure seemed to be the few times we'd talked. There was always the chance somebody would notice three teenage girls on their own – but I could call Luna, and Vera, my mother-in-law . . . Then I thought of another salient point: waiting weeks could mean that this killer could kill again – or leave town and we'd never find him.

'We don't have weeks,' I gently reminded the chief.

'We can get the fingerprints back pretty quick-like,' he said. 'I'm taking this,' he said, indicating the sheathed straight-razor, 'back to the shop now. Mary Mays is our fingerprint expert. She went to the academy in Austin to learn all about it. I'll give it to her.'

And with that, the chief was out the door and Willis and I were once again on our own. I could smell good smells coming from the kitchen. Lunch! I thought and smiled. Then sobered. One, my jeans were getting tight, and two, was now the time to mention to Miss Hutchins that someone was definitely in her attic but it was a live someone, not her daddy's ghost? Then we went into the dining room and I saw the steaming tureen of some creamy soup and a platter of breads and cold-cuts. Maybe after lunch we'd talk about it, I thought.

Lunch was even better than that first glance had promised. The soup was homemade cream of mushroom, thick with mushrooms, bacon, onions and other goodies I didn't recognize. It was ambrosia. The breads – white, wheat, and sour dough – were homemade, as was the mayo and the mustard. How this old lady had time to do all this, I'll never know. The only store-bought items on the table were the cold-cuts, and they certainly weren't the packaged kind. These obviously came from a meat market and were cut thick – ham, turkey and roast beef. I kept myself to only one sandwich, but allowed myself two bowls of soup – and of course some of the fruit

264

salad Miss Hutchins had so lovingly provided. Even so, by the time I stopped eating, I had to unbutton my jeans and suppress an unladylike burp. I also rethought my scenario about telling Miss Hutchins about the person in the attic. I was afraid on such a full stomach it might give me indigestion. I had no idea how she would react, and, truthfully, right now I didn't want to know.

So I went upstairs and took a nap. I do some of my best thinking while asleep.

BACK HOME

'Coach?' Logan called out.

Coach Robbins whirled around, staring glassy-eyed at the three kids, with no recognition on his face. Logan walked up to him and the coach seemed to shake himself.

'Logan? You OK, man? What are you doing here?' he asked.

'I'm asking you the same thing!' Logan said, his fists clenched at his side. 'Why do you care what's going on with Harper Benton? How did you even know she was here? And who the hell do you think you are, you sick son-of-a-bitch!'

And then Logan took a swing at the coach, who blocked it easily with a big, meaty paw covering Logan's fist. 'Whoa, boy!' the coach said, just as the doors swung open again and a small woman came running in.

'Is she OK?' she said, rushing up to the coach. 'Can we see her? The baby? Is the baby OK?'

Coach Robbins let go of Logan's fist and Logan backed off. 'This is my wife, Cathy,' the coach said.

265

All four kids were now totally confused. If the coach had raped or otherwise had carnal knowledge of Harper Benton, why was his wife involved? Unless these people were really, really sick.

'You better tell us what's going on,' Alicia said, walking up to the coach.

All four had been in one class or another of Coach Robbins over their four-year high-school careers. He'd been Logan's basketball coach for the past three years; Bess had taken sophomore biology from him; he coached Alicia's girls' volleyball team; and Megan had dabbled for a semester in his wood-working class. And they all knew that Harper had been on the same volleyball team as Alicia – the one led by Coach Robbins.

'You kids need to get out of here!' the coach said, his teeth gritted. 'This is none of your business!'

'Our next-door neighbor is a lieutenant with the Codderville police department,' Bess said. 'I'm thinking this might be her business!'

The coach, big and beefy and outweighing his much smaller wife by at least one hundred pounds and standing a half-foot taller, took a step toward the assembled teenagers, hands fisted by his side, but his wife stopped him.

'Honey, don't,' she said, a small arm out to restrain him. It did the trick. He stopped and just stared at them.

Then the door to the bowels of the ER opened and Mrs Benton came out. She saw the coach and his wife immediately, but didn't even glance at the kids. They weren't sure whether she saw them or not.

'She's OK,' Mrs Benton said, her hand on Cathy Robbins' arm. 'And the baby's fine.' Mrs Robbins wrapped her arms around Mrs Benton's neck and burst into tears.

'Thank God!' the coach's wife finally said.

'You're sure the baby's OK?' Coach Robbins asked, grasping Mrs Benton's arm.

'The doctor said everything is just fine. He said the cramps were probably brought on by stress' – and at this point, she turned and glared at the kids, which led them to believe that maybe she had noticed them – 'and they're going to keep her overnight, but everything's fine. They've got the monitor on her now, if you want to go in and see the baby,' she said, smiling at the coach and his wife.

'Oh, yes!' Mrs Robbins said, her face almost bursting from the smile displayed on it.

'Yeah, definitely,' the coach said, and Harper's mom went to the nurse who buzzed the door open and the Robbinses went in.

Once they were inside, Mrs Benton turned on the four teenagers. 'What in the hell do you think you're doing?' she hissed at them.

'What's going on?' Logan demanded. 'Was Harper having an affair with the coach?'

Mrs Benton stopped cold, stared at Logan, then she laughed. 'Oh, my God! No!' She put her hands on her hips and looked at each in turn. 'Could you people be any more clueless?' she said.

But then the doors to the parking lot opened

once again and Tucker Benton came rushing in. And Mrs Benton stopped laughing.

We had a clue – a real live clue. But I had to agree with Chief Cotton – if the fingerprints on the straight-razor came back to Norris Hutchins, I'd move to Florida with him. Norris Hutchins was long dead, of that I was positive. Mostly. Ghosts and goblins and things that went bump in the night were all well and good on the big screen, or even the little one in the living room. They were even OK when written by a Steven King or a Dean Koontz. But they didn't fit well into reality.

I knew as well as I knew my own name that Diamond Lovesy and Humphrey Hammerschultz were frauds, out to take Miss Hutchins for every dime she had. But that didn't tell me anything about who might have killed the pair. If you take the reality of what they were up to into consideration, really the best suspects would be Miss Hutchins or Willis and myself. Miss Hutchins' daddy, if alive, could be a suspect, if you considered a man near one hundred years of age as viable. I didn't. Besides, he was dead. Miss Hutchins had the letter from the War Office and her father's dog tags to prove it.

And then I sat straight up in bed, the need for an after-lunch nap totally forgotten. What Miss Hutchins didn't have was any proof of the death of her father's youngest brother – Elmer, Edgar? Something like that. I jumped out of bed, disturbing my husband who was lying next to me with a book on his chest and his newly acquired reading glasses on his nose. I appeared to rouse him from a deep sleep.

'Wha?' he said.

'I have an idea!' I said, slipping my shoes back on my feet and heading for the door to the hall.

'Is it a good one?' he asked.

'Let's find out,' I suggested and headed out the door for the stairs.

Miss Hutchins was nowhere to be found in the common rooms of the house. I figured she'd followed my lead and gone to her room for a nap. Instead of disturbing her, I went to the shelf where she kept her family's picture albums. I'd noticed one of those albums had loose papers shoved in the back. She'd shown me one – the letter from the War Office about her father's death on D-Day. I took that album back to the sofa and sat down, Willis next to me.

'What now, Nancy Drew?' he asked.

I gave him a withering look, then said, 'We have proof of Norris Hutchins' death, right?' I said.

'Right,' he answered.

'But what about his younger brother? Elmer?'

'Edgar, I think.'

'Whatever,' I said. 'Miss Hutchins said he died in the Pacific. Let's see if we can find anything in here that proves that.'

'You think Edgar's still alive? He'd have to be in his late eighties at least, right?' Willis said. 'So how's an eighty-year-old running up and down two flights of stairs, sleeping on a bedroll in the attic and doing all this so silently we barely hear him?'

'We did hear him!' I insisted. 'Dragging what-ever it was down the hall that night.'

'Whatever was being dragged down the hall was heavy, E.J.,' he said. He shook his head. 'I doubt it was some eighty-year-old geezer.'

'You're an ageist!' I accused.

'No, I'm a realist. Mom's in her late seventies. Can you see her doing any of this shit?'

I had to consider that. No, I couldn't see Vera, Willis's mother, climbing up two flights of stairs and/or dragging large pieces of furniture or what-ever down the hall and down a flight of stairs. And she was very fit for her age. Hell, I couldn't see myself doing any of those things either. I'm not saying I *couldn't* do it – only that I probably wouldn't want to.

I ignored him and went through the papers in the back of the photo album. And there it was – another letter from the war department, this one addressed to Clayton Hutchins at an address other than that of the Bishop's Inn. Possibly the father of Norris and Edgar? And Herbert, of course. Can't forget Uncle Herbert.

'There goes that theory,' Willis said, glancing at the letter.

I read it through. 'No, now read this! It just says he's missing in action. This is *not* a death notification!'

Willis pointed at the letter. 'In the Philippines in 1943? It's as good as a death notification. Ever hear of the Bataan Death March?'

Vaguely, I thought. I wasn't the World War II buff that my husband was. Rosie the Riveter was my WWII hero and about as far as I got into that particular part of history. The rest was too awful to contemplate. 'Does that mean no Marines made it out of the Philippines?' I asked dubiously.

'No, of course not! But if he was missing in action, then chances are about ninety-nine point ninety-nine percent that he's long dead. Just like his brother,' Willis said.

I stood up and took the album back to the shelf where I'd found it. Turning to my husband, I said, 'That gives me point zero one percent that I'm right,' I said. 'I've worked with less.'

BACK HOME

Tucker Benton stopped short when he saw the four teenagers – particularly Logan – standing by his mother.

'What the hell are you doing here?' he said, fists clenched as he moved slowly toward his prey.

Bess moved in front of Logan, but Logan pushed her gently aside. 'Not again, OK?' he whispered to her.

Bess had to consider that this might be a guy thing – he had to prove his manhood or something – so she stayed by his side.

'Tucker!' Mrs Benton said sternly. 'Leave him alone. And by the way, your sister is OK. And so's the baby.'

Tucker hadn't taken his eyes off of Logan. 'Hear that, asshole?' he said to Logan. 'Did you do something to try to get rid of the evidence?' he said, his teeth also clenched, his fists like ham-hocks at his side.

'Tucker!' Mrs Benton said again. 'He's not the father!'

Finally Tucker looked over at his mother. 'What?'

'This boy isn't the father! You need to just leave this alone!' she said.

'Yeah!' Megan who could never keep a secret said. 'Looks like Coach Robbins is the proud papa!'

Tucker whirled around on Megan. 'What the fuck?' he shouted. 'Who the hell you think you are, accusing one of the greatest men I've ever known of doing something so . . . so . . .'

'Rotten?' Megan supplied. 'Evil? Disturbing?'

Alicia grabbed Megan's arm. 'Stop!' she whispered.

'Why?' Megan asked, breaking away from Alicia's grasp. 'Is he gonna try to beat me up now? You big bully!'

Tucker turned to his mother. 'Mom?'

Mrs Benton just shook her head, a look of total defeat on her face. It was at that moment that the locked doors to the depths of the ER opened and Coach Robbins walked out. Tucker took one look at him then walked up and cold-cocked him.

If Edgar Hutchins didn't die in the Pacific, then what happened to him? I thought. Could he still be alive? *Could* an octogenarian have done these things? Maybe. Maybe not. But he could have had help! I decided. Yes, he certainly could have had help. Like another relative – a son or a daughter! That could be it! But a son or daughter would probably be in their sixties. Could two

272

relatively old people do all this damage? Kill two very healthy specimens like Diamond and Humphrey? What about another generation? What about a grandson or granddaughter! Eureka! I think I might have stumbled on it. Of course, all this rested on one fact I didn't have: did Edgar Hutchins survive the war in the Pacific?

1972–2004

So Edgar, known to his wife and son as Don Winslow, moved into the apartment his son was renting. Several months later he found a job at a discount store acting as a greeter. He knew he couldn't go to any of his old gambling hangouts, even if they still existed. He might not look at all like 'Don Winslow' anymore, but considering he'd killed a man at those old hangouts, he didn't want to take a chance. Besides, twenty years inside had lessened his desire to gamble. Every day inside had been a gamble, and he figured coming out of that alive was the best pay-off he was ever going to get.

But he couldn't stop thinking about the house on Post Oak Street back in Peaceful, Texas, and the treasure buried somewhere within. He kept the fantasy to himself until the day, five years later, when Chet took him to the ER because of a dark red stain on Edgar's pants from an accidental peeing incident of which Edgar was unaware.

'God, Dad!' Chet said, having decided almost immediately upon finding out that Edgar really was 'Don Winslow,' his long-lost father, to call him that. 'That's disgusting! You peed your pants!'

273

Edgar looked down at his crotch. 'I don't pee red, boy! I musta spilled something.'

Chet leaned down and took a whiff. 'Gross! No, Dad! That's pee!' Then he looked up at his father. 'You been pissing blood lately?'

Edgar shrugged. 'Every now and then,' he confessed.

That's when Chet loaded him up and took him to the ER. Edgar ended up in the hospital for several days until all the tests came back. Chet was with him when the doctor came in with the bad news. Bladder cancer. Too far along. Maybe a few weeks left. And then he was gone and Chet and Edgar both stared off into space. Finally, Edgar said, 'Son, I got something to tell you about a place called Peaceful, Texas, and a house on a street called Post Oak.'

And that's when Chet learned who his father really was, about his half-sisters in the Philippines, but mostly about Helen and the treasure in the old Victorian. Edgar failed to mention that he'd sliced Helen's throat with the straight-razor he was to leave his son in his will. That was about the only thing of any value – as little as it may have – that Edgar owned. Only that and the secret of the treasure on Post Oak Street.

Chet buried his dad on a payment plan and left town, figuring they wouldn't chase him down for the remainder of the bill. He moved to Jackson, where things were really happening, and found a friend who needed somebody to move weed for him. Chet had traded his old Valiant in for a VW micro-bus in pretty good condition and his friend thought that would be just the ride they needed

274

to get in and out of Mexico. Chet spent two years hauling weed from a little town in Mexico back to Jackson, Mississippi, and made a lot of money doing it. Like his father back in his Shanghai days, Chet spent his money on women and gambling. And he inhaled a lot of the profits, too.

It was one stormy spring night crossing the border from Nuevo Larado to the Texas side that Chet saw a border guard with a dog who was sniffing away at the cars as they passed through. Chet was riding shotgun, his friend Elias driving Chet's VW. He looked at his friend, looked at the dog sniffing away and jumped ship. He heard later through the grapevine that Elias got sent down for ten years at Huntsville and was looking to mete out some justice to his old buddy, Chet. Which was why Chet moved back to Biloxi. Once there, he discovered that his mother, Rita, was in bad health and died shortly after he got home. She, too, left him nothing but bills.

Chet was worried about how he was going to handle all this, since he hadn't exactly saved any money back in his heyday, and now didn't even have a car, as the VW micro-bus – which was never exactly in his name – was confiscated by the state of Texas. It was while looking over used cars that he met Lola Montgomery. Lola worked at the dealership and gave him quite a deal on a used Chevy Bellaire. The fact that her daddy owned the dealership – one of the largest in Biloxi – may have played a part in the deal. Lola had a one-year-old daughter, Darlene, father unknown, who was an embarrassment to Lola's family. So Chet married her, gave Darlene the last name of

275

Winslow (he'd found it would cost money to change his name back to Hutchins, and Chet wasn't big on spending money on things that didn't get him high or laid), and got a job selling used cars at his father-in-law's dealership.

In the winter of 1980, his wife, Lola, gave birth to a son, who Chet named Edward in secret honor of his old man. Big sister Darlene was smitten with her younger brother, a reality that lasted all of her life. As far as Darlene was concerned, Eddy could do no wrong, although Eddy liked very much to do wrong. He liked to pull the wings off flies when he was just a tyke, and graduated at the age of nine to killing neighborhood pets. When anyone ever got close to finding out what Eddy was doing, big sister Darlene would cover for him. Her parents never knew what Eddy was up to, and he sure wasn't into confessing his sins. By the time he was in high school and Darlene, still living at home and going to a junior college, was in her early twenties, she discovered that her little brother got caught trying to rape a girl under the bleachers at a football game. The boys who caught him beat the shit out of him, and it was only by the intervention of a school guard that Eddy made it out of the situation in one piece. Darlene sold her car to pay off the girl he tried to rape. Eddy didn't really notice.

Chet was as enamored of his son as his step-daughter, Darlene. In Chet's mind, the boy could do no wrong. And when Eddy turned sixteen, Chet told him the tale of the treasure in the house on Post Oak Street in Peaceful, Texas, and Eddy's true family history and true name of Hutchins.

276

'So why didn't you ever go for it, Dad?' Eddy asked his father.

Chet shrugged. 'I dunno. Just never got around to it. Maybe one of these days.' Then he smiled real big. 'Hey, maybe you and me, huh, boy?'

Eddy smiled at his dad. 'Sure, Dad, that sounds great.' Eddy knew he'd be going after that treasure, but he sure wasn't taking dear old dad along with him.

Seventeen

BACK HOME

Coach Robbins was sitting on the floor of the ER waiting room, rubbing his jaw while Tucker Benton towered over him, his face blood red. 'How could you?' he yelled. 'You were my friend! My goddam hero! And you raped my little sister?' And then he kicked him.

Coach Robbins scrambled out of the way and made it to a standing position. 'Hold on a minute! What in the hell are you talking about?' He turned to Mrs Benton, a confused look on his face. 'Nancy? What the hell?'

Mrs Benton sighed. 'He doesn't know, Les. I wasn't sure how he'd take it . . .'

'Ha!' Coach said, with little humor. 'Oh, he seems to be taking whatever *this* is just fine!'

'What are you talking about? Mom? What's going on?' Tucker asked, his face still red, his fists still clutched by his side.

Mrs Benton looked around the waiting room. There were only a few people in there, and one side was empty. She ushered her son in that direction. The coach followed – as did Logan and the Pugh girls. Uninvited but still involved. Well, at least Logan was, and since he was holding Bess's hand, she had to go, and where one Pugh girl went, they all went.

'Les?' Mrs Benton said.

'What about them?' the coach asked, pointing at Logan and the girls.

Mrs Benton shrugged. 'They may as well know the truth. It's better than what everyone is thinking.'

The coach nodded his head and rubbed his face. 'Cathy and I have been trying to have a baby for almost five years. We've tried everything. Then the doctor suggested a surrogate. We were opposed to it at first, but . . .' He looked at Mrs Benton.

She took a deep breath and said, 'Cathy told me what they were going through. I wanted to help.' She stiffened her shoulders and said, 'And we needed the money—'

'Mom, what the fuck—'

'Don't talk to your mother like that!' the coach said.

'Don't tell me what to do!' Tucker yelled at the coach.

'Tucker! He's still the same man who got you through four years of football! The same man who got you that scholarship! It's not his fault you didn't fulfill your end of the bargain—'

'Mom!' Tucker whined. 'I can't help it if I got bad grades!'

'If you'd studied instead of going out drinking every night—'

'People!' Megan said. 'Enough. So, Harper's carrying Coach and Mrs Robbins' baby, is that what you're saying?'

Mrs Benton straightened her shoulders again. 'Yes, that's what I'm saying.'

'I'm not real clear on the law, but isn't Harper

underage and isn't this like, you know, illegal?' Bess asked.

Mrs Benton fidgeted in her seat, and Coach Robbins stared out the window. 'It's not cut and dry,' she said in a small voice.

Coach turned back around. 'She'll be eighteen before the baby's born,' he said defensively, then sighed, his shoulders drooping. 'We weren't sure ourselves at first, Tucker, but . . . well, Cathy was desperate—'

'Mom, you, like, sold Harper's womb?' Tucker said, his voice louder than necessary. The people at the other end of the waiting room looked up.

'More like rented it out,' Megan said. Bess kicked her sister, who said, 'Ouch!'

'That's not how it was!' Mrs Benton said, turning red in the face; Bess thought that might be more from embarrassment at being caught than anger.

'What the hell you need the money for?' Tucker demanded. 'I've been sending you half my pay every week since I joined the army!'

Mrs Benton took hold of her son's hand. 'And I thank you for that, honey,' she said. 'But that and my small salary and dwindling tips, even with Harper working part-time at the clothing store, just hasn't been enough. They were going to repo the trailer. I needed a big chunk of money, and Les and Cathy offered me enough to pay the trailer off. Now all I have to worry about is the land it's sitting on. But with Les's help, I renegotiated the loan and got a lower payment, so it's all much better now.'

Tucker pulled his hand away from his mother's

grip. 'So why didn't you tell me any of this? I'm gone two years and this happens and you don't even mention it?'

'What were you going to do? Go AWOL or rob a bank or something? This seemed like the only alternative,' she said.

'And Harper? What about her?' Tucker demanded. 'She's seventeen, for God's sake! And she's gonna have a kid that isn't even hers? And she,' he said, pointing at Bess, 'says it's illegal! Is it? Did you make my sister break the law?'

Mrs Benton squared her shoulders and said defensively, 'Like Coach said, she'll be eighteen before the baby's born. And she wanted to do it, truly, Tucker. After everything Coach has done for us . . .'

'What has that got to do with anything?' Tucker demanded, standing up. 'Jeez, you people! Did she really want to do this? Or did you guilt her into it?'

His mother stood up too. 'Coach got her a scholarship to UT, Tucker. A scholarship she couldn't have gotten on her own. And *she'll* study! Unlike some people!'

'Here we go again,' Megan said under her breath.

'Shhhh!' Bess said.

'This is disgusting!' Tucker said, making a beeline for the outer door of the ER. But once there he turned and looked at Logan. 'Sorry for the beat-down, man,' he said, and walked out.

I called the chief. 'Anyway we can get a rush on DNA?' I asked him. 'Like, by tomorrow?'

281

'Hell no,' he said. 'If I knew somebody in Austin at the lab, maybe, but I don't. And why are you in an all-fired rush for the DNA? I thought we were gonna go with the fingerprints?'

'Fingerprints won't tell us if there's a familial match,' I said.

'Ya lost me.'

'What if Edgar Hutchins didn't die in the Pacific?' I asked.

'Who?'

'The youngest brother! We don't have a death notification on him – just a missing-in-action notification. So what if he made it back to the States? What if he's the one who killed Helen Hutchins?'

'OK, so what if? What's that got to do with who's hanging around now?'

'OK, it probably isn't Edgar who killed Humphrey and Diamond, but what about his kin? Like a son or a grandson? DNA could tell us if it is!'

'But we ain't got any DNA on Edgar, do we?'

'No,' I had to admit. 'But we do have DNA on Norris. And there would be some connection, wouldn't there?'

'Hell if I know,' the chief said. 'But still and all, no way I can get a rush on it.'

'Let me call Luna,' I said. 'She's got a buddy in the APD. Maybe we can go that route.'

'Give it a try.'

'Any word on the fingerprints?' I asked.

'Gave the razor to Mary and she's down in the lab with it now,' he said.

'OK. I'll call Luna and call you back.'

I hung up and dialed Elena Luna's office at the Codderville police department. She answered on the second ring. 'Lieutenant Luna,' she said.

'Hey, it's me,' I said.

'You still in Pleasantville?' she asked.

'Peaceful,' I corrected, 'and yeah, I am. You have a friend at APD, right?'

There was a moment of silence, then she said, 'Maybe.'

'Yes, you do! Anyway, can you call her and see if she can get some DNA expedited?'

Luna laughed. 'Are you out of your mind? The backlog on DNA is like close to a year. And these are for open cases in Austin. And you think they're gonna drop everything to rush a job for some hick town nobody's ever heard of? I ask her that, she won't be a friend for long!'

'Yeah, well maybe I won't be a friend for long if you don't!' I threatened.

Again, she laughed. The nerve! 'From your lips to God's ear,' she said and hung up on me.

I seriously was never going to speak to her again.

BACK HOME

Mrs Benton and the coach turned and looked at the four kids left – Bess, Megan, Alicia and Logan. 'I'd be very grateful if you didn't mention any of this,' Harper's mom said.

'And so would my wife and I,' the coach said. 'Logan, you interested in a scholarship?'

It was time for Logan to square his shoulders. 'Are you trying to bribe me, Coach?' he said, a frown on his face.

'No, of course not—' Then the coach stopped short. 'Yes,' he said. He heaved a great sigh. 'I'm sorry.'

'I don't need a scholarship. But Alicia could probably use one,' Logan said.

'Oh, no!' Alicia said, shaking her head vehemently. 'I'm not taking a bribe either!'

'Look, after what Harper's done for us, it's the least I can do,' the coach said and smiled at her. 'I'd rather y'all didn't tell anyone about our arrangement, as much for Harper's sake as ours. But that's up to y'all. The scholarship is yours even if you print the whole story on the front page of the *BCR Times*. You're a foster kid, right, Alicia?'

She nodded her head.

'Might not be UT,' he said. 'But I've got connections all over the place. I'll see what I can do.'

Alicia looked at her sisters, both of whom took a hand each. 'Do it!' Megan said.

'It's a great opportunity,' Bess said.

'I wouldn't tell anyone anyway,' Alicia said to the coach and Mrs Benton. 'As long as that's what Harper wants. I think we should talk to her. If she's as OK with this arrangement as y'all think she is, then, yes, a scholarship would be very nice.'

The coach sighed. 'Even if you find out she's not, the scholarship is still yours,' he said.

Alicia nodded her head, then looked at Mrs Benton. 'May we go in and see Harper?' she asked.

She nodded, said, 'She's in room four,' and walked up to the nurse's station.

As the girls were buzzed in, Alicia, heading for the door, stopped herself. 'Oh!' She turned to Mrs Benton and pulled the woman's car keys out of her pocket. 'I parked your car for you. It's in the lot toward the back.'

Mrs Benton smiled. 'I did sort of abandon it, didn't I?' She took the keys. 'Thanks,' she said.

Logan stayed behind as the girls went in to see Harper. They passed Cathy Robbins on her way to the waiting room.

Harper was lying on a high bed in room four, a light blanket over her legs, a hospital gown over her torso, her hands massaging her belly.

'What the hell do y'all want?' she demanded on seeing them.

'Don't get upset,' Bess said, touching Harper's arm. 'We're not here to hurt you in any way.'

'Like you could!' Harper said.

'Your mom and the coach told us everything,' Alicia said.

Harper looked from one to the other. Finally, she said, 'OK, so?'

'So we just want to make sure all this is really OK with you,' Bess said.

'Yeah, I'm fine with it,' Harper said, a frown on her face.

'But you got pregnant with somebody else's baby!' Megan said. 'That's like, you know, creepy!'

Harper shrugged her shoulders. 'Not really. It was just like going to the dentist, but at the other end,' she said. 'No big deal.' Then she smiled. 'And I sorta like the feeling when the baby moves around!' Then her eyes got big and she grabbed Megan's hand. 'Feel this!'

Megan let her hand be led to Harper's belly. Then she grinned from ear to ear. 'Y'all gotta feel this!' she said to her sisters, and all three girls had their hands on Harper's belly.

'Oh my God!' Bess said, a smile playing across her face. 'This is incredible!'

Alicia grinned. 'Not my first kicking fetus,' she said, 'and I hope it won't be my last! It's so cool!'

Megan removed her hand, frowned at Harper and said, 'But are you still a virgin?'

Bess quickly removed her hand, too. 'God, Megan! What a question!'

'No,' Harper said, shaking her head. 'It's an OK question. I wondered about it, too. But technically I still am. I mean, they had to break my hymen but other than that, I mean, yeah, I guess.'

'Wow,' Alicia said. 'Another virgin birth! Maybe you'll become a saint!'

Harper laughed. 'I doubt it.'

It was getting late in the afternoon and I was afraid we weren't going to hear back from the chief in regards to the fingerprint results. So I said to Willis, 'Let's go to the station.'

'Why?' he asked.

'Because I want to!' I said.

'Why do you want to?' he asked.

'OK, fine, I'll go by myself!'

He sighed and stood up. 'I'll go with you because obviously you're up to no good, or you'd tell me! I need to be there as a buffer.'

'Some buffer,' I grumbled and headed to the

door. Once in the car, I said, 'It's no big deal. I just want to make sure we get those fingerprint results. That the chief isn't clue-blocking me.'

Willis laughed. 'Good use of the word blocking,' he said.

'Thank you,' I said.

It took us five minutes in my Audi to get to the station. It was after five, but the front door to the station was unlocked, even though the gray-haired lady was no longer behind the counter. I went up to the counter and leaned down to the small opening. 'Hello?' I called out.

Willis went to the locked door and knocked. After about a minute, I saw the chief come out of his office. Seeing me with my nose pressed against the glass of the reception window, he got a slightly unpleasant look on his face. Then he sighed and walked to the reception desk and buzzed us in.

'You get anywhere with your friend Luna?' he asked me.

'No,' I admitted. 'What about the fingerprints?' I asked.

He shrugged. 'Far as I know Mary's still workin' on 'em,' he said.

I looked at my watch. 'For three hours?' I asked.

He frowned. 'Doesn't usually take that long,' he admitted. 'Come on, let's go see.'

So we followed him to the back of the station, through a door marked 'employees only,' that led to a staircase going down. We followed him down the stairs to a warren of offices and labs. 'We only got the one in use anymore,' he said, pointing at all the doors. 'Cut-backs, ya know.'

We agreed that we did. He opened the door marked 'Lab' and we followed him inside. There was no one there. 'Mary?' he called out, but received no response.

He walked up to the desk and looked at the top of it, moving papers here and there. 'Hum,' he said. 'Don't see anything.'

He turned and headed out of the lab and back up the stairs. The gray-haired lady was coming out of the bathroom. 'Where's Mary?' the chief asked her.

She shrugged. 'I dunno. Saw her go out the back about an hour ago,' she said.

'Why didn't you tell me?' the chief demanded.

'Why would I?' she asked.

Well, she had him there, obviously, because he gave no response. We followed the chief back into his office.

I took the one visitor's chair while my husband leaned against the wall. 'Where do you think she is?' I asked the chief.

'She probably went home a little early, that's all,' he said.

'Without telling you?' I asked.

He shrugged. 'Usually would, yeah,' he said, frowning.

'Is that straight-razor down in the lab?' I asked.

'Didn't see it,' he admitted.

'Would she store it somewhere?' I asked.

'Yeah, in the evidence locker,' he said and stood up. We followed him back downstairs.

The evidence locker was small and with good reason. There was hardly anything in there. A few handguns labeled and tagged, a baggie of weed, and some white powder that could have been anything from cocaine to speed. In small-town Texas I was pretty sure it was the latter. But no sheathed straight-razor.

'Why would she take it with her?' I demanded. Again the chief shrugged.

'That's not normal procedure, right?' I asked.

'No,' he said.

'So what do you know about Mary Mays?' I asked him.

He whirled on me. 'That she's a fine officer! That's what I know!' he said. 'I've been knowing that girl since she was a child! Her parents and me and the Mrs go to the same church! I know her history! Hells bells, I know *her*!'

'Then why did she take the evidence?' I asked, my voice soft.

He shook his head. 'Hell if I know,' he finally said.

'Maybe we should just call her,' Willis suggested.

The chief looked at me and I looked back at him. 'Maybe we should drive over there,' he said.

'That might be best,' I agreed.

So we got in the chief's squad car and headed out of town to a white-frame farmhouse with acres of plowed fields around it. A man was on a tractor doing something farm-like when we pulled up. The man was close enough to the driveway to cut off the tractor's engine and call to us.

'Hey, Rigsby!' he said. 'What can I do you for?'

'Hey, Clifford. Looking for Mary!' the chief called out from the open window of the car.

'Why you looking here?' Clifford Mays asked. 'Mary don't live here anymore! Didn't she give you her change of address? Like maybe six months ago?'

'Hum,' the chief said. 'I just figured she still lived with y'all. Didn't think to check with Mildred.' He turned and looked at me. 'My clerk,' he said in an aside.

'I don't rightly know her new address,' Mary's father said. 'But she lives in that new apartment complex over by the high school.' He leaned forward and laid on the horn of his tractor. A woman came to the porch of the white-framed farm house, drying her hands on a dishtowel, an old-fashioned apron covering her from neck to groin.

'What in the hell—' she started then spied the chief's car. 'Well, hey there, Rigsby! To what do we owe the pleasure?' she said, smiling wide. She was a pretty woman, and it was obvious who Mary Mays favored.

'He needs Mary,' Clifford said. 'What's her apartment number?'

'If you ever went over there to see her, you might know!' his wife chided him. Looking at the chief, she said, 'It's that apartment complex near the high school. Apartment 2304. Second floor, near the rear.'

'Thanks, y'all,' the chief said, smiled, honked his horn briefly, and headed out of the driveway.

He didn't speak again until we were parked in the back parking lot of the aforementioned apartment complex. 'So now what?' he asked, not looking at either Willis or myself.

'I guess we go knock on the door,' my husband said. I was glad he said it and I didn't have to, because the look the chief gave him wasn't friendly.

'Y'all stay in the car,' he said, opening his door.

'You know that's not going to happen,' I said, opening the shotgun side and letting Willis out of the back.

Chief Cotton sighed. 'I'm beginning not to like you, ma'am,' he said.

I grinned. 'That must mean at some point you did!'

'Shut up,' he said, and led the way up the stairs.

Apartment 2304 was the second in from the stairs. The chief knocked rapidly on the front door. It took a minute but the front door opened and Mary Mays stood there, out of uniform, wearing cut-offs and a tank top, her hair down and flowing. She was much prettier and much thinner than the uniform would have you believe.

'Chief!' she said, and the look on her face was one of fear. She tried slamming the door, but Chief Cotton's foot kept that from happening.

'You wanna tell me what's goin' on, Mary?' he said, his words clipped.

'Nothing!' She looked back over her shoulder and tried again to shut the door. That's when a bullet whizzed through the wooden door of the apartment, hitting the chief.

2004–2014
Eddy got caught when he was sixteen stealing a car. He ended up in juvie until his eighteenth birthday. Upon release, his sister Darlene picked

him up and took him back to her apartment in Biloxi. His parents had gotten a divorce while he was inside and Mom was shacked up with a guy only slightly older than Eddy, and dear old Dad had turned into a serious drunk, living in and out of halfway houses. So it was Darlene who gave him solace, who nurtured him and took care of him, feeding him and housing him while he sat around and did nothing but play video games, the more violent the better.

No one but Darlene knows if she ever really reacted to her little brother's penchant for violence. Maybe because he never used it against her, she really didn't care. Who knew?

In 2008, Darlene, with Eddy in tow, moved to Houston, Texas, following on the heels of the only man who'd ever paid much attention to her. Eddy knew this guy had no romantic interest in his sister, not even a purely sexual interest, but he didn't let it bother him. In fact, nothing that didn't affect Eddy directly ever bothered him. He was like his grandfather in that respect. And, as it turned out, in other respects as well.

Being in the state of Texas brought to Eddy's mind his father's story of the town of Peaceful and the old Victorian on Post Oak Street. He wondered sometimes, when trying to fall asleep, what the treasure might be, and if it truly existed. But Dad had said his father was adamant, that he knew for a fact there was a treasure in the old house, and that's why Grandpa's older brother had married that Bishop girl in the first place, to get his hands on the treasure and keep Grandpa Edgar from it.

This pissed Eddy off. If Grandpa Edgar had been able to get hold of that treasure way back when, how different could Eddy's life be now? Way different, he figured. He'd be one of those boys he hated so much at school – the ones born with the silver spoons in their mouths. But Eddy would have been better than those guys – mainly because he was way smarter to start with – and by now he could be a multimillionaire, maybe even a billionaire. Maybe he could invent *video games instead of just playing them, and his would be way better than any of the ones he played now. Ha! He thought. Maybe* real *violence! Like snuff films he could turn into games. He liked the thought of that, and the thought of all the more money he could make – if he just had that treasure to start with.*

These thoughts nagged at him so hard day in and day out that, three years after moving to Houston, Eddy stole a hundred dollars from Darlene's purse, grabbed her keys and her car, bought a map and headed to Peaceful, Texas.

Eighteen

BACK HOME

The kids got back to the Pugh house a little after six. Holding hard to Bess's hand, Logan turned to the other two and asked, 'Can y'all figure out something for dinner without Bess?'

'Of course,' Alicia said, while Megan said, 'Not any worse than if she was here.'

'Why?' Bess asked, not letting go of Logan's hand, but looking up at him with a slight frown.

Looking down at her, a small smile playing across his lips, he said, 'Because I thought maybe it would be OK if you came home with me for dinner. What do you think?'

'What would your mother say?' Bess asked, terrified of the idea.

'I already called her, when y'all were getting the car at the hospital. She said that would be great. She really wants to meet you.'

Bess gulped in air. 'Oh,' was all she could think of to say.

'Go for it!' Megan said.

'Definitely,' Alicia agreed, smiling. She stopped smiling when her cell phone rang and she saw the caller ID. Turning her back on the others she said, 'What?' into the phone.

'Hey,' Graham said.

'What do you want?' Alicia demanded.

'I think we need to talk,' he said. 'Meet me at the Dairy Queen for dinner?'

'No,' she said. 'Some place more expensive.'

'Hey, I'm just a poor student, you know,' Graham said.

'Then maybe you should stop going to the movies,' Alicia said with some heat.

There was silence on the other end of the line. 'Diego's,' he said, naming one of the fancier Mexican restaurants in town. 'Half an hour.'

'Maybe,' Alicia said. 'Or maybe not.'

She came back to the group who'd been standing around staring at her. 'Who was that?' Megan asked.

'Your brother,' Alicia said. 'He wants to talk.'

'Oh, shit,' Megan said. 'I'm sorry.'

Bess rubbed Alicia's arm. 'Me, too,' she said.

Alicia shook them both off. 'No biggie,' she said. 'It is what it is.' She took the keys to the minivan from Megan's fingertips. 'Looks like you're on your own for dinner, Megs,' she said and walked to the minivan, which was blocking Logan's car and would have to be moved anyway.

'You want to come with us?' Bess asked Megan, hoping her sister would say yes. She wasn't sure she was up to meeting the parents. She'd heard stories . . . lots and lots of stories. Most of them not turning out so well.

'Are you kidding?' Megan said. 'You forget you never did eat your leftover steak, nor did you throw it away.' She grinned. 'Dinner!' And with that she turned and walked into the house.

Bess and Logan moved onto the grass as Alicia backed the minivan out of the driveway, then

Logan walked her to the shotgun side of the car and opened the door for her. She crawled in while he went around and got in the driver's side. Life as she knew it was about to change. For her and Alicia both.

Willis and I ducked down, Willis grabbing the chief's legs and dragging him away from the door. I grabbed the chief's gun from its holster and held it *Cagney & Lacey* style. Willis took it out of my hand. 'The safety's on,' he said, with a look on his face indicating he thought I was a ninny. Under the circumstances I let it slide.

'Give me my goddam gun!' Chief Cotton said, using one arm to rise himself from the second-floor balcony.

'You right-handed or left-handed?' Willis asked, noticing that he was favoring his right arm, the one dripping blood all over the place.

'I'm a south-paw, now give me my goddam gun!' Willis handed it to him butt first and the chief said, 'Now stand me up.'

Willis got him to a standing position and I took a look at his arm. 'We need to call an ambulance,' I said.

'In a minute!' he said, irritated. Again, under the circumstances, who could blame him for a little irritation? 'They still in there?' he asked.

'Nobody's moved,' I said.

'Is there a back door to these places?' Willis asked.

'Probably not,' the chief said. 'They put these up in about a week, week and a half tops. Cheap shit like this don't usually have extra doors, do they?'

'Probably not,' Willis said.

The chief, gun in front of him in a one-handed stance (personally I prefer the two-handed *Cagney & Lacey* style, but he did have one arm out of commission), headed back toward Mary Mays' front door. Standing to the side and leaning against the wall he called out, 'Mary! You need to come out, hon! Ain't no need for this. Who's in there with you? I know you didn't shoot at me, girl, so you're OK. Somebody's making you do this, right, hon? I know this ain't your style. You're a good girl, always have been. This is just a little hiccup, so to speak. We'll get it worked out. But whoever's in there with you needs to put down their gun and come out with their hands up. You tell them to do that, OK, Mary, girl?'

'Shut up, you old fool!' came a male voice. Then another shot came through the now closed front door.

'Mary, you OK?' the chief called out. 'I'm worried about you, girl. Whoever this asshole is, if he's willing to shoot at me, what's he gonna do to you? Answer me that!'

'Chief, go away!' Mary called out. 'Just leave us be!'

'Who is this guy's got you so wrapped up, honey? Your mama and daddy know about this? You know it's gonna crush 'em. You don't wanna do this!'

There was a shouted but feminine 'No!' from inside the apartment, sounds of a struggle, then silence. Gingerly the chief pushed open the door.

Mary Mays lay on the floor, her head bleeding. When the chief, with gun drawn, checked out the one bedroom in the back of the apartment, he saw a window open wide, the screen gone, and a man running full tilt down the street.

2012–2014

Eddy was not charmed by the beauty of Peaceful, Texas. In fact, he hardly noticed it. He found a cheap motel on the outskirts of town and, after depositing his one piece of luggage, got back in the car and drove by the house on Post Oak Street. To a boy raised in a two-bedroom duplex, the old Victorian was huge. He wondered how in the world he was going to be able to search the whole place. There definitely was an attic – he could see that just by looking. And maybe there was a basement, too. He knew people didn't go in for basements too much in the South, but a house this old and this big . . . maybe this was the exception.

But he couldn't just sit in his parked car outside the house indefinitely. Someone – like a nosy neighbor – could get suspicious. So he drove on and decided to treat himself to lunch at the Dairy Queen. Once inside, he noticed a woman looking at him. Unfortunately for him, that woman was in uniform – a police uniform. He tried not to look her way, although it was his tendency to check out good-looking women whenever possible, and this one was a real knock-out, even in her bulky uniform. He couldn't help wondering what she might look like out of it, but then he wondered that about most every women he encountered – fat, thin, young, and sometimes even old.

He was sitting there minding his own business, chomping down on his D-Q Dude, when the woman ambled over to him. 'Hi. Haven't seen you around before,' she said.

Eddy looked up. 'Just visiting,' he said, wondering if he was going to have to take off before he even saw the inside of the house.

Then she smiled at him and he immediately recognized it. She wasn't interested in him as a possible threat to peaceful Peaceful, she was interested in him like a woman to a man. He smiled back.

They hooked up that night at his motel. After she left – he found out she lived with her parents and had to get home before they noticed she was gone – he drove his car a block down Post Oak Street from the old Victorian and walked down to what should have been his family home. It was late, way past midnight, and the street was empty, lights off in the houses he passed. There were a few porch lights blazing, and a streetlight, but it was half a block away from the old Victorian, leaving it in shadow. He found his way into the yard and began a slow progress around the house. He knew what the outside of a basement door should look like, but didn't see one in his perusal of the house and grounds. He ignored or didn't even notice the well-kept grounds with its flowers and trees – not that he could have seen much in the dark even if he so desired. He was almost to the back door, up on the porch, ready to try the door, when the porch light came on and the door *swung open, revealing an old lady in her night-clothes. She opened her mouth as if to scream, then stopped, her eyes big.*

'Daddy?' she asked.

Maybe a bit quicker on the uptake than his old man – taking more after Grandpa Edgar – Eddy said, 'Hush, honey. Go back to bed.'

And Miss Hutchins, sure she was dreaming, did exactly that.

Nineteen

Willis used his cell phone to call an ambulance for both the chief and Mary Mays. She was unconscious and her head wound was bleeding like – well, a head wound. I found a dish towel that I held to her head while we awaited the ambulance. The chief was sitting on the floor, next to Mary's body, shaking his head.

'Can't believe she's mixed up in this!' He looked at me, a pitiful expression on her face. 'She did real good at the academy. Top of her class.'

'Whoever this guy is, it's all his fault,' I soothed.

'Well, yeah, of course. But I thought Mary was smarter than fallin' for some jerk-weed bad boy!' he said, again shaking his head.

'Did you get a look at him?' I asked.

'Naw, just the back of him,' he said. 'Couldn't even tell how tall he was from up here. Not fat's about the only thing I'm sure of.'

Willis, who had been out on the balcony that surrounded the second floor, stuck his head inside. 'Ambulance is here,' he said.

I helped the chief to stand up. 'Hope she's gonna be OK,' he said, looking down at his officer. 'She's a good girl. Really.'

'I'm sure she is,' I said in a more patronizing tone than I'd intended. Considering the way she'd treated Willis and me lately, and the fact that she

301

might be involved in the deaths of Diamond Lovesy and Humphrey Hammerschultz, I doubted she was *that* good a girl. I was thinking she was a stone-cold bitch – but I didn't mention my opinion to the chief.

The ambulance attendants came up with the gurney and, after checking out Mary Mays, got her on it and out onto the balcony and down the stairs to the waiting bus. The chief was right behind them, holding tightly to the railing of the stairs. Willis was already down, waiting by the ambulance, as I came down after the chief. I saw the chief hand Willis a ring of keys.

'Take my squad car back to the shop, OK?' he said. 'I'll get a ride back after they patch me up.'

Willis nodded, patted Chief Cotton on his good arm and helped him into the back of the ambulance, where he sat down next to the stretcher that carried Mary Mays. I almost felt bad about Mary, seeing the look on the chief's face. He looked ten years older than he had when we first met, and very, very sad.

Willis and I headed back upstairs to Mary's apartment. The chief was otherwise occupied – both physically and mentally – and obviously hadn't even thought about securing the scene or getting a forensic team in to check it out. Not that he actually had a team – there'd been that one lady with the bag at the Bishop's Inn when we'd found Humphrey, and I'd seen the same lady at the scene of Diamond's murder.

'Maybe we should call the station and get that forensic woman out here,' I suggested to Willis.

He nodded, pulled his cell phone out of his

pocket and went to the balcony to put in the call. I headed into the bedroom. If there was anything left of Mary's 'bad boy,' I figured this was where I'd find it. And there was. Trying not to touch anything, I went back into the kitchen, found some tongs in a bowl of kitchen tools on the stove top and took them back into the bedroom with me, using them to move away scattered clothing. Some of the items were definitely larger than Mary's clothes and looked more like those of a man than a woman. And there were male toiletries in the bathroom. I'm not sure what that told me other than the 'bad boy' was indeed shacking up with Mary, but I'd already figured that.

Willis came back in. 'That old lady at the station—'

'Mildred,' I supplied.

'Whatever. She kept bugging me to tell her what happened, but I didn't!' he said, like a little boy proud of his first major accomplishment. 'She did say she'd send the forensic woman out, but kept insisting I tell her why I was calling instead of the chief.'

'So what did you say?'

'That he asked me to call,' Willis said, and grinned. I hoped he was finally beginning to understand my penchant for things mysterious. Changing the subject, he asked, 'What did you find?'

I shook my head. 'Not much. A guy's been living here, all right. There's men clothes in the bedroom and a few toiletries in the bathroom, but nothing of any significance.'

Willis frowned. 'Were they all new?' he asked.

303

'Because we found the same crap in Miss Hutchins' attic.'

My eyes got wide and I grinned at my clever husband. 'You're right!' I said. 'Let's go see.'

There were a couple of shirts hanging in the closet with the tags still on them, and all the toiletries, when lifted with the tongs, seemed fairly full. Willis borrowed the tongs to open the only drawer in the bathroom. And there, staring up at us – if it had eyes, which of course, it didn't – was the sheathed straight-razor that Mary Mays was supposed to have fingerprinted.

There was no noise, just possibly a shadow passing between the bedroom light and Willis and me still in the bathroom. That was the only thing that made me turn around. When I did, I grabbed Willis's arm. There was a man standing there, pointing a gun at us. I had no doubt this was Mary Mays' bad boy. Surprisingly, though, he looked like the same guy who'd been in the picture with Diamond Lovesy, and the same guy Miss Hutchins had called 'daddy.'

'So,' I said, putting on a braver face than I felt, 'you're Miss Hutchins' daddy, huh? You're kinda young.'

He grinned at me. 'Not for a ghost, huh?' he said.

'You look pretty substantial to me,' Willis said.

'Oh, I am. Substantial enough to blow a hole through the both of you!'

'You're Edgar Hutchins' grandson, right?' I said.

The grin left his face and he frowned at me. 'What makes you say that?' he asked.

'Who else could you be? You're too young to be his son. The family resemblance, the destroyed pictures so no one would know about that resemblance, Miss Hutchins seeing you all those times and believing you were her father. Personally,' I said, 'I don't believe in ghosts, so I figured it had to be a relative. Especially when we found a picture of you with Diamond Lovesy. What was your connection to her?'

'She was my half-sister. And that stupid name is one she made up. Her real name was Darlene Winslow. My daddy gave her his name, although she wasn't really his kid. And he never let her forget it, either,' he said with a grin.

'So your name is Winslow?' Willis asked. 'Not Hutchins?'

'Ol' Grandpa Edgar changed his name when he came out of the Philippines,' he said. 'Least, that's what my daddy told me. Actually named me after the old coot. They call me Eddy. But ol' Edgar went AWOL, so he couldn't very well use the Hutchins name now could he?'

'I don't understand what you're doing here,' I said. 'Why are you harassing the old lady? What's in it for you? I can't see you doing anything that doesn't profit you somehow.'

The grin was back on his face. It was a lovely grin, full of straight, pearly white teeth and a dimple in his left cheek – just no sparkle in the eyes. Actually, there wasn't much of anything in those eyes. No spark, no shine, no depth, no life. They were as cold as the proverbial witch's tit.

'Profit? I guess you can say that. I don't mind telling y'all, since you're going to be dead in a few minutes anyway. It's a treasure. Real treasure. No fooling around.'

'Is that what all the banging around has been about?' Willis asked. 'By the way, what were you dragging down the hall Saturday night? Sounded like something heavy.'

'Oh? Y'all heard that? Sorry to wake you,' he said, the grin even wider than before. 'It was an old chest. Had a strong lock on it. Figured if I tried to get it open up in the attic I'd be heard. So I dragged it outside and into my car. Opened it up there. It wasn't all that heavy.'

'No treasure inside?' I asked.

He shrugged. 'Just some old clothes. Mary, the dumb ass, said they were worth a mint – real vintage, she said. But who in their right mind would buy old clothes?'

'You'd be surprised,' I said.

'So what happened to Humphrey?' Willis asked.

Eddy shrugged. 'That asshole! Darlene – Diamond to you – knew about the treasure I was after and told Humphrey. For some reason she thought he was her true love. He couldn't see her for nothing. Actually, I think he was more interested in me than her. But he's the one who got her into this whole psychic scam bullshit and made some decent money. I told her I knew where we could get some real money and she could dump his fat ass. But then she told him!' He frowned. 'The bitch! She was supposed to be on my side, but she goes and tells that dipshit!'

'That must have been annoying,' I said, edging closer to the drawer where the straight-razor still resided in its sheath. I had no idea what I was going to do with it, especially up against a gun, but it was the only thing I could think of.

'Annoying shit!' he said vehemently. 'That SOB thought he could bargain with me. Came up with this plan of him and Darlene getting into the house and helping me look for it. Like he was gonna *share* the treasure with me when he found it! I've been in and out of this house for months. I know where everything is! Still, I didn't mind helping Darlene a bit at first – not enough to bother me, mind – then that stupid Hammerschultz gets stinking drunk and I go downstairs in the middle of the night and he's all, "When I find it, I'm keeping it, asshole, and you and your sister can shove it." So I grabbed him and sorta twisted his head. Didn't really mean to kill him,' he said. Then he grinned again. 'But it sure made a neat popping sound when I broke his neck.'

I thought I was going to throw up in my mouth. This guy was one of the sickest people I'd met – and in my hobby of finding killers, I'd met a few true sickos. But this one took the cake. 'You moved the chest *after* you killed him?'

'Well, I was gonna get him to help me, but when he said what he said . . .'

'So you're the one who wrote the reservation in Miss Hutchins' book?'

He said nothing, just grinned at me.

'And then you shot your own sister?' I asked.

He straightened his shoulders and got an indignant look on his face. 'Hell, no! That's family! You don't kill your kin.' He stopped and thought about it, then said, 'Mostly. But no, I didn't shoot Darlene. Ol' Mary Mays did that. Darlene was really pissed about Humphrey and she asked me to meet her to talk, but I was busy, so I sent Mary. And Darlene's all shook up, tells Mary she's gonna turn us both in for killing Humphrey, and get this, Mary says she said, "the love of her life!" That squirrely old fag!' He laughed out loud. 'She wasn't joking, though. And she shook Mary up so much that she just lost it and shot her.' He shrugged. 'I had nothing to do with that.'

'Why did you come back here?' Willis asked him.

'To the apartment, you mean?'

Willis nodded.

'Well, there was Mary – before she grew a fuckin' conscience and wanted to confess everything. But then I saw them take the policeman away in the ambulance. Thought you two would be long gone. I just needed one little thing. If you wouldn't mind, lady, open that drawer behind you and hand me that thing in the red velvet bag.'

'You mean your straight-razor?' I asked, doing as he said. But I didn't hand it to him. Instead, I hefted it in my hand. 'Family heirloom?' I asked.

'Guess so,' he said. 'It was Grandpa Edgar's. Now hand it over.'

'Put down the gun,' came a voice from behind us.

Eddy whirled around to stare at the forensic lady standing there with her bag in her hand. She held no weapon, so he shot her. Luckily, he wasn't a very good shot and the bullet only grazed her, but my husband, bless him, took that opportunity to jump into action and managed to knock Eddy to the ground, pushing the gun away. I grabbed it while Willis continued to knock Eddy around a bit. I really didn't blame him – I mean, we were both pretty high on adrenaline.

Epilogue

BACK HOME

'I didn't mean for any of this to happen,' Graham said as he sat across from Alicia at a quiet booth in the Mexican restaurant. They both had iced teas in front of them, along with chips and salsa. None of it had been touched. The menus sat unopened on the tabletop.

'How long?' Alicia asked.

Graham lowered his gaze. 'A while,' he said.

'How long?' Alicia asked again, her voice raised.

'About three weeks,' Graham finally said.

'About the time you decided we needed to start seeing other people,' she said – a statement, not a question. 'I take it you were already seeing her before you made this announcement.'

'I just saw her at the library at school. I didn't go out with her or anything—'

'My, aren't you the righteous one!' Alicia said.

'You hate me,' Graham said, looking up to stare into her eyes.

'Yes, I do,' Alicia said. 'And I hate her. Doesn't bode well for family get-togethers in the future, does it?'

'We can work this out—'

'I don't think so,' Alicia said, standing. 'I've lost my appetite. Please call ahead whenever you

309

decide to come to your parents' home. That way I can leave before you get there.'

Graham stood up, too. 'Alicia!' he called, but he was talking to her back as she left the restaurant.

The dinner at Logan's parents' house went fairly well. Logan's mother was a little stand-offish but his father was friendly and warm. The mother – 'call me Angela' – warmed up as the evening progressed, and Bess managed to remember her manners and use the right utensils. She didn't offer much by way of conversation, but answered politely when spoken to and smiled at the proper moments. On the drive back to her house, Logan declared the evening an unqualified success.

'You did great!' he said.

'I hope so,' Bess answered.

'How do you think Alicia's doing with your brother?' he asked.

Bess shook her head. 'Probably not nearly as well as I did with your parents.'

'Speaking of parents, when are yours coming home?'

Bess shrugged. 'I have no idea. Haven't heard from them today.'

They pulled into the Pugh driveway and all thoughts of Bess's parents went by the wayside as Logan took her into his arms.

We called the girls as soon as we got back to the Bishop's Inn. Megan was the only one home and we told her we'd be heading back the next day. 'Cool,' was her response. 'See you then.' And that was it.

Then we found Miss Hutchins and asked her to have a seat in the living room while we explained the situation to her. 'Uncle Edgar was alive all these years?' she said, incredulous. 'And he never came back to visit?'

'I think he did,' I told her as gently as possible, taking her hands in mine. 'I'm pretty sure he's the one you saw standing over your mother's body. I'm pretty sure it wasn't your daddy who did that.'

Miss Hutchins nodded her head. 'I always wondered why he would do it. They were real happy before the war. Very loving.' She sighed and tears formed in her eyes. 'And all these years I've blamed him for Mama's death.' She shook her head. 'How can I ever forgive myself?'

'It's not your fault!' I assured her. 'He wanted you to think he was your father, right? He said he was, right? And you were just a little girl! It's not at all your fault.'

Seeing Willis take something from his pocket, her eyes got big. 'Oh, my goodness! Where did you find that?'

'This?' Willis asked, holding up the sheathed straight-razor.

She reached out for it. 'This was my daddy's! Look at this!' she said, pointing to faded lettering on the bottom of the sheath. 'NMH. Those are Daddy's initials: Norris Manford Hutchins! Where did you find it?'

'Edgar's grandson had it.' I took her free hand and squeezed. 'I'm sorry, Miss Hutchins, but there's a good chance that's what was used to kill your mother.'

311

Instead of dropping the thing like a hot potato – as I would have done under similar circumstances – she just looked down at it. 'So sad,' she said. 'You know, Mama went with Uncle Edgar before she met Daddy.'

'No, we didn't know that,' I said.

'Maybe it's one of the reasons why he killed her,' she said.

'That and the treasure,' Willis said.

'Treasure?' Miss Hutchins asked, looking up at him.

'Yes, the guy who's been living in your attic said Edgar told his son, Eddy's dad, about this treasure here in the house, and he told Eddy—'

'Oh!' she said and smiled slightly. 'The treasure! Well, of course.'

'There *is* a treasure?' I asked, surprised.

'Oh, there certainly was one. A million dollars. But Mama and I used it as kindling during the war years,' she said.

'You used a million dollars as kindling?' my husband asked, aghast at the very thought.

'Oh, it wasn't worth much by then,' she said. 'Confederate money didn't hold up much after the war.'

Willis and I looked at each other. 'No,' he said. 'It really didn't.'

We left for home the next day.